TO THE MOON

BO HUFFMAN

To The Moon

ISBN 979-8-9918030-3-8 (paperback)

ISBN 979-8-9918030-2-1 (ebook)

Cover art by Adrian DKC

To Benjamin,
who has swept aside all obstacles
so that I can pursue my dreams.

And to Amélia,
who now zooms faster than a Twisted Twig.

1

Best Buzzems

Best Buzzems was one of the oldest broomstick dealerships in the kingdom of Everdorne, though it could not boast of being the busiest. But it did have its regulars—some forced in by generational guilt—and its peculiar cast of employees buzzing the lot, selling broomsticks both new and used to the inhabitants of northern Citeel, the capital city of Everdorne.

The New Brooms showroom was impeccably upkept, every bit of it curated to entice its customers to buy. From where the brooms were displayed down to the smell of the place, which was a carefully formulated scent of citrus and pine that suggested an adventure awaited on any one of these brooms. Some broomsticks hung from hooks on the wall, generously spaced out, while others were suspended from above by clever levitation magic to show them in motion. It invited customers to imagine themselves astride it, their hair and cloaks whipping behind them in the wind. There were no price tags in New Brooms, not even on the Customization Wall, which displayed all sorts of accessories for upgrades.

Different bristles—any and every high-end twig imaginable—in a variety of thickness and colors.

Mountable seats, saddles, and cushion sleeves for handles for that guaranteed (but only for five years) no-slip grip.

Tiny stardust lamps, all the new rage, to install for night flights.

Baskets, both leather and woven, their buckles charmed by anti-smudge protection.

There was also an assortment of cleaning and repair kits, varying in complexity for the first-time owner to the more advanced, do-it-all-yourself rider.

Despite all the products, the space didn't feel crowded at all. Everything was cleverly arranged so that customers only ever focused on one broom at a time, the one they were being sold right in front of them, discouraging wandering eyes.

"Anything new, Dutch?"

Dutch Brown peered over the top of his copy of *The Harking Herald*. He was a gnome, which made him shorter than all of his coworkers. He was also much older than everyone else, far past his prime, and his hunch didn't help. His hair was receded to mere tufts over his pointed ears holding up a thick pair of glasses. He adjusted them on his wart-riddled nose to get a better look at Bane Woods, the twenty-five-year-old Used Brooms Salesman who looked every bit his age, from his perpetually wind-whipped mass of curly, unkept hair to his precariously tied boots. "Just the usual. The coronation and whatnot."

"What of it?"

Dutch rolled his eyes and flipped his paper around to show Bane the page he'd been interrupted from reading. "The coronation!"

"What. Of. It?"

"I don't know! You didn't let me finish reading it," Dutch snapped and turned the paper back around.

Aeryn Void approached the coffee machine and nodded to Bane. He and the rest of the dealership personnel were human. Most of the citizens of Citeel were. Aeryn was as tall as Bane; all the salesmen were, except Dutch, but he had been tall once, for a gnome. Aeryn was in his late 20s. His hair was impeccably manicured, his face freshly shaved, his shoulders pinched back as if he were permanently proud. Really it was from all the deadlifts he did. "Bane. Dutch. What's new, Dutch?"

"For gods' sake!" Dutch stood, crumpled the paper in his hand, and tossed it on his desk before storming out the door to go take a lap around the practice lot.

Once he was out of earshot, Bane and Aeryn looked at each other and erupted into laughter. Bane dropped into the chair and, moving aside the flask, the box of snuff, and the vials of anti-compulsion potions, spread the paper out so they could both read it.

"What's new?" Ezra Novic asked, walking over. He and Aeryn were the only other New Brooms Salesmen besides Dutch, and he was the youngest, having just turned twenty. He was gangly, not quite filling out the uniform shirt that Bane wore comfortably and Aeryn's biceps threatened to split at the seams. His hair was always cut once a month, no exception. He once tried to be Aeryn's workout partner and couldn't keep up, so instead they bonded over their mutual hobby of pub hopping.

For these two salesmen, looking good was a point of pride. Though the once-strict grooming rules were no longer enforced, everyone but Gerwin, who grew a beard three months ago, upheld them. Bane tried his best, but he just couldn't keep the same standard as all the rest of them. He went through razors at an alarming rate, and even though he shaved every morning he had a shadow of stubble dusting his face by late afternoon.

It was this same ritual, every morning. Dutch trying to read his paper or sitting with Gerwin discussing the latest dragon racing bets they would be placing, while the younger employees—Bane, Aeryn, Ezra—streamed in at their leisure, knowing full well that showing up hours before the first customers did would make no difference. Eventually Bane got shooed back across the lot to Used Brooms, where he and Candor were the two lone employees.

"I think they're avoiding their wives," Aeryn once said.

"Who would marry them?" Ezra asked and Bane snickered. Though he shouldn't have. None of *them* were married, so what did they know about the woes of long-term commitment? He and his girl Lusine were going on almost three years, but he knew full well that was but a drop in the bucket compared to a lifetime.

"Says here the coronation's taking place this weekend," Bane read aloud.

"Already? Didn't they just get married?"

"Last summer, so it's been a few months. But apparently tradition dictates the coronation to always take place the following January."

"Tradition? When was the last coronation? Thirty some years ago?" Aeryn asked.

"Oy, Bane! Get on over to the other lot!" Gerwin shouted, spotting the Used Brooms Salesman in his New Brooms showroom. "And stop drinking my coffee!"

"Tastes like fairy piss anyhow," Bane grumbled, getting up and stuffing Dutch's newspaper under his arm. He saluted the other salesmen and gave a little curtsy to Gerwin as he passed his boss. He barely felt the cold as he pushed out the door and trudged across to the Used Brooms showroom.

In the hierarchy of salesmen at a broomstick dealership, Bane was dead last in the pecking order.

At the top was Gerwin Vault, Owner and General Manager. Next was Mic Void, the Finance & Enchantment Manager of both lots. No deal was approved without his stamp, and he earned a commission from any deal made at the dealership.

Then there was his son Aeryn, and Ezra and Dutch, the New Brooms Salesmen who prowled the lot like dragons hunting for sugar. When they got too old or lost their good looks or had too many consecutive bad sales months, they would be banished across the practice lot to Used Brooms, where Bane spent his days playing cards with Candor Newman, Used Brooms Manager, who was so old he remembered the last coronation.

The Used Brooms building was a fraction of New Broom's size, and all the brooms were displayed leaning sadly against the wall, each with a price tag lassoed around its handle. No fancy floating brooms. But also no haggling, no clever sales tactics, and no pressure. Also no fat commission checks, but Bane was in no position to complain.

Bane started in New Brooms two years ago, but after missing too many workdays around the full moon he nearly lost his job. Instead, he was reassigned to Used Brooms after six months and served as overnight security once a month as a compromise. Bane, who had burned through an awful lot of jobs in the last five years, gratefully accepted. It was hard to keep a job as a werewolf, even in such a metropolitan city swirling with all types of peoples.

While the other salesmen his age were friendly, they were quick to ignore Bane when they were hunting a sale. It wounded Bane's ego a bit, because what did they know about a hunt? *He* knew about the blinding need that came on after the catch of a scent, the ecstasy of that first bone-crunching bite...Bane shook his head to clear it and quickly turned to the back of the newspaper, where Lovetta Fox's daily horoscopes and moon phase were listed. Sure enough, the full moon was approaching.

Bane jumped as a stack of parchments dropped onto his desk. He looked up to see Honey Vault, her lips in their usual tight pinch. Oh, how could he forget Honey, the owner's daughter? In her tight-fit dresses, her waist pinched in extra small under her corset, the hem swishing just above the ankles. She saw everything and was always everywhere and nowhere at once. She manned the front desk, placed orders with the broomstick manufacturers, and, most importantly, distributed pay each month.

"Give these to Candor when he gets in."

"What are these?"

"If they were for you, I'd tell you," Honey snapped. She clicked away in her impossibly high heels, hurrying as if staying in Used Brooms would soil her reputation.

Bane rolled his eyes, picked up the stack of parchments, and dropped them onto the only other desk in the office.

No one really bought used broomsticks unless it was a parent buying a first broom for their young child. Even then, most magical folks enchanted their own broomsticks for amateur flight around the front yard or in the park. Then when their children lost interest, they retired the broom to sweep the porch. At the dealership, most of the used broomstick inventory consisted of new brooms that never sold but had provided one too many test rides to honestly still advertise as new.

Recently, the broomstick industry had exploded. Where before pigeons made the majority of deliveries in the kingdom, the recent union strike between the new king and P.U.K.E. (Pigeon Union of the Kingdom of Everdorne) created a rift that let trickle in an opportunity for private delivery services.

Suddenly, anyone could hop on a broom and make deliveries, and there was nothing P.U.K.E. could do to stop the competition until they renegotiated their contract with the Crown. As they waited in the lounge for their broomsticks to get serviced, these deliverymen often shared their stories with Bane, who was blown away at what all people would order: food, clothes, and sometimes even emergency contraception potions.

Bane heard the most stories from Mel Bone, who came to service her Extra-long Wayclean whenever it lost too many bristles. She delivered groceries to the elderly and always complained about what lousy tippers they were.

"Can't you deliver to anyone else?"

"Yes, but these clients are reliable. They don't trust just anyone to pick out their apples. And once they decide they like you, they insist on only calling you," Mel explained. She had three teenage sons and an underpaid accountant for a husband. She picked up these extra gigs to supplement their income and keep busy while she awaited the birth of her fourth.

The dealership of course had its very busy Service Drive, manned by Doc Turner and his son, Son Turner. They polished and unbent wooden handles, restrung bristle strings, replaced lost bristles, and re-infused magic into the broomsticks. There wasn't a nick nor scratch they couldn't buff, and bristle replacement was complimentary for the first year after the purchase of a new broomstick. Mel had bought so many broomsticks over the years that they just added bristles for free to thank her for her loyalty. Mel always assured them it was much obliged.

"Better get out there," Candor called, stomping his boots on the doormat. He was nearly seventy, the oldest only after Dutch, whose people lived a lot longer than humans. Candor had been a professional broomstick athlete in his youth and his lean frame still hinted at it. He retired early thanks to a busted knee and two broken wrists and was escorted into the sales profession by a whole host of fans who kept showing up wanting to meet him. "Someone's trying to sell a broomstick."

"You're the buyer," Bane insisted, though that wasn't always true, not when Candor was home with the aches or his once-a-year head cold at the beginning of winter. Bane just really hated negotiating purchases.

"Go start the process. Let me unfreeze and I'll be out there to help ye."

Bane let out a groan, grabbed his scarf, and stormed outside.

He could immediately tell the fellow was anxious; it didn't take a wolf's nose to smell the nerves on him. These weren't unusual, the sellers who were selling what they didn't want to sell because the winter holidays had put them into debt.

"Bane Woods," he said, striding up with as much confidence as he could muster. "Welcome to Best Buzzems. How can I help you?"

"Hallo," the man said, accepting the hand he was offered to shake. "I've got this beauty I need to part with."

"Sure, let me take her for a spin and I'll let you know what we can offer you." Bane was already swinging his leg over the handle when the man began to protest.

"No need, she rides fine."

"I'll bet, but I still need to see *how* well so I can give you the best deal."

Deal.

Value.

Guarantee.

He learned these buzzwords in New Brooms sales. They were rarely uttered on this side of the practice lot since hardly anything over here had value and the only thing they could guarantee was a mildly bumpy ride home. Bane wasn't much of a rider anymore, but he had raced in his youth. When he tested a broomstick, he was mostly making sure it could make the lap around the lot, sensing where it needed fine tuning. Then Candor and Doc got together and figured out an offer price. First, Bane had to make sure the thing could leave the ground.

"It's broken," the man hurried to add. "I think I left it out in the sun too long. Won't work."

Bane paused, already straddled. "Alright," he said carefully. "Mind if I take it inside? Say, why don't you go next door? The coffee there is excellent. Have a cup while you wait."

"I just need a few golds for it," the man insisted. "Quick sale. Don't have much use for it."

"Mhm, I understand, it's just policy..." Before Bane had fully dismounted the handle, the man grabbed the broomstick and yanked it out from under him. "Hey!"

The man jumped on and kicked off, but the broomstick bucked and swerved, trying to rid itself of its rider. It narrowly avoided collision with the family Ezra was showing the latest Cloud Sweeper to. Eventually the broom got airborne, but it flew as if it had a nail stuck in its side.

"Stolen broomstick," Candor muttered, making Bane jump. The old man slid around the lot like a shadow, and he often startled Bane. "It'll do that if it's not properly disenchanted and then reenchanted by the owner."

"What do you mean?"

"Each broomstick only responds to its rider. It's a new safety feature they introduced a few years ago. Now it's mandatory on all new models. Spells are put on every new broomstick to only allow riders that have been given access to it. When a broom is sold, Mic goes and reenchants it so that only the new rider can ride it. Uses their thumbprint like a key."

"What about test flights? We're not taking thumbprints from prospects for those."

"Every broomstick can be ridden as far as the end of this lot before it drops out of the sky," Candor explained. He motioned around them. "Invisible perimeter set up. Clever magic. As for those used brooms, most take them to a sorcerer to unlock before they bring them here to sell. Cheaper that way. Mic charges too much, says it's a waste of his time. Anyway, if it's not unlocked and someone else tries to ride it, it'll try to buck off the thief like it did that man. It'll still go, but it'll fight the whole way. Yerp, that broomstick was stolen. Got to watch out for those."

"Why did he think he could sell it?"

"There are shops that will buy it," Candor assured. "We're not one of them." He set his hand on Bane's shoulder, ready to guide him back inside where it was warm, but they paused when they saw a team of pigeons above approaching the lot carrying a long, narrow wooden crate. All of New Brooms, including Honey, ran out to greet the exhausted pigeons, crowding around as they lowered the box to the ground. Gerwin barked orders to get the box inside as he took the parchment from one of the pigeons, who transformed into their human form, to sign. "Yer lucky," he said to Gerwin. "This is our last delivery before we too join the strike."

Bane narrowed his eyes. "Hold on, is that…?"

Candor shoved Bane in the direction of New Brooms, and they took off after everyone else clamoring back inside. They got through the door just as Aeryn and Ezra ripped the box open to reveal the newly released Twisted Twig.

The broom was a masterpiece of craftsmanship, the handle hewn from basswood that twisted naturally in a graceful spiral. The wood was polished and glossy and looked so smooth it seemed hands would slip right off, but the grooves were impeccably whittled to ensure a safe grip. Enchantment wove through those grooves like threads of stardust, pulsing with subtle power. The broom's gold-capped birch bristles were fanned out elegantly to catch and ride even the faintest breeze.

The room went silent in awe.

And though she had no right, Honey was the first to step up and touch the broomstick. She took the Twig off the model holder and held it out, did a turnaround it as if it were a loving dance partner. Outside of the box, the threads of stardust pulsed to life, thrilled to be touched by a warm hand. The handle permeated a faint scent of petrichor, a sign of the protective spells woven into its core—wards against storms, hail repellant, and a cushioning charm to make even the roughest landings feel like touching onto a cloud. She looked at her father and whispered, "It's beautiful."

The room erupted in chaos.

"I want to hold it!"

"Me first!"

"Not with yer grubby hands!"

Gerwin let out a ferocious whistle to silence them. "Not before Mic enchants it," he barked, and nodded to the sorcerer. Mic took it gingerly from Honey and carried it to his workshop as if it were made of glass. Everyone else scattered in a panic to ring their prospects.

"Maybe they'll let us give it a test spin?" Bane asked, already feeling Candor's hand pull on his collar.

Candor snorted. "Dream on, wolfie."

2

Copper University

There were about a dozen Copper Universities in Citeel, brought on by the sudden craze for caffeine that was introduced to the city by Baroness Eugena Copperton, the daughter of the Head of the Copper Mint. Her father was an artist who wanted his children to also find a passion, and while his son became a pastry chef, she became a coffee connoisseur. Eugena Copperton traveled the continent and discovered all sorts of strange new nuts and beans, including one called a coffee bean, which was roasted, ground, and brewed like tea, spotted with milk and spiked with sugar. The locals taught her this process, showing her how it also paired well with vanilla and chocolate and even a drizzle of caramel. Through her own testing back home, she discovered that essence of hazelnut delighted the tastebuds and a dash of peppermint extract on a cold day tantalized the mind and warmed her up right down to the toes.

And the aroma of roasting these nuts! It was rich, inviting, and earthy, a scent that reminded many people of simpler times, of places beyond the cramped city center. Every Copper University roasted its beans in-house to ensure perfectly balanced flavor. The first store was a wild success, dominoing the opening of a whole chain of them. Now the coffee chain's logo—a copper mug with steam curling into the shape of a quill pen—was instantly recognizable. The shops hired just about anyone and fired them for just about any reason. The lounge always smelled of roasted coffee and whatever the last drink the barista had made. Customers could drizzle as much sugar and cream into each cup as they pleased, and the toilets in the back were the modern, flushable kind. Best of all, the entrance fee only cost a copper, the price of a cup of small black drip coffee.

Citizens flowed through these shops every morning. Some went right in and right out after shooting back a quick espresso at the bar. Others arrived, drank their drink, used the facilities, and then were off to work, feeling as if they'd already accomplished something big that day. Still others took seats in the over-cushioned chairs and lounged for hours, being either retired, unemployed, or feigning sick that day. There were students who came after classes to study either solo or in obnoxiously loud study groups. Mothers met to lament and seek advice, bouncing their babies on their knees, stuffing bits of crumb cake into drooling mouths while constantly pushing their mugs out of chubby fingers' reach. And of course, there were always the tormented poets and hopeful writers, who spent the least and stayed the longest.

Bane was an ex-employee. His friend Dante still worked at the one on Swan Dive Drive. Dante was a demon, accidentally summoned by a child playing with a forgotten spell book in his grandmother's attic. After they both stopped screaming, the demon jumped out the window and ran until he stumbled through the front doors of this exact coffee shop. Lucky for him, Jaymie Lloyd the franchise owner was something of an activist. It was easy to be one when her husband owned a bank. They had no children. Her calling became to employ the needy, and nothing screamed *charity case* like a discombobulated demon.

"Are there many of you? What's the underworld like? That is where you're from, is it not?"

It had been the least conventional and perhaps a totally illegal job interview, but it got him the job and so Dante never complained. He had no memory of anything before he was summoned and had no idea where he came from. As far as he knew, he'd never had a job interview to compare it to and so didn't know any better. He was here in this strange new place, but at least he now had a job and a place to stay. He quickly acclimated to city life, starting with wearing conventional clothing that Jaymie gifted him from her husband's overflowing closet.

This explained why Jaymie tolerated ex-employees loitering in her shop and drinking coffee for cheap. Or in Bane's case, free—from those Dante "accidentally" made extra.

"You'll drink me out of house and home," Jaymie scolded, seeing Bane take a seat at the bar facing the drink-making station, over which he could easily chat with the baristas. She kept in shape with morning laps in her private swimming pool and always showed up to work perfectly made-up, from her colored red hair to the mole she drew just above her lip, though the corporate-issued apron and the rubber-soled black shoes did little to help her look desirable. Dante manned the massive espresso machine, which was all heat and steam and skin-scalding splashes, which didn't bother him one bit.

"Oh no! Another unclaimed cinnamon caramel latte!"

"Extra hot!" Bane shouted over the whistle of the steam.

"No, you don't," Jaymie snapped. "It's black or it's out the door for you."

"But I made it too hot! Here you go." Dante dropped the mug in front of Bane before his boss could swipe it into the sink. "Waste not, Jaymie, there are demons freezing to death out there."

It was a saying Dante shamelessly used too often. It made Jaymie gulp and go quiet. She went off to go slam the ice box door a few times.

"She'll be alright," Dante assured, pushing the mugs aside and dropping his elbows onto the bar in front of Bane. His jet-black hair was pulled back into a low ponytail and his ears were studded with gorgeous hoops that trailed all the way up their elegant curve. His crimson eyes trailed on Bane. "Her husband's been working extra-long hours trying to get that newly minted coin distributed in time for the coronation."

"What coin thing? The one in the papers?"

"That a-one. Banks are giving them out to their customers as tokens to use at the festival booths this weekend. Then the Crown is going to collect them from vendors and reimburse them. It's supposed to encourage spending at the festival, but people are already trying to use it around the city as free money."

"What are they worth?"

"Absolutely nothing. They're made of fool's gold. See here?" Dante went over to the mug by the register and tipped the cup so Bane could see inside. "Someone even tipped me with one."

These coins were the same size as the other coins minted in the kingdom but were exceptionally shiny. Bane plucked it for closer inspection. All of the official coins had the emblem of the royal seal on one side (two river otters swimming around each other in a hexagon, the motto "Fides Et Sapientia" smiling up from the bottom) and the creature that represented their respective mint on the other; for gold it was a chimera, silver a unicorn, nickel a rabbit, and copper a tabby cat. The fool's gold Bane held had the faces of the king and queen, one on each side, and the date of the coronation stamped on it.

"I don't even have a bank account," Bane grumbled and tossed it back in the mug.

Dante's eyes lifted to look over his friend at the customer waiting to be served. "Sorry love, didn't mean to hold you up. For here or to go?"

"For here, please."

Bane looked over his shoulder at the woman wearing a purple cloak. She was actually a harpy but was currently in her human form, tall with a serious face, hooked nose, sharp grey eyes. Her hair was shorn short on the sides and left long in the middle, styled so that it plumed up fashionably. It made him think of the feather crest of a cockatoo, if it were a black so shiny it almost looked blue. She stepped up to the counter, but before she could speak again, Dante had an enchanted quill aimed at the order slip. "Can I get a name for the order?"

"Harper. Leewood."

"Like from *The Harking Herald*?" Dante gave a little laugh, recognizing the name. It wasn't uncommon for people to give aliases here. As long as they picked up the right drink, he didn't care.

"Precisely." She gave a knowing smile. Dante's face went slack with shock.

"Not joking? I love your stories! What are you working on next, now that the baking competition is done and over?"

Wasn't that the million-gold question? Harper had been wrestling with it for weeks now, since her editor Eldron refused to let her back into the gossip section. She gave what she hoped looked like an indifferent shrug. "Who knows? Maybe if you let me pay for my coffee with one of those fool's golds, I'll have something to write about."

"Sure, I'll let you."

Harper's eyebrows shot up. "Really?"

Dante nodded enthusiastically. "Sure, just drop it in quick before my boss notices."

"Dante, you clumsy newt! Why'd you spill that..." Bane dropped his voice. "Quick, what did he spill?"

"Um, er..." It took Harper a few seconds of glancing between the two young men to realize what they were doing. "A flat white."

"The loveliest flat white you ever did brew!" Bane finished shouting. They heard a cabinet's doors smack in the back, and he snickered. "Every time."

"Will two coins do?"

"You set the price," Dante said, giving Harper a wink.

This delighted her so much she pressed two into his hand and dropped a third into the tip mug. "I hope tomorrow I don't find out I could have bought a sandwich with that, because those were the only coins I had."

"Could you imagine? Buying a meal from fool's gold? It would throw the banks and mints into chaos," Bane mused. Then he shrugged. "I imagine. I don't know much about trade...commerce..." In truth he didn't know much about money at all, never having enough of it. He didn't have much to his name at all. Broomstick commission was a tough competition, and *used* broomsticks...well, if there wasn't a base monthly salary, he would have come back to working the milk frother a long time ago.

Dante playfully covered his nametag. "Just keep me off the record, will you? This sort of thing...it could be seen as insider trading."

It was a bad joke, but Harper forced a laugh and took her drink. "Don't worry, you'll be one of my many trusted nameless sources."

Dante threw his rag over his shoulder, watched her go take a seat in the far corner. Then he dropped back down to eye-level with Bane. "You think she'll write about us?"

"Do you want her to?" Bane glanced over his shoulder where, sure enough, she had a quill racing over a fresh piece of parchment. "You won't get anything out of it."

"Glory, my friend!" Dante reached over and gave his friend's shoulder an enthusiastic squeeze. "I came from nowhere, nothing, and now I'm being quoted in *The Harking Herald*! Ah, I love this city!"

Bane envied his friend. Dante loved life, and yet he had even less than Bane had. Bane at least had a girlfriend, the flat he shared with her, and dinner dates once in a while when he could afford them. Dante lived in the attic of the shop, keeping vermin away and basically working for free, dusting and cleaning and tidying when he wasn't pulling espresso shots. But he loved it, and Bane envied him for that.

"I'll bring you the paper tomorrow if it's in there," Bane promised, finishing the last of the sweetened froth, and set his drained mug in the dish return bin.

"Tell Lusine I said hello!"

Bane waved over his shoulder and pushed the door open, headed home. He had meant to vent to his friend, but he already forgot what he had been upset over. Was he upset? All he could remember now was the arrival of the new broomstick, and he looked forward to telling Lusine about it.

3

Making Plans

Bane was cooking supper when Lusine Glowry arrived home, hunched over from the weight of her knapsack filled with books. The thick, dusty, moldy-smelling ones that bored most people to tears and had no pictures. Bane knew this; he had checked each one.

She walked to the calendar tacked to the wall and checked the date and corresponding phase of the moon. Only then did she move further into the room. Their furniture was sparse but sturdy, heirlooms gifted by their parents who seemed rather relieved to get rid of them. Nothing matched, not in shape or color or size, but the cushions were wonderfully worn in and the tables at least were level. It was also immediately obvious which pieces had come from Bane and which from Lusine, though Bane had crossed his fingers behind his back and told his mum they were equally nice, impossible to tell apart.

Lusine dumped her sack by the lumpy sofa, which was where she would probably be burning the cheap candles until her eyes drooped so low she literally wouldn't be able to read any more. She was in her final year of law school, and every bit of stress showed on her. She felt as if law text oozed from her pores, as if exhaustion permanently glazed her eyes. Sometimes, she felt she wore a halo of righteousness like a crown on her silver-haired head. While some babies were born a blonde that darkened, hers lightened over the years into moonlight threads. Her silver hair with her smooth, youthful skin was a startling contrast. It was what Bane had noticed first about her, and he loved to unpin the bun from her head after supper and brush out the frazzled tangles. He felt as if he were pampering the moon. Sometimes Lusine wouldn't let him, because it made her drowsy, but sometimes it did exactly what he hoped it would, and it turned into foreplay.

He kept her brush in his apron pocket just in case, so it was always in easy reach.

Lusine came up behind him and wrapped her thin arms around his waist, snuggled her cute button nose into his neck. His hair smelled freshy washed, and when she spotted the brush, she felt a tingling in her instantly.

Bane nodded to the carrots he prepared for her. They were wonderfully fragrant, roasted in plenty of butter and a few sprigs of rosemary, which he had snipped from a potted bush in the corner by the window. He had also dusted, folded their laundry, and topped off the oil in their lone lamp before she arrived. "Dinner is ready." He lifted her steak—medium-well—from the pan and tossed his on. He held it there for thirty seconds, flipped it over for another thirty seconds, then joined it on the platter beside Lusine's. After a few weeks of watching him devour raw meat straight from the ice box, Lusine finally begged that he at least give it a little color on the outside. And since he would do anything for her, he happily obliged.

He also went back to using a knife and fork. Though he still refused vegetables, he always prepared a side dish for her, for she once claimed, "Women cannot live on meat alone." She had rolled her eyes at the plethora of jokes he made at that.

They were absolutely mad about each other. Bane found her brilliant, beautiful, and liked her rules and regulations, the order with which she organized her life and brought him into it. Lusine thought he was outrageously handsome, easy to care for, and didn't mind that he was a werewolf. In fact, she saw it as a bonus. His lack of career drive didn't bother her either, as it let them have the power dynamic she preferred; their routines would revolve around her job as a lawyer after graduation, and Bane would adjust his schedule to hers. He put her on a pedestal, and she flourished on it.

Bane had wanted to propose to her within months of them meeting, but over dinner one night Lusine explained her carefully crafted roadmap of her remaining years of law school. She said without saying that she had no intention of throwing a wedding into the midst of it. They did move in together six months into their relationship, into the tiny loft above an ink and parchment shop in the heart of the city. They immediately molded to one another's schedule as if already a married couple.

Now that her diploma was fast approaching, Bane found himself admiring rings on women's fingers, peering into jewelry shop windows, and trying to discern how much money he needed to save up for a band. Seeing as how his coin purse was perpetually empty, he was getting a bit anxious about the approaching unstated deadline. He never disclosed to her how rocky his finances were, and because he always paid his half of the rent, she never asked.

It was a point of anxiety for him, not having any money. Sometimes Bane worried Lusine would leave him once she was making lawyer money, however much that was. He had a suspicion though. He saw the gold-embossed plates outside the nicest buildings in the city, advertising that *lawyers* were inside. He figured he would have to work hard and make enough money to afford the lifestyle she deserved. He told her only then would he get her a ring, which he often promised was coming.

"You idiot, you'll never catch up to me," she scolded. "I'm going to be an animal activist lawyer. I'm *leagues* ahead of you. You knew that when you gave me that free drink!"

He did know that, back when he was a barista at the Copper University, because he had read the cover of her book *The Codex of Claw, Paw, and Feather* before he interrupted her to ask, "What are you reading? And will a spiced apple cider pair well with it?"

It had, as did the bartender who served it to her. She had meant to settle in for a long study session, and he had meant to finish his shift up until his scheduled time, but neither succeeded. He went looking for a new job the day after he met Lusine, because she would never settle for a barista. *No offense, Dante,* and of course Dante didn't take offense. Nothing could offend that man.

On their third date, Bane decided it was time to come clean. He figured they had had two wonderful dates; she laughed at his jokes, he paid for both meals, and she hadn't commented on his aversion to vegetables. This was the time to confess. Let her back out now, before either one got too tangled up in the other. "What's an animal attorney?" he asked.

"It's exactly what it sounds like."

"Hardly. Do you represent dragons? Or shifters who turn into animals? Do you..." Here Bane gulped, tossed his luck into the ring. "...represent were-wolves?"

There was never a good time for Bane tell the girl he liked that once a month he got a crazy raging hankering to rip his clothes off and gorge himself on raw meat under the light of the full moon, preferably after running around like a maniac in the woods.

As it turned out, Lusine also got like that once a month, but the hankering was for chocolates rather than cold steak.

"I don't think I've ever met a werewolf. But I assume if they get in trouble, I'd be the one to help them out," Lusine said, not quite catching his drift.

"I...*I'm* a werewolf."

"Are you also in trouble?" It came out as a joke. But when he didn't say anything, she looked down and poked her meat pie and the gravity of what he said sunk in. She looked up and asked, "Well, are you?"

Bane shook his head. "I know the rumors," he said. "But werewolves don't just go around biting people."

"Were you born a werewolf?"

"Not exactly." Not at all. "Not...at all."

Bane's heart hammered in his chest. This was different than when he had told his mother. He told her angrily, defensively, insisting this was right, the way to prove his love for Selene. Now he had to tell the fall-out version of that love story.

"I...well, I fell in love with a werewolf." Bane grabbed his goblet of water and lapped it down. He watched Lusine's eyebrows shoot up, then catch themselves, realizing they were being tested. She carefully brought them back down.

"Oh?"

"Yeah, I was young..." That was what he was supposed to say, right? Young and stupid? But really, how much stupider was someone just a year ago? So he fudged the timeline. Actually, he omitted it completely, at first. "She was my first love. I didn't know better. She told me I had to convert if I wanted to prove my love for her, if I really wanted to assimilate to the pack lifestyle. She told me she needed to be with another werewolf who understood her ways. That's why I let her bite me." He shrugged. "Apparently, I still wasn't alpha enough. Shortly after, she broke it off."

Lusine gawked at him. The waitress came by then, offering to top off her pint, and Lusine looked at the woman as if she had offended her. Turning back to Bane, Lusine asked, "And there's no antidote?"

"Would you like there to be one?"

"I can't tell if you're the one joking now. I know nothing about werewolves other than the fact that they're allegedly dangerous, transform against their will by the light of the full moon, and live in packs."

"I live with my mum, I'll occasionally kill a fly when I'm on my A-game, and yes, I definitely transform once a month and get a ravenous appetite."

"Is that all?"

"Would you like to stick around and find out?"

She had. Because she studied animal law or because she liked him, he wasn't sure, but it blossomed into a very sweet romance. And so far, he'd kept away from her during the full moon.

Lusine wondered why. If their relationship was progressing as it should, should she not be there for him during his transformations? She felt the distance there, something telling her they couldn't be truly established as a couple if she hadn't seen him at his worst. When she brought it up, he joked that his worst was first thing in the morning, with his morning breath in her face.

"I went by the bank today," Lusine announced, sitting down at the table to their steak and carrots meal. "Got some of those fool's gold coins."

"Does everyone have a bank account except me? What happened to dropping coins in the teapot in your gnome cabinet?"

Lusine blinked at him in surprise. "You don't have a bank account?"

"When have you ever seen me go to the bank?"

"I assumed you just went on your own time." Lusine tried in vain to unscramble the look of disappointment that was clearly on her face.

Bane changed the subject. "Aren't those coins just commemorative?"

"We can spend them when we go to the festival." She pulled her plate in close and unfolded her napkin. "I was thinking we could all go. Take your mother. The festival is being held in the palace courtyard. They so rarely open it up to the public, and your mother always reads the gossip section of *The Harking Herald*. She's always telling me how she wants to get into the palace and see how the *other half* lives."

Bane snorted. "It's hardly half. Like, one percent."

"Do you work this weekend?"

"I mean, there's not really a schedule..."

"Can you ask to be off work?" Lusine asked, rephrasing and reemphasizing what she meant.

"Yes. Of course. No one's buying broomsticks this weekend anyway. Can I borrow your mirror to ring Mum?"

Mirror communication was all the rage right now. When once it took parchment and a quill to send a message, now all it took was a few runes drawn on the surface of a mirror to scry someone. It was ancient magic, once coveted, now popular thanks to the previous king's push to place a mirror in every home, business, and pocket. King Varundil went so far as to orchestrate a royal bake off that anyone in the kingdom could watch, but only via enchanted mirror. The demand for enchanted mirrors sky-rocketed, and now it seemed everyone in the kingdom had one except for Bane.

"It's time you get one." Lusine fished her compact mirror from her pocket. "Everyone has one."

"Who am I going to ring? These didn't exist before the royal wedding last year and now all of a sudden letters by pigeon are no good!"

"Mail delivery is tied up now with P.U.K.E. being on strike."

"The *what*?"

"The Pigeon Union of the Kingdom of Everdorne! They're in negotiation talks now with the new king. It's in a bit of a deadlock since we're in-between reigns right now, but they should settle on terms after the coronation. It's in the paper if you'd only read it."

"I don't need to read the paper. I have you to summarize it for me." Lusine rolled her eyes. "Mum's headed out to Bambrough for the winter next Monday. I suppose this will be a nice way to spend the weekend with her before she goes," Bane said.

"Are you house-sitting?"

"No. In fact, she's asked me specifically to stay out, because she's showing it. She said if she gets the right offer, she'll sell it." Bane's mum had been threatening to sell ever since she found out her son went and got himself bitten in the name of love. Bane wasn't sure if she really meant it. He and his mum were close, as close as mother and son could be who still, a decade and a half on, tiptoed around the death of Bane's father.

Marmie Woods kept busy with her Spells for the Elderly classes and gardening club and dragon spotting on the weekends, a club she was in with Lusine, who joined specifically to get to know her. Bane often worried about her, wondering how her health was, if she found herself lonely. She was getting on in years, having met her husband later in life and having had her first and only child when she was forty-five. The big city was harsh and loud and merciless, and Marmie so loved the months she spent in the little resort town on the lake by Superstitious Mountain. When Bane broke into her house during the last full moon and ate all her chickens, she'd confiscated the key from him and only let him in by invitation.

"Are you not worried about her moving?" Lusine asked, spearing a perfectly tender carrot with her fork. Bambrough was about a day's carriage ride away if the horse pulling it was spritely. Far enough away from Citeel that it took some planning to get out there, and never on a whim.

"Not really, but she's never actually alone. She's got friends she's made down there, and she always makes more wherever she goes. And I have you here. I'll be alright. I figure she has a few good years of independence left, and I want her to spend them wherever she likes before she has to move into our spare bedroom." He said this last bit teasingly, because obviously they didn't have a spare room now, but he also wanted the gravity of it to stick. For Lusine to know that he would be taking care of his mother in her final years, and Lusine would have to be okay with that, as his wife.

They did this to each other—dropped nuggets of truth like this. Little tests. Trying to gauge how the other felt without it being a direct, immediate confrontation. For Bane, it was always the impending threat of taking care of his aging mother, as her only child. Lusine clapped back with promises of long hours at the office. If Lusine was never around when Marmie was there, what did she care? Luckily, Lusine rather liked Bane's mum, and Marmie adored Lusine almost as much as her own son, if not perhaps secretly a bit more.

"Don't threaten me with a good time," Lusine joked, pulling the dessert brandy from the cupboard. She poured them each a thimble's worth and handed Bane the impossibly tiny glass. "Cheers. To another perfect meal."

"To us."

While Lusine enjoyed the burn in her mouth, Bane went ahead and poured himself a few more mouthfuls.

"Why do you do that? Isn't one enough?"

"Maybe for your metabolism. I'm over here growing fur inside of me and pumping blood at twice your speed. I hardly even wear a cloak this time of year."

"I noticed," she murmured, referring to the moon calendar she had consulted. She looked him over languidly. "You won't have to choose, you know. Between me and your mum. I like her. And you love her. She'll be my mum, too."

Bane nearly choked on the last mouthful of brandy. His eyes glazed over with sentimental shine. "Lusine, darling. Nothing moves me like the moon, and no one has moved me like you do."

"Moved you how?" Lusine teased, because Bane so rarely got sentimental.

"In...my heart?"

"Are you asking me?"

Bane grabbed her hand and put it nowhere near his heart. She giggled and groped and hurried to finish her glass. It barely made it into the sink before he swept her across the room to their bed, where they shucked their clothes and hurriedly made love. They stayed huddled under the covers, whispering lazily until they fell asleep, Lusine's final words scolding Bane for forgetting to scry his mother. "I'll ring her tomorrow," he promised, but Lusine was already fast asleep.

4

The Festival

Marmie Woods was a serious woman, most of the time. She raised her son on her own since he was ten and she liked to tell everyone that his teen years nearly broke the both of them, but didn't he grow into a handsome boy? She pinched his cheeks still whenever he was in close enough proximity, and she was most proud of his height and the thickness of his hair, which she knew was prized by all the women and envied by all the men. She herself didn't have much that she prized or that others would look twice at.

She had been a teacher in the city and helped the poorer citizens learn to read, write, and block curse spells. She looked the other way when the girls in her class poured together syrups and salts in the cafeteria and tried to hawk them as love potions. But she didn't tolerate bullying, fighting, or outright stupidity, and every child in her class walked the stage for graduation. And yet, her son had proven to be her greatest challenge.

First it was the bullying, because he was the scrawniest, then it was the depression from the death of his father, then it was the explosion of puberty where he seemed to stretch and grow at the speed of light and nearly ate her out of house and pension. He snuck out to be with friends though she always suspected it was to be with girls, which flattered her nervous son so much he let her think that and took the punishment gleefully. Then it was dating, trying to get him to focus on finding someone kind and smart when before he couldn't get anyone to look twice at him. All of a sudden, he was tall, handsome, and had hair so thick the calvary could lose its finest in it. Then there was that girl, and this whole throwing his life away to be a werewolf business. Marmie began to pray again in earnest when Bane met Lusine. *Gods, let this last*, she begged at any and all temples that crossed her path.

Marmie found no peace except to literally escape her life, which she began doing three years ago. It started with a girls' trip, her and a few other retirees. Then she found a cottage she rather liked, which she rented until the owner offered to sell it to her, which she felt obligated to do. Now she felt obligated to visit annually before the bitter cold of the city settled in and to enjoy the peaceful seaside life. She never invited her son, who her friends got her to realize was the source of her angst, to her dismay.

Old enough to solve his own troubles, they insisted, and Marmie finally decided they were right. She had left Bane the key to her home until the chicken incident, which was the eureka moment she needed to realize that while she loved her son, she needed a life beyond being his mum.

She still spent plenty of time with him, especially when he invited along that new lady of his, who was so smart and pretty and about eight rungs too high up the ladder for him. Marmie prayed often that Lusine wouldn't catch on. Marmie was thrilled at the festival invitation they extended her, and she put on her furs, her new boots, and her fine leather gloves in preparation. She had the official commemorative coins (OCCs) she received from her bank in her pocket, but she decided on the way to the palace that perhaps she wouldn't spend them. They would be nice to use as betting chips when playing cards with the girls in Bambrough. It would be sentimental, too, marking her last winter here in the city. She plucked up five more of the coins casually discarded in the streets while on her walk. It seemed no one else found any value or sentiment in them.

She told Bane that she *might* sell the house, but it was leaning more towards probably. The shingles liked to shake off too often and the houses on either side had already been sold twice over while she lived there. They had been fixed up each time, and both looked so fresh and proper next to her aging home. Marmie thought once she retired she would spruce her house up if the pension allowed, but she quickly abandoned the idea; it was sturdy and aside from looking about as tired as she felt, there was nothing wrong with it. But it was time. The cracks in the corners had gotten too wide, the windows no longer held out the city noise, and the place was haunted by memories she was ready to let go of. She had given her agent the lit candle to take an offer even half decent.

Marmie waved to the handsome couple she approached. They had offered to drop in and pick her up on their way to the festival, but Marmie liked the feeling of independence as she walked the streets of Citeel. Each day she strode alone was a win for her, and she wasn't yet ready to be feeble. That day she waved at people she knew, nodded at acquaintances she bought her weekly goods from, and in general enjoyed the bit of calm before the madness that was the coronation festival.

And madness it was.

All the drawbridges were lowered over the moat and foot traffic streamed in and out constantly, a colorful river of fine clothes, expensive jewelry, polished shoes, and wool-lined coats and cloaks. Bane gripped his mother's hand in one of his and Lusine's in the other, studied the pattern, and jumped into the stream when he saw a gap. It was thrilling, that moment when they weren't sure if they would collide with someone or a horse or a cart, but Bane had good instincts. Caught up with the swarm and careful not to get poked by any rogue sword sheaths, they crossed the bridge. They funneled onto the lawn where tents were erected, banners were strung, and signs pointed to the main attraction in the courtyard, where a whole city of brightly colored tents stood. Smoke and the smell of foods cooking wafted their way, goods stalls shouted at them, trying to hock their wares. Commemorative this, memorabilia that. Marmie lunged into the first tent, dragging her accomplices in after her.

Vests, scarves, vases, saucers, pins, flags of every size jumped at them from overflowing shelves. Trinkets, trinkets everywhere!

Marmie couldn't help herself—she started grabbing it all. She reached for cloths on shelves way over her head. Bane hurried to help and cringed when the orc shopkeeper noticed and beat him to her.

"The best price! You like? Is this what you like?"

Bane looked at Lusine and rolled his eyes. She ducked her head, hiding a giggle. He leaned in and whispered, "We're never leaving this tent."

"She's got to get hungry at some point."

"She can go days shopping instead of eating," Bane lamented. He sauntered over when his mother beckoned and became a living shopping shelf to store all the things she wanted.

"Mum, this is only the first stall," Bane protested. "What if we make a lap around the grounds, see all there is to see, and then if you still want these we'll come back? You never know, there could be a better deal out there—"

"No better price!" the orc snapped. "Are you calling me a swindler?"

"Go take Lusine on round and have something on me." Marmie reached into her pocket, pulled out an OCC, and handed it to him. Bane resisted the urge to roll his eyes again. What was he going to get with fool's gold?

"How am I going to find you?" he asked his mother.

"The coronation will be broadcast in one of those big mirrors. I'll meet you at the one closest to the bridge we crossed."

"Are you sure? You won't get distracted and forget?"

"So what if I do? I'll be having fun. Aha!" Marmie laughed and grabbed the stack of trinkets from him and shoved them at the owner before giving her son a dismissive wave. "Go. Have fun. I know I am!"

Bane wasn't about to argue. He snatched Lusine's hand and whisked her out of there as fast as he could, following his nose to a massive grill station.

"Wasn't the whole point that we were going to spend time with your mum?" Lusine asked, trying her best not to sound like she was complaining, because she really wasn't. She liked Marmie just fine, and she was great fun to play cards with, especially once she'd broken out the gin and it became impossible to tell if she was bluffing or if it was just booze confidence.

"You heard her, it's her choice," Bane said. He raised two fingers. "Two meat sticks, one rare. Bloody rare."

"Oy, don't be impatient," snapped the chef.

"I'm not cussing, I mean literally bloody. Give it just the tiniest scorch, would you? And do you take these?" Bane held up the fool's gold.

"Sure. One for two sticks?"

"Done." Bane slapped the coin into the man's hand. When they were ready, he accepted the sticks of meat and handed the cooked one to Lusine. "Thanks, Mum."

Lusine barely had her teeth sunk into the mystery meat before Bane grabbed her hand again and whisked her out of the warm tent and back into the cold, the skirt of her blue dress swishing behind her. *On to the next one.* She didn't mind being led around. She would have also enjoyed hunting through souvenirs with Marmie. What she really wanted to do was find a rowdy crowd in one of the mead tents and eavesdrop on their opinions on the state of the Crown. Did they like the new king? What were his *real* policies? She heard he was trying to eradicate dragons from the kingdom, is that reasonable? Ethical?

Lusine loved Bane, and they were good together because he cared about things she didn't and vice versa. Initially she thought that made them round each other out, then she worried if perhaps the overlap of interests wasn't wide or deep enough. Bane didn't mind hearing his news secondhand, whereas she read *The Harking Herald* provided in the school's lounges and watched the unofficial news channels in her mirror, sometimes letting it run in the background as she studied. She understood though that the basic necessities that Bane worried about—holding down a job, finding a place to hole up once a month with enough food to last the full moon's night, taking care of his aging mum—took up so much of his waking time that he viewed being worried about the troubles of strangers as a luxury. But he enjoyed her being his source of worldly information, and she loved to sit in his lap in an oversized chair and pet his hair and tell him all the things she had heard and learned that day. He did not contradict her or try to tell her an even more fantastical story he had heard. When they spoke, they shared information, and it was valuable, no matter who it came from. Their lack of interest overlap gave them both so much to share with one another by the end of the day. And at the core, they did care about the same things and wanted similar futures.

They would be able to live out their fantasies of comfortable lives because, despite Bane's money troubles, Lusine secretly had plenty of money. Her family lineage was full of scholars; old, forgotten aristocrats who didn't need to work and so studied whatever they liked and lived comfortably in obscurity. She had a title as well, a minor one, one she didn't advertise and hadn't yet told Bane about. If he ever cracked open a history book on Everdorne he would have easily been able to find her family's name in it, but he never did and probably never would. Not unless it had pictures. This let her be a bit incognito, to be whoever she presented herself to be to him, and it thrilled her. He liked her because of who, not what, she was.

Despite the sack of coins in her dress pocket, Lusine pulled out the three OCCs she'd gotten from the bank and pressed them into Bane's hand because she knew how he would react.

"We're rich!" he exclaimed and pulled her in for a kiss. "Let's get you a wacky scarf or maybe a tapestry of His Majesty!"

There was no shortage of tapestries or wacky scarves, but they all cost far more than the OCCs. They demanded real money to be bought, and Bane grumbled, wondering aloud who would honestly work hard to make money to then waste it on the face of someone they didn't even know. Lusine laughed; that was one way to think about it.

They ended up spending the OCCs on a plate of oil-drenched noodles and a small heap of charred chicken. Bane didn't complain as they ate and made sure Lusine had her fill before he scraped the leftovers directly from the plates into his mouth.

They wandered back to the bridge as the announcements were made, passing the repetitive tents popping kettle corn or peddling beauty potions, lopsided hand-sewn pointy hats, or crystal bracelet-making kits. At every festival there were always a handful of these, the latest flare of work-for-yourself marketed businesses, packaged in boxes and sold mostly to mothers who wanted to make an income on the side but didn't have many marketable skills.

Bane and Lusine almost didn't find Marmie under her stack of packages. She would have begun unwrapping each one and showing them off immediately if her son hadn't insisted that she could, later, once they were home. Bane put one arm around his mum's shoulder, the other around Lusine's waist, and they watched the massive mirror flicker to life and broadcast the coronation.

"Say what you want about the royal family, being alive to see a coronation is great fun," Marmie announced once the mirror flickered off, revealing the staring, blinking crowd reflected back at them. They shuffled away, embarrassed, and Bane grabbed his companions' hands and once more ducked into the channel of travelers streaming across the moat bridge.

The sun was setting and the walk to Marmie's house was full of the spectacle of drunks running around, waving flags, bellowing in song, "Maybe this Crown! Maybe this will be it? Long live our king!"

"What are they hoping for?" Bane asked. "He spoke of bettering the health of the kingdom and the end of the dragon reign of terror. I feel fine and I don't think dragons are so bad."

"It's because I raised you right," Marmie said, and hiccupped. Lusine eyed the bottle of golden mead in Marmie's hand, something that had been handed to her by a friendly stranger right after they crossed the bridge. She was meant to share a mere swig but never returned it, and so they had brought it along, taking turns passing it back and forth. It was nearly empty, and Lusine gingerly pried it from Marmie's hand, deciding she had had enough.

"That you did." Bane pressed a kiss to his mother's temple and helped her up the few steps to her front door. It was one of the few neighborhoods that wasn't built above shops. Though the house had been purchased for a reasonable price, the value had since shot up exorbitantly. Bane didn't dare ask by how much, though if he had asked his mother in that moment, she would have gleefully shared the price she listed on the market.

They piled into the living room with its ancient, well-used furniture. Every cushion was permanently sunk in, not a single spring willing to uncoil after all the years of wear. There was a healthy layer of dust on every surface, not in thick coats as if it was never dusted, but as if the spans between dusting were simply stretching more and more of recent late. Things were tidy but cluttered, room for them to be "put away" long having run out on all the shelves in all the cabinets. Bane dropped the two massive sacks of purchases onto the floor. Lusine went to grab them the pitcher of water and came back to find Marmie on the couch, directing Bane as he gingerly unwrapped one package after another and set them on the table, admiring them each with an appropriate amount of feigned enthusiasm.

Bane looked up and raised the teapot embossed with the newlyweds' faces above his head. "Look, Lusine, for us!"

"I was just saying we need a very nice teapot," Lusine lied, joining Marmie on the couch. She echoed the praise parade until all the tchotchkes were unwrapped and were found homes around the house. Bane wanted to yell that these would just be more things they would have to rewrap and box if and when his mother moved, but he kept that to himself.

Finally, Marmie stood up and retrieved the OCCs from her pocket. "Thought about spending these but thought better."

"Why? They're not worth anything now," her son said, seeing not coins but skewers of delicious meat he could have enjoyed.

"They can become a collector's item, you never know!"

Bane looked around the room full of bookshelves that hardly held books, the overcrowded mantle above the fireplace, the cupboards in the kitchen that didn't all house dishes. All open space had been taken over and crowded with trinkets, including many from the last coronation over thirty years ago. Commemorative dishes on plate stands that Marmie claimed would grow in value, that she could someday sell in a jam, but never had. Instead, they all tragically turned sentimental. Bane took in his inheritance and tried not to cringe. "They won't be worth anything, Mum."

"You never know. Maybe if there's an assassination?"

Lusine let out a laugh. "Maybe. But then they'll just make commemorative plates from that. Remember the scenes that were painted and sold everywhere of that dwarf returning the dragon egg to its mum? They were wild and completely made up. One was of him hiding behind his shield as a massive stream of fire poured out of her mouth. In truth he was wielding a rolling pin and meat cleaver!"

"Yes, well, you never know," Marmie huffed. She stood up and walked over to her new teapot on the mantle—the one that matched the one she gifted Bane and Lusine—and dropped the OCCs inside. "We'll use them when you come over to play cards. And we'll always remember what a nice time we had at the festival."

"Definitely," Bane promised. He asked his mother if she was hungry, and when she said no, he motioned for Lusine that it was time to go. "Are *you* hungry?" he asked, stepping out the front door.

"Always," she lied, wrapping her commemorative scarf around her neck and stealthily dropping a few real coins into Bane's pocket for him to find. He did and kissed them with excitement.

"I forgot I had these! Come on, we deserve a feast." He led her to one of their favorite little meat pie shops which was open late, served beer warm, and offered a vegetarian option.

They huddled in a booth recounting the day, giggling over the teapot they were gifted, which sat watching them on the table between them.

"I'm going to make tea in this every morning," Lusine threatened.

"Don't. We'll get some sort of mystery paint poisoning. Are you finishing that?"

Lusine pushed her plate to him, watched Bane gobble the rest up. She smiled. *A slice of pie, a slice of life.*

5

Coffee for Coin

Bane thought the article about the coins would simply turn into an inside joke that he and Dante and a sort-of-famous journalist shared when the article still hadn't come out the day of the festival. He checked Lusine's copy of *The Harking Herald* when they arrived home that night. There was no paper Sunday, but when, on Monday, he overheard Dutch yelling about buying a cup of coffee for fake coins he jogged across the lot to ask, "What are you going on about?"

"It was in the paper this morning." Dutch sniffled, rubbing his red nose. "Some idiot at one of them Copper Universities took fool's gold as payment. So now they're equating those coins to be worth something like five coppers."

"Come off it, a cup of coffee's no more than three," Ezra countered. He had his hands hidden under his cloak, also shivering from the cold, kicking at the dead, crunchy grass under their boots.

"Still. If I had gone through the fair ground and picked up every fool's gold coin on the ground, I would be able to finally retire from this shite hole," Dutch muttered.

"So why don't you?" Bane asked. "Go back there and pick them all up? A bit like fishing in the fountain, isn't it? You could, but you'd be looked at as a looney."

"No, it's illegal," Ezra countered. "Upsets the royal fish or whatever."

Bane looked at him as if he were mad. "What fish? Royal fish? In the pond in city center that everyone always shakes their pockets into for the name of love and luck?"

"That money goes to the poor," Dutch snapped. "It's charity. Can't steal from the poor, or you become poor, by the gods."

"There's no curse from picking up OCCs from the ground." Bane thought he'd sound a bit fancy, calling them by their official name. Maybe this made him sound like an expert on them.

"OCC?" Dutch asked, eyebrows furrowing.

"Official commemorative coins." It annoyed Bane that this didn't impress the other two like he thought it would. "That's their name. It's what they're called."

"Doesn't much matter does it, because everyone's used them or tossed them by now," Ezra said.

"Nah, my mum's kept some in a teapot for commemorative reasons." Bane rolled his eyes. "Suppose she holds onto them long enough she could retire."

The other two chuckled, agreeing this was silly, that it would all blow over.

If only they knew what mayhem was coming their way.

"Mel's here," Honey shouted from the door. She didn't bother coming out. She didn't bother doing much, to be honest, but it was her right, being the owner's daughter. It wasn't fair, just like it wasn't fair that everyone else wasn't born a royal, but Bane tried not to let the rage of that work itself up to his head most days. Lusine for whatever reason defended them, saying it was all luck, no one could help to whom they were born.

"So strip them of their title and the bags of money and let them work it out like the rest of us have to," Bane had said. "We're all born naked all the same, why not even the playing field?"

When Lusine hadn't responded, he assumed it was because she agreed with him. Not because she was secretly harboring a title herself.

"See ye, lads." Bane jogged over to catch the door Honey didn't bother holding open for him. He assumed she was rude to him because she had a crush on him. In truth, she thought he smelled funny, but that was only a projection because she was one of the few at the dealership who knew what he was.

Mel Bone was an imposing woman, tall and sturdy. Her dark hair was cropped short, which showed off her cartilage piercings and a tattoo behind one ear that was so old and faded it was hard to make out. She had three boys in their teens and now, twelve years after her last son was born, found herself pregnant with her fourth, a baby girl she hoped. Unlike her, Mel's husband was a quiet man, an accountant who preferred numbers over people. It was a good profession, an honorable one even, but it didn't pay nearly as much as people assumed; just because one touched gold didn't mean that it somehow rubbed off onto the handler.

Mel was there getting her Extra-long Wayclean serviced. One of the boys was trying to learn to ride, and she had insisted they buy him a used broomstick. Her husband Homer countered this and said they already had a broomstick, a perfectly good one. Never mind that it was long enough for two to sit comfortably astride, three when the boys were younger. To no one's surprise, her eldest backed it right into the mailbox, which had their pigeon roosting in it. Old Peter tumbled out of the nest, transformed, and gave such a gibberish swearing at the boy that Joyce burst into tears and nearly snapped the broom in half trying to run with it through the door to his mother. Mel had to console everyone and beg the pigeon not to leave, not in his old age, where would he go? Who would deliver mail as dutifully as he? Then she shot Homer a glare, grabbed the broom, and had a very precarious ride around the edge of the city to Best Buzzems.

Most of the bristles had snapped to the side and would need a full replacement, Son explained to Mel, who was upset, but not upset at him.

"He's going to work this off, alright," Mel told him, though Son wasn't sure whom she was referring to. She pushed through the door from the Service Drive into the New Broom's showroom to wait in the lounge. This had been tactfully designed so that salesmen could casually engage with waiting customers to offer upgrades to newer models: *Don't you get sick of the way the wood starts to splinter after a few years? Let me show you the new Dashing Duster while you wait. Get a grip on that!*

"Oh, hello Bane. I've had a morning." She accepted the coffee he offered her and followed him to take a seat in the lounge that was becoming more or less her home away from home.

"Did this happen this morning?"

"Aye. At least it happened today, and not yesterday or tomorrow. Mondays make it worth it, eh?"

Bane raised his own cup in a toast. "To Mondays."

As if on cue, the front door opened and a jolly, "Hallo!" rang through the showroom. "Turkey legs! Half off!"

"I love it when he's early." Mel jumped up off the couch. She wobbled a moment from the momentum, placed a hand on her tummy to steady herself. "Toby! My friend!"

"Mel, my friend!" Toby, who was a shifty, scrawny man about half of Mel's imposing height, took her hug greedily. He lifted the lid of the rolling box he dragged after him and the smell of perfectly roasted meat spewed up like a mushroom cloud. "I have salt & pepper, smoked paprika, and honey glazed. And plain, of course, but you're not a plain lady."

"Never. Bane! Which one do you want?"

Bane walked over and peeked inside. He wanted all of them, but the coins in his pocket were light until next payday. He needed to make his coins stretch until then. But half-off turkey legs? How could he resist?

Many solicitors trickled in throughout the week; there was the hot drinks cart, the sausage on a stick man, and then there was the pretzel lady with her crucifix of pretzels: *plain, salt, or cinnamon sugar, love?* Toby was always their favorite though, and always he insisted his turkey legs were half off, but they had no idea when they were full price. Never here, that was for certain, since he only ever came on Mondays. Surely it was a sales tactic, and from one professional to the other, Bane had to take his hat off to the man.

"I buy six of these and it keeps my boys fed for at least half a day. Absolute animals, the way those eat. No offense," Mel said as she counted out her coins.

Bane laughed. "None taken. You make a fair comparison."

Mel was also one of the few who knew, because she liked to talk and even more to listen, and she spent an awful lot of time at the dealership. She took the legs wrapped in wax paper and stuffed them into her own box, which always traveled on the back of her broomstick, usually full of meals to deliver or groceries.

"Just a salt & pepper for me, Toby," Bane said. He took his turkey and followed Mel back to their seats, where they wouldn't be bothered by the circling salesmen. She was a loyal woman, to her husband of two decades and to her beast of a broomstick for the last six. She had made it abundantly clear early on that she wasn't interested in upgrading until her broomstick literally broke in half under her.

As they munched their turkey legs, Mel answered the chimes on her personal mirror. Orders for this, for that. Check-ins from anxious clients who needed assurance that yes, their groceries would be delivered on time this week, same as every other week.

Mel finally returned her mirror to her pocket. "That's enough work on my day off."

Bane took her stripped bone along with his and walked to the trash to drop them in. Gerwin always complained that the stink of food would deter customers, but Dutch finally lost it on him and said they wouldn't work while starving, and there hadn't been an incident since. "It must be nice, not having to wait for a pigeon to get orders," he said, finding his way back to Mel.

"Downside is people expect things instantly now, but I can't just toss groceries through the mirror, now can I? Not like they have a choice with the pigeon strike now. It's either me or it's nothing. Not even my own pigeon works anymore."

"It's not strange, having a pigeon permanently?"

Most people made away with hired help as fortunes dissolved, were gambled away, or divided up amongst many children's inheritances rather than passed down to just one. Footmen, maids, and personal pigeon messengers eventually had to find jobs amongst the masses, in factories or storefronts instead of serving one master. Pigeon shapeshifters suffered especially, and those who lost permanent employment banded together and, through the help of merciful King Argo, formed P.U.K.E., the kingdom's sole official letter mail delivery system.

"Why, because he's a shapeshifter? Old Peter hasn't transformed back into a human in five years. Well, not until the incident this morning, and that was out of sheer terror. He's old, he's tired, and he doesn't like fussing with clothes anymore, turns out. I think the boys will be in shock for the next few years. But he's not going anywhere. He's been with me and my family for fifty something years now. Private hire, back in the days when loads more people had butlers and maids and footmen. He's old-school. He was loyal, so now we're loyal. That's why we got him the mailbox. It's cute. Homer built it, the boys painted it. Any day now he'll die in it."

"Do you worry what will happen to the pigeons once everyone turns to mirrors?"

"I doubt we'll phase old methods out completely," Mel insisted. "We'll always write on parchment with quills and use coins to buy our turkey legs."

"What about this pigeon union? It doesn't affect your job?" It wasn't until recently that broomstick delivery began to take off, literally. Mel and other large-item deliverers provided a wonderful service to the city for those who could afford it.

"I'm self-employed, a freelancer. My own boss. I'm not part of any union. I'm definitely no pigeon. Besides, there's all this trouble with the negotiations with this new king. I heard he's bringing in the big guns, the Hawk."

"Who's that?"

"Some expert negotiator." She shrugged. "I get hired because of who I am. It's all about the customer service. People like to see the same face over and over, build that trust. It's the reason I come here instead of to the shop closer to my house. If I'm going to kill half my life waiting in a lounge, let it be here with you fine folks." Mel gave Bane a knowing nudge with her elbow.

Bane rolled his eyes sheepishly, then remembered the exciting news he had been itching to tell her. "Did you hear? The new Twisted Twig arrived."

"Shut it! Let's go see!"

Bane jumped up and led Mel, giddy with excitement, over to the new broom that was displayed on a raised podium, a velvet rope around it. Stardust landers shone light from below, making the broomstick look like some sort of king on his throne.

"How much is it?" Mel asked, visibly fighting with herself to keep from reaching over the rope to touch it.

"If you have to ask you can't afford it," Aeryn said, stepping up to the pair. "Gerwin's already calling all the rich folks on his contact list to offer them rides."

"Oy, you're not only going to let them take a ride on it, are you?" Mel asked, her eyes pleading.

Bane and Aeryn exchanged a look. Aeryn took two steps and peeked into the general manager's office. Then he went in, grabbed the ring of keys off the desk, and trotted over. He pressed the key into one of the gold orbs holding the velvet rope and that section of the rope recoiled, allowing entry. He tossed Bane the keys and gingerly lifted the Twig. When he turned, he saw every pair of eyes in the room locked on him.

And because he was Aeryn, the golden boy, he glared right back, daring any of them to ask what he was doing. They did not, and the salesmen shuffled their customers away to look at more reasonably priced broomsticks in their budget.

Aeryn handed Bane the broomstick. "You hand it to her. If anything happens to it, it'll be on *your* head."

"I trust Mel." Bane locked eyes with Mel, who seemed infinitely more sure of herself than the two men were of her.

"Don't worry, I'm not one to fall off sticks," she joked, patting her belly. It was hard to see because of her winter cloak, but under there was the swelling of a second trimester belly.

Aeryn burned with embarrassment. Bane shook his head and turned, led them outside.

Bane pressed his hand to the place on the stick he knew had an inconspicuous button and the twigs, which were pressed tightly together into a bundle, flared apart with a *poof*. Ready to ride.

"You go first," Mel insisted. "I know yer dying to as much as I am. If they ask, tell them I needed a demo."

Bane hadn't grown up riding broomsticks. It was a rich person's sport, like horseback riding or sailing. His mum couldn't afford him a pet dragon, much less a broomstick. But he had gone to the school his mother worked at, which had been a prestigious school, a mix of smart students and rich ones, and he made enough friends that several of them owned broomsticks and let him ride around the grounds before and after classes. He eventually became a pretty good rider.

Gerwin said it wasn't a job requirement, riding broomsticks to sell them, but it definitely helped land the job. Bane had no sales experience, no celebrity fame like Candor to pull in potential customers, but he rode very well, which impressed Gerwin. Lucky for Bane, when he rode a broomstick, he made it look so effortless it was the selling point—ease of use—that made most of his sales. To him, everything was easy to ride, but he convinced his customers that *this* specific broom they were eyeing was the smoothest one in the lot.

"Here goes nothing." Bane straddled the broom and kicked off. The Twig took to the air with ease and was completely at its master's command. It felt as if it anticipated Bane's intentions, turning the moment he thought to turn, gliding easily through the frigid air. Broomsticks were only as good as their physical craftsmanship and the enchantment that motored them, and it was clear that this model was the love child of both beauty and brains.

Bane marveled at the ease with which he glided around the lot, grass blades yellow, dead, and frost-bitten beneath him. There weren't many others braving the cold to buy brooms this time of the year, but some liked to exchange their models for nicer ones for the new year or felt there was luck in buying right at the start of the year. Bane whizzed around these prospects easily, so close over their heads some reached up to check if something had landed on them. Bane wondered if maybe the broomstick picked up on every twitch of his body, every squeeze of the muscles in his wrist and legs as he made a final lap, curving his flight path to the shape of the lot with minimal effort.

Perhaps there was a mind-reader spell in this one.

Bane landed soft as a feather in front of Mel, who was just about salivating.

"She's an easy ride," Bane began to explain, but Mel didn't need any more convincing. She cut him off with an eager, "I saw you ride, it sold itself." And then she was off. Mel let out a whoop of pure joy as the broom leapt into the air and did a swan dive as if it did a million of them a day. Mel did a quick loop-de-loop, pulling up then back sharply, which was unfortunate because the booger she had been trying to keep in flew out and slapped itself across a cheek.

The broom leveled out perfectly immediately. She landed almost as gracefully as Bane and wiped the snot from her face. "Got lots of interest in this one?"

"Loads," came a voice behind them. They turned to find Gerwin sauntering onto the lot. Bane froze, but his boss didn't look upset. He looked...proud, actually. "Already had Honey show it off in the mirror. I'm only offering rides by appointment. You're the lucky first." Gerwin winked at Mel. "How was it?"

Mel gave a happy sigh. "Have you tried it?"

"Sure, sure, but I have owned the last three models. This one's gorgeous, but I'm more of a Swift Saddle for the everyday commute."

"It's amazing," Mel gushed.

"Good. Well, if you decide you're ready for one, you let me know. In the meantime, your broom's ready. Doc will cash you out at the register. Bane, won't you put this back on the podium?"

"Sure thing, boss." Bane took the broomstick and led the way inside. Gerwin peeled off with Mel to escort her to the counter while Bane went to the podium. When the Twisted Twig was safely back on its resting ledge, he headed into Gerwin's office to deposit the keys.

The office wasn't a large room, but it had its not-so-subtle luxuries. Real leather seats. A desk so long Bane could have slept on it comfortably, made of ancient oak sourced from somewhere definitely outside the kingdom, maybe an elf forest. The wall behind the desk was a honeycomb of cubbies to store important parchments, all the deals done over the years. Gerwin didn't spend as much time here as Honey did, who, when she wasn't manning the appointment desk, came in to do the accounting. The salesmen had overheard through the door plenty of arguments between father and daughter, Gerwin always wanting to order the newer luxury models while Honey insisted that they weren't built for that sort of inventory, they were too north in the city for that. The southern dealerships did the luxury brooms, toys for the rich to jet off to their summer homes in a hurry.

Their dealership was more for the everyday commuter like Mel, or for athletes wanting to go professional. But over the years Gerwin, who had grown very wealthy, had met plenty of rich men with pockets deeper than Bane could ever fathom. And so every once in a while, a broomstick as beautiful as the Twisted Twig arrived.

Since Gerwin didn't spend so much time in his office, it didn't have any personal, fun touches. No tchotchkes, no expensive cigars lying around, at least not since the last time Bane and Aeryn went snooping through the drawers. But it had been a while since then, and if Gerwin was planning on making a sale as big as the Twig, surely he had bought a new box? Gerwin never said anything when a cigar went missing, but he never hid them in the same place twice. It had turned into a sport on the lot, flashing a stolen cigar to the others, enjoying their envy at the win.

Naturally, Bane went for the place he had found them last time, and of course they weren't there in the top drawer. *If he doesn't want cigars going missing, he ought to lock these*, Bane thought, not for the first time. There were parchments stashed in there, enough that Bane decided to pull them out to check under them, just to be sure. Nothing. He moved to put them back when the title at the top gave him pause.

Contract for Real Estate Sale.

Bane scanned the document, then flipped to the next page and did the same. And the next. He checked the dates on the signature line and looked up, squinted at the wall calendar across the room to confirm. Finally, he shoved the papers into the drawer and stormed towards the door. He nearly collided with Aeryn as he stepped through the doorway.

"Woah! Watch where you're going!"

"Come here," Bane growled and grabbed Aeryn by the collar, pulled him into the general manager's office, and shut the door.

"Are we snooping again? You're out of luck, I already checked this morning while you were stinking up the lounge with that turkey leg. You might want to consider eating some fiber every once in a while. It hurt just watching you eat that thing. Oh hey, do you have the keys to the Twig? I figure if you got to ride it, I should get to too before Gerwin sells it."

"He's selling the dealership."

Aeryn frowned. "No, he's selling the Twig."

"*No.*" Bane went around to the drawer and pulled the parchments back out. He splayed them out on the table and jammed a finger to the date line. "They're closing next week. We're about to be unemployed."

Aeryn looked at where Bane was pointing, then took another moment to scan the rest of the document. Then the next one. And the next one. "Huh. Gods, I think you're right." Aeryn looked up at Bane. "Well, what are you going to do?"

Bane balked at the question. "What do you mean?"

"I mean, now you know, so what? Are you going to stop it?"

"I can't. It's signed. It's done."

"*Exactly.*" Aeryn collected the papers and tossed them back into the drawer. He clasped a firm hand on Bane's shoulder and steered him out of the room. "Not your business, not your business. Now. Hand me the keys to the Twig. I've got to go clear my head."

Bane handed the keys over and stood by the door, dumbfounded, until Dutch shouted for him to get back across the lot, Candor was calling.

"Get a damn mirror," Dutch grumbled. "I'm not your messenger."

"Candor wants you," Honey called as Bane passed her desk.

"I know. Dutch told me. Isn't that *your* job?"

"Woah, watch your tone," she snapped, matching his annoyance.

As riled up as this discovery made Bane, maybe it wouldn't be so bad, no longer working with Honey, assuming she was leaving with her father. Unless he wouldn't be working there at all.

6

Women in Business

"Irma?" Mel called, pushing open her sister's front door.

Irma always insisted to "put it wherever" when Mel inquired where to park her broomstick, but her cleaner Cinthy always fussed over it. Cinthy wouldn't be happy unless it was parked outside on the street, but in the heart of the city, Mel was reluctant to do so. Even if her sister did live in the nicest, wealthiest neighborhood in all of Citeel. There were loads of amateur wizards who were good at unlocking broomsticks. It didn't take a sorcerer to pick pockets and jimmy locks.

Mel had tried putting the broomstick in the broom closet, but while Irma's house had vaulted ceilings many envied, they didn't extend into the broom closet, which housed fur coats instead of the intended brooms. So Mel parked her Extra-long where she always did, on the floor in the hall; since her sister's last pet dragon died, nothing would come along to munch on it.

"It's a tripping hazard," Cinthy had protested.

"Then don't trip over it," Irma snapped, and that had been the end of that.

"Irma?" Mel wandered deeper into the house, following the sound of muffled voices, her shoes clicking on the expensive marble floors. She noticed new paintings on the walls and wondered if they had been from the latest student artist auction. Irma never missed those. The drinks were always free and stirred with the most expensive liquors to attract patrons, which of course she was. Irma was the member of so many boards it was hard for Mel to keep track. Or she rotated through them, maybe that made it easier. All Mel knew for sure was that her sister was always buying a new outfit for something or donning jewels for a ball or planning some party or function.

The house was still lit with gas lamps, an extravagance compared to most people's oil lamps and candlesticks, but they hadn't been upgraded, like the rest of the neighborhood, to the new stardust lamps. The carpets were old and faded, though impeccably clean and in decent shape, since the only footsteps that regularly padded on them were Irma's and her live-in housekeeper's. Mel used to come around when the house was newly purchased and she and Homer were still just a couple, to attend the parties her sister threw to show off the many rooms of the four-story townhouse. They came once when the boys were little, when Irma decided she wanted to host Winter Solstice, but that resulted in a terrified pet dragon, one scorched curtain, countless mystery stains on the furniture and carpet, and two sisters that squabbled all the way into the new year. Irma stopped inviting Mel to parties, which Mel didn't want to go to anyway, not as her clothes grew plainer and more practical. The sisters now saw each other a few times a year when Irma dropped by to drop off birthday presents and to sit rigidly for a single cup of tea and ask Homer how much money an accountant made these days.

The voices amplified and grew clearer as Mel rounded the corner and stepped into the kitchen, where she'd never actually seen food prepared. Her sister was in there arguing with her long-time housekeeper.

Irma kept shouting as if she didn't notice the intruder, but Cinthy turned to Mel and jabbed finger behind her at her employer. "She's gotten into the bottle again, that one."

"What's all this about? What did you ring me for? You said it was an emergency," Mel insisted.

"She's trying to pay me with fool's gold." Cinthy slammed a handful of festival fool's gold on the polished island counter.

Irma crossed her arms. Nearly forty, she was very beautiful, and still very spoiled. She looked like a rigid, deflated version of Mel. Their eyes and noses matched, but they didn't quite sit the same in their different features. They rivaled each other in height, although the chairs didn't moan under Irma the way they did under Mel, pregnant or not. "Why not? I read in the paper it's worth money."

"Money's worth money," Cinthy snapped. "Now pay me what you owe, and you'll never see the backside of me again."

"Come off it Cinthy, she's been paying you for years," Mel pleaded. She whirled on her sister. "You're drunk, aren't you? Who brought you booze? Roy knows not to sell you any. Cinthy?"

Cinthy threw her hands up defensively. "I know she won't pay me back if I did."

"Let's go." Irma grabbed her coat and motioned for Mel to follow.

"Me? I'm not going anywhere. I've come to Cinthy's rescue and now I've got to get home."

"You promised!" Irma wailed. "You promised that Monday, *today*, you'd come with me to the Women Empowerment Meeting!"

"I agreed to no such thing."

"The Women *in Business* Empowerment Meeting," Irma corrected, adding in the magical words she sensed Mel needed to hear.

"Oh. Is that today?" Mel pulled out her pocket watch and frowned. "I've got to be back for when the boys get home from school."

"Cinthy can watch them."

"I don't watch children."

Mel dug through her coin sack and pulled out two silvers. "Won't you? Take the leftover booze from this house. You don't even have to feed them, they'll fend for themselves." When Cinthy snatched the coins and reached for the kitchen cabinet, Mel added, "Take the broom, it's in the hall. They'll be let out of school in an hour."

Thrilled to be paid for such an easy assignment, Cinthy gave a little wave. "Don't be out too long!"

"Let's go then." Mel grabbed her sister gruffly by the laced sleeve, but Irma jerked away. "Don't. You promised you'd keep an open mind. For me. For our futures."

"My future is fine." Mel leaned in for a whiff and made a face. "It's rotting you from the inside. You'll keel over dead if you keep up the pace."

"You have no idea what it's like," Irma wailed. "Working at the university is a bore. No one's hiring witches in this city! They all want Crown-certified sorcerers. Everyone's trying their hand with finding a patron to sponsor them through the mirrors by showing off their spellcasting skills *for free*. I wrote books about spells! You remember that, don't you?"

"I remember you writing *one*, and you're drinking away the royalties. Watch, soon you'll have to clean your own flat. Maybe that will sober you up." Mel marched ahead but shortly realized she hadn't a clue where she was going. She stopped long enough for her sister to catch up and grumbled, "Lead the way."

Irma Warmwood never married, never had children, and made her fortune young as the author of the best-selling spell book of her generation, *The Joys of Spell Casting*. Since then, she used her fame to never pay for anything again in her life, except her house, which was tall and narrow and squished between other perfectly upkept, colorful houses. It was located in the coveted Artists' District adjacent to the university campus, just across the moat from the palace.

That was until all of her suitors got married and had wives to purchase things for instead, and the taxes on her property rose and rose as it gained value. Irma finally got a job as an honorary adjunct professor at the university. They didn't actually hire anyone who wasn't a man, but with her reputation and looks it certainly had the students flocking. It was supposed to be temporary while she finished her second book of spells, but eventually she took on more and more university work until she was finally made a tenured professor without even meaning to be one. This upset a lot of the other staff and alienated her, because no one wanted to hear, "I don't know how I got it, I didn't even try!" while the rest dedicated their days and nights slaving away to earn that coveted position.

Irma lamented her work woes to Mel. Mel listened dutifully and decided to keep her opinions to herself. It was hard for Mel to feel sympathy for her sister, walking around the pruned lawns kept perfect even in the midst of winter. Where her sister never saw money as a problem, it was all Mel could think about lately. Her husband's job as an accountant was comfortable, safe, but with the new baby coming, everything had to be repurchased since they had gotten rid of all the baby essentials a decade ago.

Signs announcing the Women in Business Empowerment Meeting were posted on the university doors. The sisters joined the stream of other women, both human and plenty of non-human, filing into the building. The university only recently opened admissions to everyone else who wasn't male to counter the stagnation in student enrollment. Lusine Glowry was the first woman to enroll in the prestigious law school, and the sisters passed her student portrait hung proudly on display as they funneled in. Heads were heads as long as tuition was paid, the new university chancellor argued. And so Princess Damora passed an ordinance to allow any type of student—any gender, race, religion—to be allowed entry into the university. Even The Royal Confectionary Apprenticeship was finally forced to accept every sort of applicant, though they were the last to open enrollment. Today's event was meant to entice prospective students to see where their future could lead, if only they attended university!

Once inside, the sisters found themselves lost in a chaos of booths, everyone shouting over each other to be heard. Pamphlets were thrust at them, samples were punted in their direction. Mel looked around confused while Irma looked as if she absolutely survived on this sort of mayhem.

"What is this?" Mel asked, doing her best to avoid those beckoning behind the tables. "I thought you said this was a conference."

"It is." Irma looked at her, confused. "For women and witches in business."

"I see the businesses, but is there going to be perhaps a motivational speaker? This looks like a job fair. Do you need a job? Or do you have a booth?"

Irma understood Mel's confusion and let out a laugh. "No, it's for you! You said you need a new job, so here we are!"

"I have a job," Mel insisted, looking around herself again and recognizing several of the banners as the odd-jobs mothers did from their homes. Businesses that needed a little up-front investment ("Ask your husband to be your very first investor!"), self-motivation, and an endless commitment to restocking inventory.

The top contenders included Lovely Handmade, which sold beaded bracelet kits and encouraged sellers—er, *bosses*—to hold beading parties. Some sold the kits, some sold the completed bracelets themselves in haphazardly assembled booths at festivals. Teachers were absolutely sick of receiving the hideous bracelets as appreciation gifts.

Then there was Smelly Candles, cheap wax candles that came in every scent under the sun. Put them in every room of your house! Your neighbors' houses!

Pretty Potions was having its moment; beauty potions for hair, skin, acne, nail growth. Did they work? Those peddling the bottles swore by the stuff.

And of course Healthy Herb, to be brewed in tea and sprinkled into any soup for a slimmer waist and better gut health! There wasn't a single mother in all the kingdom who didn't secretly try the stuff at least once.

"I've picked up broomstick delivery," Mel reminded her sister.

"Yes, but you want something stable, don't you? Now that you're an empty nester?"

"I'm literally pregnant, Irma!"

Irma glanced down at her sister's belly. She squinted. Mel rolled her eyes and pulled apart her cloak to reveal the bump under her dress. "Well, you hide it well."

Before Mel could protest any more, Irma took her sister's arm and led her around, pointing out colleagues they passed, whispering their secrets into Mel's ear for entertainment while she picked up pamphlets and inconspicuously stuffed them into Mel's cloak pocket.

They passed a few booths representing different deity temples. Mel looked at them quizzically. Her sister noticed and whispered, "Temples are all just businesses, if you whittle it down."

An announcement directed everyone to file into the auditorium. Mel, who had grown quite flustered by now, told her sister she had to go relieve Cinthy.

"We still have an hour," Irma insisted and pushed her sister through the double doors.

The seats were rigid, uncomfortable, and reeked of the boredom that had seeped into them over the decades of putting on amateur theater productions. They were also not as wide as Mel would have liked, and she felt the armrests digging into either side of her.

"Stop fidgeting," Irma snapped.

"I don't want to be here," Mel shot back as the lights above dimmed.

Newly upgraded stardust lamps came to life at the edge of the stage. A spotlight snapped on. A moment later, a witch in a gorgeous gown glided to center stage to the drumroll of applause.

Mel looked around to see some of the women around her weeping. She gripped the armrests, terrified.

"Thank you, thank you! Sit, please sit! I'm sure all of you already know who I am from my mirror appearances. For those who don't, my name is Eleanora Knobs. Entrepreneur, mother, devoted wife, and your host for this evening."

She paused to allow the appropriate length of shouts and whistles to shower down on her before tapping the voice-amplifying crustal at her throat once more.

"It is my sincere pleasure to see so many women in business. Look at you! A round of applause to you!"

Everyone obliged. Mel got an elbow in her side from Irma, prompting her to clap on command as well.

"We have spokespeople from all these amazing businesses from around our kingdom, founded or run by women just like you. How many of you are your own bosses today, sponsored by Pretty Potions?"

A roar of excited shouts thundered through the room.

"Smelly Candles?"

Roar.

"Healthy Herb?"

A smaller *roar*, but with just as much gusto as the last two.

Eleanora nodded encouragingly. "It's about finding *your* community. That includes your fellow businesswomen believing in the same products as you. It's about your support system at home, including the person who helped you invest in the initial start-up costs. And of course, your customers, without whom there would not be a business. Yes, yes!" Eleanora shouted as the auditorium erupted once more into impassioned applause.

"This is a cult meeting, isn't it?" Mel whispered. Her palms were starting to hurt from slapping them together so long. "Irma, why are we here?"

"Oh, it looks like someone has a question!"

A second spotlight appeared and swiveled to shine right on Mel. She blinked against the blinding bright light before putting her hand up to shield herself. "No! No questions."

"Please stand up and tell us what you do."

"No, I'd rather not, thank you."

"Can you please speak up? Those in the back can't hear you."

"That's because I'm not here to speak."

Irma, horrified, spoke up instead. "She-she has her own business!"

"Gods, shut up," Mel hissed.

"And what is it you do?"

Mel cleared her throat. "I make deliveries."

"Deliveries?" Eleanora let out a chortle and a ripple of agreeing giggles echoed her. "Don't we have pigeons for that?" When Mel didn't respond, she pressed. "Tell us about this business. Are you self-employed?"

"I am."

"And it pays well?"

"It pays enough."

"And how do you make your deliveries? On foot?" Eleanora pointedly looked at the scuffed shoes poking out from under the hem of Mel's dress. Mel pulled her feet up ever so slightly to hide them.

"By broomstick."

"It's a great broomstick," Irma interjected, envious that her sister, a non-believer, was getting all the beams of attention from her hero.

"I'm sure. So you are here...because you are starting a business!" It wasn't a question, and in fact it garnered applause, which confused Mel because no, she wasn't going to start her own business. She *was* her own business. She wasn't going to start anything except the long march home in just a moment.

But Eleanora kept talking, kept commanding the room, weaving some sort of enrapturement spell as she spoke. "I bet you're here to rally supporters, aren't you? Well, you have come to the perfect place. Look around! Look at all the eager women wanting to build you up, support themselves by supporting you."

Mel narrowed her eyes, trying to see what Eleanora was trying to do here. From the smile that teetered on a smirk, Mel had a suspicion she knew where this was going, but it wasn't she who had the amplifying crystal. She wasn't the one with the hypnotic voice, gliding on the stage arresting everyone's attention. And so she could do nothing as the axe fell with the next words.

"Everyone, be sure to meet Mel in the lobby after we conclude our meeting here. She'll sign you right up for her broomstick delivery business. Oh! It looks like she has to leave early, duty calls! No worries, you'll be able to find her via her mirror rune."

Mel wasn't sure if Eleanora was the sorceress or if she had one working behind the backdrop somewhere, but the mirror rune to summon her suddenly appeared as a hologram beside Eleanora. "This is criminal," Mel seethed. She shoved her way out of the aisle, trying her very best not to bump her belly in everyone's face and already feeling her pocket mirror chime ceaselessly.

"Good luck!" came Eleanora's call at her back.

Outside the auditorium, Mel just about ran for the door. She huffed and puffed and pushed the doors open, which had been closed to seal out the bitter cold. The wind slapped her hot, burning face, and it felt deliciously refreshing. With the sun dipped below the horizon, the wind was picking up and the air was turning more frigid. The walk to Irma's and then the flight home would be brutal, but it would let her work her rage out of her system. Then she remembered her broom wasn't at Irma's house.

"You're not mad at me, you're mad at yourself," Irma called, running to catch up to her sister.

Mel whirled around. "This isn't what I bloody signed up for."

"You wanted to be your own boss!"

"I *am* my own boss. Apparently now I'm your boss and everyone else's mother's boss!" Mel pulled her cloak tighter around her. "I'm not going to start some business. I'm going to make my deliveries and scrounge up some change so that we can afford this baby some nice things. A new crib. Decent winter clothes. Maybe a university education someday. I'm not here to change the world, Irma. That was always *your* dream."

Irma frowned. "What about after this baby is born and grown? What will you do then?"

"I suppose I'll move into the Artists' District with you and get bloody drunk all day and yell at my maid and do nothing at all!"

Mel turned and stormed off, headed for home. She spotted and hailed a carriage. It immediately screeched to a halt, one of the many perks of this neighborhood. She gave the driver her address and settled into her seat. Then she remembered her broom, which Cinthy was probably riding back to Irma's house at that moment. Mel decided she would get Homer to pick up the broom in the morning, or she would beg Cinthy to return it. Her eyes fluttered shut, and she resolved to put the broom out of her mind. She was cold, tired, and in need of a toasty fire and some soup. Mel ignored her mirror, which chimed incessantly the whole ride home.

7

Brooms for Sale

There was a new column in the finance section of *The Harking Herald* the next day. It was a slim little sliver on the edge of the paper, a tiny thing really, easy to miss if someone never looked in the section and even if they did devour it every morning.

It had the last price of OCCs and the projected future value.

That day it was:

OCC Value: 5 silvers.

Proof: Five rounds of four drinks (valued at a total of 5 silvers) were purchased at Badger & Bard with 1 OCC.

Future Value estimate: 6 silvers.

"Isn't Badger & Bard that student pub? With experimental brews?" Dutch asked, leaning back in his chair, feet up on his desk, the paper a tent over him.

Bane went over to him, curious to see why he was asking. "I think so." Bane never went to university and so didn't patron the pubs around there, but he knew four drinks for a silver was a good deal. Maybe he ought to take Lusine there, especially if they were accepting fake coins. He lifted the paper to see what Dutch was reading.

"Wait until after I'm done," Dutch snapped and slapped the page closed.

"But you always crumple it before you toss it! Why can't you just set it down when you're done?"

"Because half the joy is crumpling it in a ball and tossing it into the bin from across the room."

"Want me to start buying you the paper?" Aeryn asked, walking over with a fresh mug of coffee.

"No," Bane grumbled, but what he really wanted to say was *absolutely yes.*

"That bit's outdated anyway," Aeryn said. "Just this morning a wand was sold for OCCs."

"How many?" Dutch asked, eyes narrowed.

"I don't know, I was just flipping through my mirror on the way over here and saw a bit of the news clip. *The Harking Herald* can be a bit slow."

"So how much are OCCs worth now?" Bane asked, loving that they were now calling them OCCs.

Aeryn shrugged. "Maybe a gold or two. I think it was just a publicity stunt. Everyone's always trying to one up each other in those mirror channels, trying to do something outrageous."

"Or maybe they just set the new price," Bane said, eyes wide with excitement.

"Candor wants you over there," Ezra announced, poking his head into Dutch's office. "He's been trying to call you all morning."

"He doesn't have a mirror," Aeryn reminded him.

"Sure you do," Ezra said to Bane. "Your work one."

"Gods, I keep forgetting I have it." Bane ran around the desk. "No one ever calls it!"

Bane didn't have to make it all the way across the lot to see the group of women milling around. As he jogged up, he tried to read the situation, but it wasn't clear if they all knew each other or not. They were very friendly. Maybe it was the joint experience of buying a broom that was giving them all a sense of comradery?

"Bane! There he is. He'll be more than happy to take you around the room. When you find one you like, just point it out and he'll prepare it for a test ride." Candor walked up to Bane and added, under his breath, "I've already got three deals waiting on my desk. You get as many commitments as you can, and we'll knock these out."

"What's happened? Why are they here?"

"What's it matter? It's a new year's miracle!" Candor just about danced into his office. They didn't have to worry about commission, since no matter who sealed the deal they split it, 60-40 to Candor. It wasn't like New Brooms across the lot, where it was nearly a bloody battle to get new prospects and seal the deal. There wasn't nearly as much money to be made in Used Brooms, the broomsticks all costing a fraction of the price of new ones and fighting over the few customers who did come in would cause unnecessary tension. Tension that the other lot thrived on. Dutch and Aeryn and Ezra shared jokes around the coffee pot but would sell out their closest relative for a sale. That was why Bane could be friends with them—he posed no threat.

Bane gestured for the women to come inside and tried to project his voice as much as possible as he led them on a tour of the available units. He was surprised they weren't across the lot, but from the chatter he picked up, he understood that these were all homemakers, mothers on a budget.

"Ooh, this is nice. I like when there are prices," one said, picking up a Hover Rod. "They don't have prices in the new lots."

"There were a few," someone retorted. "But some dealerships don't have prices *at all*."

Because if you have to ask, you can't afford it, Bane thought, not unkindly. It was a mantra he had learned and was constantly reminding himself. "It's because there's no hidden tricks or fees here. What you see is what you get, and the price on each is the one you'll pay."

"There's no wiggle room?" another asked, sounding disappointed. Bane glided over and replaced the Quick Bark in her hand with a Tiny Tidy. "What is the main purpose of your new broomstick?"

He meant this question to be directed at the woman he had just handed the Tidy to, but they all exploded with excitement. "Deliveries!"

"Yes, we'll be making deliveries!"

"It's a new business, we're so excited."

"Very lucrative, from the sound of it."

"Bane!" Bane looked up to find Candor poking his head out of his office. "Pick it up already, will you? Mel's been calling all morning." Candor tossed the hand mirror, which sailed expertly across the gaggle of heads. Bane snatched it mid-air. "Really? What does she want?" But Candor didn't answer and was already ducking back into his office. Bane opened the mirror and traced a rune on the glass to answer it. "Mel?"

"Gods, I've been ringing you all morning! I've been trying to warn you—gods, are they all already there?"

"You sent them?" Bane looked over his shoulder, then back at her, eyes wide with awe. "I owe you my commission!"

"Actually, I'll take you up on a favor instead." She too looked over her shoulder to yell at her son that if he didn't like the breakfast, he could make something himself, she gave him two hands for a reason. She let out a huff and peered back in the mirror. "I need you to go get me my broomstick from my sister's. Or send someone to fetch it, I can't think of all that right now. The house is a mess and I'm due to make my first delivery in an hour."

"Where is it?"

"Artists' District."

Absolutely not. "Mel, are you not seeing this?" Bane raised the mirror and did a panorama of the room. "I'm swamped."

"Don't you have other salespeople?"

"Did I not just tell you we make commission?" Candor really would kill him if he left.

"Please!"

"Mel, can't you send your pigeon to fetch it?"

"He's old! He can't carry a broomstick!"

"What about hiring a different bird?"

"How would that look?" Outsourcing her job to a pigeon was preposterous.

"*I'll* send it by pigeon," Bane snapped, making up his mind. "Tell me your address."

A few calls later—with them all on strike, it proved a challenge to find a freelance pigeon for hire—he had arranged the pickup and delivery of the broom. He also had five women ready to test out their broomsticks, so he led them outside. He nervously squeezed the mirror in his pocket as he watched them kick off, clearly amateur riders, all wobbly on their sticks.

A mirror was handy, but it was a luxury. No one would contact him, except maybe his mother, but she wrote, and Lusine, but he lived with her. Bane got the sense that people with mirrors were glued to them, and he really didn't have the spare time. But maybe, at the rate today was going...maybe a cheap one, a used one would be good after all. Maybe he'd buy one on credit and pay it off when he received the commission for today's sales. *Takes money to make money,* Gerwin always barked, but that never made sense to Bane before. Now it sort of did.

Meanwhile, even more exciting things were happening across the lot.

8

A Splendid Sale

Used Brooms hit a new record: 20 sales in one day. Bane and Candor stayed late to finish up the last of the deals, and even got cocky and sold some insurance to nearly all of them, which would tack on a nice bit of extra to their bonuses. For a Used Brooms lot that sold fifty broomsticks on average *all year*, this was something to celebrate.

"I need to call Lusine and let her know I'm running late."

"Use the work mirror."

"Isn't it against policy to use it for personal reasons?"

"I don't think he'll mind this time," Candor said, referring to Gerwin. He was already pouring the celebratory spirits into two glasses for them to toast. Bane ducked out of the office and flipped open his work mirror to find it already buzzing. He swiped the glass to unlock it to find Ezra's face, flushed red with excitement, filling up the frame. "We did it! We sold the Twig!"

"Oy, they sold the Twig," Candor called, apparently also just getting a call from someone, probably Dutch if Bane had to guess.

"Come over and celebrate!" And then Ezra's face was gone. Bane shouted, "Want to celebrate over there?"

"Oy, I've already poured two out here. Let's drink to us first, then we'll shuffle over and celebrate the cocky bastards."

Bane couldn't keep the grin off his face as he rang Lusine. When she appeared, her chin was in her hand, elbow resting on a stack of books, her braid messy from a busy day, the candle beside her nearly two-thirds gone. She let out a yawn before she said, "Where are you?"

"I'm still at the dealership. We've had a nutso day. You're still up studying? You won't mind if I celebrate a bit with the boys before I head home?"

"What are you celebrating?"

"Everything. Loads to tell. I'll see you soon? I won't stay out too late."

"Stay out as long as you like, I'm about to head to bed. Won't make a difference if you come in an hour or in the morning." She forced a smile. "Have fun."

Bane told her he loved her before tossing the mirror onto his desk and joining Candor. "To retirement," Candor declared, which gave Bane pause. He watched Candor shoot back his drink. "What? You're retiring?"

"After today? Yes. And after the news we're about to receive when we're over there? Definitely."

"What news?"

"Drink up."

Bane downed his mystery drink. "Now tell me what you mean."

"You already know. You went snooping," Candor accused, cocking an eyebrow. "You and Aeryn. You're not very discreet."

Bane winced. "How do you know?"

"Honey sees everything, lad. Remember that." He poured another drink for them. "That was to my retirement. This is to tonight's good work."

Bane drank when Candor drank. "That's how I know, but how do *you* know he's selling the dealership?"

"I have been threatening to retire for years now. I was asked to hold out just a bit longer. Gerwin hasn't officially told me, but I suspected it. And now you've confirmed it."

"Gods, I'm sorry. I didn't mean to steal Gerwin's thunder."

Candor let out a bark of laughter and slapped a hand on Bane's shoulder. "It's alright. He won't be striking thunder here much longer. Let's go."

Crossing the lot, Bane looked up at the moon. The day of the full moon was approaching and the pull of it had already begun. Candor knew, of course, but he didn't say anything. It didn't bother him because he was never around when Bane transformed. No one was around; just Bane, the moon, and the stockpile of meat he enjoyed between laps around the lot.

It was extra pocket money, doing security one night a month. That was the night Terry from Finance & Enchantment came and did inventory of every broomstick. It was also the day before payday, and it was up to Bane to make sure no one showed up in the morning to rob Honey of the gold she brought from the bank. Once he was relieved of his shift, Bane would go home, catch a few hours of sleep, then enjoyed the rest of his day off. Usually he took Lusine out, the one time a month he could afford to do so.

Bane enjoyed the side job and wondered if he would still have it when the new owners took over. If he would have any job at all. If it weren't for the slight buzz from the booze, he would have been a nervous wreck, following Candor into the lobby of New Brooms where everyone was assembled. Gerwin stood on the empty podium where the Twig had been, looking rather important and full of himself. Ezra clapped Bane on the back and Aeryn pushed a mug of ale into his hands.

"Who sold it?" Bane asked.

"He did, of course." Ezra nodded at Aeryn and rolled his eyes. "Leave some commission for the rest of us!"

"Oh, it was nothing."

"Not nothing," Ezra insisted. "D'ye know Gerwin took a bag of those fake coins for it?"

Bane's jaw dropped in disbelief. "You sold the latest Twig for a bag of OCCs?"

Aeryn couldn't stop grinning. "Apparently"—here he dropped his voice conspiratorially—"Gerwin believes they'll be going up in value. He's trying to horde as much as he can now and sell at a tidy profit."

Bane couldn't believe what he was hearing. "How long is he going to hold it for? How high does he think it's going to go?

"High, apparently," Ezra said, catching Aeryn under the arm as he swayed.

Aeryn threw his arm around Ezra's shoulder and howled, "To the moon!"

Dutch, who stood in front of them, turned around and snapped, "Shut up! Can't you see the man's trying to talk?"

"Sorry, Your Majesty," Aeryn hissed and giggled along with Ezra, who was also several ales deep. "Honey told me," Aeryn added with a shrug. "She and I get drinks after work sometimes."

Their boss's voice boomed over them. "Thank you, gentlemen, for joining me here—"

"Whoo!" Aeryn let out a whoop. And because it was Aeryn, Gerwin let him get the others riled up along with him a moment before he raised his hands for them to pipe down. "I have some big news. I have decided to sell the dealership—"

Shouting erupted, an angry uproar from Doc, Dutch, and Mic.

"...and the ink is already dried and it's happeningthefirstofnextmonth," Gerwin finished as fast as he could.

"Who's taking over?" Mic bellowed.

"The...Honey, who is it?"

Honey rolled her eyes. "The Van De Besens."

Mic looked as if she had spoken elvish. "The who?"

Honey threw her hands up in frustration. "I'm not the one who signed the contracts."

"Lovely people," Gerwin continued, trying to power through. He knew he was going to get eaten alive after and was already eyeing the exit. "They have agreed to keep on the current staff. They might bring some of their own, I don't know, it's their business now. But building this business up over the last few years has been..."

Bane tuned out of the long, drawled-out speech Gerwin plunged into. His mind raced, trying to calculate how much commission they made today, how long it would last him if he got fired the day the new owners came in. There was no reason to fire him, not specifically, but in all honestly, he wasn't an especially good salesman. And when Candor left, who would vouch for him? Or maybe with Candor gone they would need him around to teach the new hires the ropes, at least for a little while. Bane sipped his ale, feeling more miserable by the minute.

At the conclusion of his speech, Gerwin, as expected, raced for the door and was already on his Swift Saddle before anyone could catch up to him, though they tried. Bane decided not to stick around and finish the ale with the others, because if he heard the actual monetary amount that Aeryn made off the sale of that Twig it would ruin his day. They say comparison is the thief of joy, and so salespeople are the biggest thieves of all.

As Bane stepped out of the dealership, Aeryn's voice followed him out, drunkenly shouting that he was a lousy friend, a piss salesman, and was ruining the fun by leaving. Bane didn't pay him any mind. He made his way across the practice lot wondering how someone even accumulated enough OCCs to purchase a lavish broomstick. And if they had, why couldn't he?

With that thought Bane changed direction, and rather than head home, stalked towards the palace. Surely there were coins still littering the courtyard, remnants of the festival, and Bane was determined to comb every blade of grass and overturn every single stone until he scrounged enough coins to quell the miserable pit growing in his stomach. Besides, Lusine would be asleep, and if he did it tonight, he wouldn't have to explain to her why he was late, where he'd been. He felt he couldn't tell her about this, not yet. Not until he had a few coins in hand, at least.

The walk to the palace was long but uneventful. It was a weekday and so the streets were quiet, not like on the weekends when the pubs had their doors flung open to invite everyone in and to easily kick the unruly ones out. When he finally arrived, Bane found the drawbridges all up, no way to cross the moat.

He kicked a rock in frustration. He told himself not to lose hope and decided to hunt through every public park he passed on his way home.

They were all empty this late at night, or so they seemed. But Bane wasn't afraid and didn't pay the shadows any mind as he rummaged through the trash bins, peeked under every bench, and crawled around in the grass, just in case. What did he have to steal? He had a few coppers on him, no jewelry, not even a gold filling. That made him brave.

He did come across a few fountains, but Bane didn't dare reach his hand in to fish around, remembering Dutch's warning about becoming poor if money was taken from them. But then, it wasn't really money, was it? So it didn't really count? Bane decided if he saw an OCC real obvious, he'd reach in for it, but these fountains didn't have more than a few coppers and algae from what he could make out, and so he didn't dare stick his hand in. He might not have anything of value, but he still had fingers to lose. There was no telling what lurked in the murky water.

The moon gave enough light that the search wasn't completely miserable, and he did pick up a few coppers and nickels for his troubles. The moonbeams guided him as he stepped over the holes beside large rocks, burrows for the Tunneler dragons. Above the bare branches swayed as Nester dragons hopped from limb to limb, gliding effortlessly between trees, hoping Bane would drop a treasure for them. Some were brave, and they came down and perched on the ledges of trash bins and even approached cautiously to beg for food. But mostly they kept to themselves, their glowing yellow eyes glowering down until they felt it was safe to come out and sniff around.

Bane finally gave up and headed home. The ale made him drowsy, and he was feeling frustrated and discouraged. He passed several temples and thought of the offerings of food and coins people left inside at the feet of the statues. He wondered if anyone had left OCCs. He didn't dare go inside; even if there were any to be found, he knew better than to steal from a shrine. He wasn't a believer like his mum, but she had raised him to harbor a mean streak of guilt anyhow. Maybe there were gods, or maybe it was all just fickle luck. Either way, he needed them all to be on his side, for once.

Bane even went to a bank, the one thought might be Lusine's bank, right before he made it home. He stood at the bottom of its very steep, imposing stairs and stared up at it, resenting it for all the riches it held in its belly. He had never been inside and wouldn't have entered even if it was business hours, wholly intimidated.

He finally made it home, exhausted, and stripped out of his filthy clothes just inside the front door. He crept into bed beside Lusine, who shifted slightly in her sleep, unaware of his arrival. He forced his eyes closed but his mind raced, making a list of all the places still left to search. The only thought that finally quelled the rising angst was to tell himself he would wake up early the next day and make it back to the palace to search the courtyard before work. Then he smashed his pillow over his head and willed himself to fall asleep.

He had every intention of carrying out that plan, but he slept right through Lusine's attempts to wake him and was nearly late for work when he finally rose. He cursed himself, he cursed his rotten luck, and he swore this wasn't the end of the treasure hunt.

9
Incorporated

Two days after the Women in Business Empowerment Meeting, Mel was back at the dealership. There was nothing wrong with her broomstick, but her house had been taken over as an impromptu workstation with these very capable women already taking orders and dividing up customers and planning delivery routes. It was practically taking off on its own. Overwhelmed by it all, Mel announced to deaf ears that the baby needed something and abruptly left.

She needed this to work. That was what Mel needed. She was suddenly in charge of a small army of very determined women who seemed to believe that Mel would lead them to financial freedom. It was terrifying. So Mel went to the one place no one expected anything of her, no snacks or orders, but also had free coffee.

"Polish it up a bit, won't you?" she told Doc, who was checked-out by the news of the dealership sale. He instructed Son to do it, not to charge her, and make it a priority.

Mel went out and crossed the field to Used Brooms to find Bane reading a crumpled issue of *The Harking Herald*. "Want to get a cuppa?"

Bane jumped up and followed her back to New Brooms. It wasn't until they had warm mugs of coffee in their hands that they finally relaxed and began speaking.

"That pigeon you sent to bring my broom back? My sister offered to pay him in OCCs and the idiot took them and then had the gall to demand I exchange them for real coins."

"I'll buy them off you," Bane said immediately.

"What? The fake bits?"

"Yes." Bane tried not to sound too eager, but it was too late. "My, um, mum, she collects them. Uses them to play cards." He wasn't about to tell her they sold the most expensive broom on the market in exchange for them. He wanted those coins, bad. Coppers would always be worth coppers, and gold would always be worth gold. But OCCs? Who knew what they were worth this minute, then the next. The thought was exhilarating, in a squeeze-your-heart-with-anxiety way.

"Does she? Well fine. I'll use them for your first few payments. If you work for me."

"You're recruiting me? To do what? Make deliveries?"

"Yes. Apparently, you're looking at the new owner of Mel's Delivery Service."

Bane frowned. "What do you mean, *apparently*? Are ye or are ye not?"

"I am. All those women who bought broomsticks? They're all my sub-contractors. Look at all these new words I've had to learn and incorporate." Mel was smart, smart as the next person at least, but she wasn't business smart. If any rich person tried to talk business with her just a few days ago, they would have called her stupid. That was why she had gone to a book shop and bought a tome on business and was trying to cram it all down, spew back as many facts as she could recall.

"Are you incorporated?" Bane asked.

"What does that mean?"

"You just used the word." Bane frowned. "I mean, are you a legitimate business? With a royal seal and everything?"

Mel squinted, thinking about this. "No...I think you only need a royal seal if you're opening a literal shop." She thought of all the women at the job fair—there was no way they all had obtained a prestigious royal seal. Perhaps it was because technically they weren't their own businesses, or even their own bosses, if they really read through the contracts they signed when they joined the marketing plots.

"Mhm, I don't think that's true..."

"Well, they're all sub-contractors," Mel repeated, certain that was the title that all those Pretty Potions and Healthy Herb women must have. "Self-employed sub-contractors. That's right!"

"What does that mean? That they're not actually your employees?"

Mel amazed herself by regurgitating one of the pamphlets she'd picked up at the fair. "They are their own bosses. They set their own hours. Their success relies solely on themselves. They use my business's name to market themselves and so I take a portion of their income as a finder's fee."

"Oh. I suppose that works out well then. Less paperwork. No payroll. But, how do you know they're paying you the right amount?"

"What do you mean?"

"Well, if they are their own bosses, do they set their own prices for deliveries? And if so, how do you know they're actually paying you the, say, ten percent you agreed on?"

"Ten percent?" She hadn't even thought of it as a percent. She just declared a flat fee and they all agreed to it. *I ought to write this down*, Mel thought, and grabbed a notebook out of her sack, another item she had bought from the shop. Red leather bound, to jot down ideas. And one of those new, ceaseless-ink quills that never had to be dipped in a pot of ink. The wrapper of the final item she bought came out as well, stuck to the notebook, but she tucked the candy wrapper back inside her sack, ashamed of it. *The baby wanted it*, she had told the clerk, laughing it off as if it were a joke. Why did pregnant women do that, begin to blame their babies for all their woes even before they were born? She wrote down *10%*, and looked back up at Bane, expectantly, as if he would keep giving her answers to questions she hadn't yet asked. When he didn't, she said, "You know about business, it seems. This is good. What else do you know about independent contractors? Are you one?"

"No, I suppose I'm not," Bane said. "But...if I were to work for you..."

"Yes?"

"Well, you ought to set prices. Deliveries based on distance, or how heavy the items delivered are. Bonuses for working extra hard. Incentives."

"You have incentives here?"

"I get commission, so yes. Making more money with each sale is the incentive."

"What if no one comes in to buy a broomstick?"

"I make a base pay."

"Who brings in business?" Mel asked. "Who advertises?"

"The dealership does," Bane said. He hadn't considered this before. Where did all the prospects come from? He had been urged to bring people in while in New Brooms, but he hadn't been around long enough to really get a prospect list going.

"Hmm." Mel scratched her chin. "I suppose it would be up to me to advertise."

"Put that into the fee you take out. They'll wonder why you take a fee, if all you do is nothing but sit around. If you are the one getting the leads for jobs, then that's what you are getting paid for. How do you get your jobs now?"

"It was just people I knew, then word of mouth. I suppose if they get leads, they should keep more of their commission."

"You could do that. That would encourage them to drive their own business."

Mel scribbled furiously. An excitement gripped her, both in the wrist and in her heart, and it was making her baby kick furiously, enjoying the dose of adrenaline that had just been dumped into the bloodstream. It made Mel feel absolutely manic. Like this might actually work out.

"Passive income," Bane said dreamily. "Think, if all you do is nothing but let people use your good name, the reputation of your business, and they do all the work, and you make money off them. That's the dream, eh?"

They both stared off into the distance, imagining what they would each do with all that free time. With all that money. *Passive income* were the magic words. Passive-income, Mel hyphenated in her notebook. There, that sounded better, didn't it? A single magical word. "Then you'll join me? Make deliveries?"

Seeing as how he might be out of a job in a few days, Bane nearly agreed. There was one hitch. "I don't have a broomstick."

"How do you not have a broomstick?"

"They're expensive! I just walk to work, like all the other people who can't afford brooms."

Mel tucked her notebook back in her sack. "I've got an idea. What if you asked your boss to lend you one? And you would use it for advertisement? Every time someone asks about where you got it and whatnot, you can direct them here. It would get the word out, and if it's a nice enough broomstick surely people will think this is a classy lot."

Bane let out a bark of laughter. "Classy? This lot? Mel, come off it."

"Alright fine, but it's not half bad. Really, I've been all around the kingdom looking for a decent Service Drive and this place takes the cake. And maybe they won't lend you the Twig—"

"They sold that."

"Did they? Good for them. But maybe another one, a mid-level nice one. A Zoom Broom, perhaps?"

Bane considered this. "There's one problem. They're selling the shop in a few days, and then I'm out of a broomstick when the new owner takes over. I highly doubt they'll honor the agreement."

"Why not? Maybe they'll also think it's a good idea. Or...maybe your little arrangement doesn't get mentioned and it's overlooked." Mel cocked a knowing eyebrow at him.

"Nah, that'll never happen. We have a whole inventory system."

"Alright, so work a few days for me and maybe you'll earn enough to buy it outright."

"In that short of a time?"

"Sure!" Mel lied. It came out of her so effortlessly, so instantly that she nearly slapped a hand over her mouth in shock. Was this what being a business owner was like? White lies all day long?

But then, maybe it wasn't a lie. Who could tell how business would look in a few days?

"Alright, I'll do it." Bane jumped up. "I'm going to go ask!"

"That's the spirit!"

"What if I don't get the broomstick?" Bane was suddenly unsure. It was happening *so quickly.*

"Make it happen!" Mel shook her fists at him, trying to get him riled up. "You're a salesman, by gods, go sell yourself!"

And he did. Bane walked back to Mel in a daze, holding an older model Fly-By that had been set aside to be moved to Used Brooms. By the time he made it back to her, Mel had received four calls, answered two, and was filling up her notebook again, this time with orders and ideas.

Apothecary deliveries.

Partnering with the Pretty Potions women to deliver bulk orders around town.
Food deliveries but charging double after dark.

She looked up at Bane and beamed with pride. "I knew you could do it!"

"I'm still fuzzy on the conditions," Bane said and took a seat beside her with the contract. Mel took the broomstick to admire it while he read over the parchment. "Alright, it says here I am leasing it, and I owe nothing on it, unless I wreck it. Expenses like upkeep and maintenance will be up to me to pay out of pocket, and I must mention the broomstick once a day to a new person or, on average, thirty people a month." Bane looked up, relieved. "I'll just take this pup to the pub two evenings a month and tell the whole room about it. Easy as pie."

"Easy as pie," Mel echoed. "Doc's waving at me, I better go. Oh, and I have your first two jobs."

"Can I get them both done today? It's coming up on that time of the month. Full moon and all."

"Oh, that's right. Yes, today's fine. Then get back to me once you're all...yourself again." Mel ripped the sheet with Bane's orders from her notebook and handed it to him. Then she gathered her things and headed to the Service Drive. Bane stood there staring at the Fly-By in his hands, not quite believing what he had done. Then he ran after Mel.

"How do I get new orders? You'll send your pigeon? Or do I need a mirror?"

"A mirror would be best. You ought to get a used one. Pawn shops have plenty."

Bane nodded. "Alright. Thanks. Boss."

Mel cringed. "Ew. That's awful."

"Get used to it!" Bane ran out the door and jumped on his broomstick. He circled the lot over and over until finally, *finally* he believed that his luck was turning around.

Oh, if only he knew what was coming.

10

Deliveries

The two deliveries Bane had to make for Mel seemed easy, and he completed the first without a hitch. A student had left his homework at his father's house and needed it delivered to his mother's house, and the pigeons—even non-union ones—had a strict no-squabbling-exes rule. The mother even tipped him, and Bane wondered if tips were included in the percentage he owed Mel. He made a mental note to ask her, then went to his favorite meat stall to pick up a family value meal to deliver.

Yoni the owner recognized Bane and greeted him with his usual enthusiasm. "I've got your order in the back, I didn't know you would be coming this early."

"I'm not here for me. I'm here for a delivery for Mel? Bone?"

"Mel! You're doing her deliveries now?" Yoni peered over the counter and noticed the broomstick, sucked in a breath. "Wow! Is that yours?" He ran around the counter. "May I?"

"Uh, sure." Bane handed the broomstick over and then realized what a great opportunity this was. "It's from my work, they're lending it to me. Bit of a promotional thing. If you're ever in need of a broomstick, be sure to stop by Best Buzzems."

"Maybe I should hire my own delivery person, wouldn't that be something?"

"And run me out of business? Already?"

Yoni gave a good-natured laugh. "Maybe for on your busy days when you can't make it out."

"I hope you become so busy," Bane said, taking the sack containing the meal and wishing his friend well. "I'll be back soon!"

"Okay! I got you extra lamb this time, I know you like it so much. No extra charge."

Bane patted his belly, a gesture that was regarded as the highest compliment to a chef. Yoni forced a kebob into his hand for the road, and Bane happily munched on it as he left the shop. Outside, he used the straps Mel gave him to secure the sack onto the back of his broomstick, making sure most of the weight was distributed on the bristles.

It wasn't until he was nearly at the drop-off location that Bane smelled the burning meat. When he finally looked over his shoulder, he saw the plume of smoke.

Panicked, Bane shoved down on the handle to make a crash landing on the cobblestone street. He nearly collided with a horse-drawn carriage rounding the corner. As he hopped out of the way, the tip of the broom smashed into the stucco wall of a house, chipping both the wall and the broom handle.

The sack of food, miraculously, stayed on. Bane did his best to hold the broom level as he kicked off to get around a corner, not wanting to be caught by the homeowner.

A live coal must have gotten shoveled in with all the meat, Bane figured, finding a spot to park and dismount. He tore open the sack to find the top box fully on fire.

Bane chucked the box to the ground and stomped on it, relieved to feel the culprit coal crunch under his heel. He peered back into the sack; it looked like the rest of the boxes had remained unscathed.

Cursing, he reached to call Mel to tell her what happened and realized that he did not, in fact, own an enchanted mirror. His work one was back in his desk office. That meant he also couldn't call Yoni and give him a piece of his mind.

Now Bane would have an unsatisfied customer and would probably lose his new job. On top of it, the bristles of the broom were singed and the nose was now crooked and chipped.

Defeated, he dropped onto a stoop and buried his face in his hands. Hands that smelled of delicious grilled meat. And now the juices were all over his face.

He looked at the box smashed into the ground. It was only one ruined of a pile growing cold, and Bane realized there was a hungry family out there who was eagerly waiting for their supper.

Bane collected his thoughts and decided the best thing to do was finish the delivery. He would apologize profusely and promise to make it right, and then pass that along to Mel, his boss, whose job it would be to fix all this. He suddenly stopped envying her position.

Right then. Bane resecured the order after giving each box a good sniff to make sure there were no more coals hiding in there. Then he swung back onto the Fly-By and kicked off. It hadn't flown anything like the Twisted Twig to begin with, and the bent nose forced Bane to put more effort in steering, but the broom still flew relatively well. Bane was relieved and flew extra carefully to his destination.

The mother who opened the door was completely flustered with a babe on her breast, a toddler hanging off her dress, and another somewhere deep in the house shouting, demanding to know if it was dinner. Bane plunged into explaining what had happened, but she quickly shushed him with, "I'm sure it's all right. Mel will sort it out." She reached out and dropped the coins into Bane's hand and shut the door in his face.

That was it? He had pumped himself up for a shouting match, had prepared himself to grovel. But he held the money in his hand, payment for the delivery. Which, a moment later, began to burn his palm.

"Oww!" Bane dropped the coins and, sure enough, saw a silver. He groaned. He pulled a shoe off, peeled off his sock, and picked the coins up with it before stuffing them in his pocket. He hopped back on his broom and wondered what sort of solution Mel had for botched deliveries like the one he had just had. There would need to be a contract if this was to be long term, he figured and began composing one in his head as he climbed in altitude and pointed the broomstick in the direction of home.

The city was an endeavor to cross if one walked it on foot, probably a good day's worth from one end to the other. Less by carriage, and hardly any time at all by broomstick. And yet there weren't all that many broomsticks being regularly ridden.

There was the learning curve that came with riding one, which some saw as a privileged skill; one must own a broomstick to learn to ride one, and they were quite expensive. Easily a year's salary even at the lowest paying job aiming for the lowest priced broomsticks. It made sense—they had to be crafted physically, and then they had to be enchanted by a very powerful sorcerer.

Then there was the upkeep. Plenty of witches and wizards pushed power into old broomsticks for joy rides, but the broom used up the power to fly and was constantly having to be re-juiced. Even those professionally enchanted by sorcerers had to be recharged, and that was a routine service every broomstick dealership's Service Drive offered. Terry at the dealership did routine juicing, but he only worked by appointments because he only had so much power to give. There were plenty of tune-up stations around town that also offered a whole host of other enchantments on their menu.

Factor into that crashes, twig loss, theft...keeping a broomstick was a hassle. Besides, no one was really in any rush to get anywhere, and walking was good enough for most people. But there were the broom hobbyists, there were the sports, there were the dragon watchers who liked to fly with migrating dragons...speaking of which, Bane looked to his left and right and noticed two dragons had joined him on his air stream, gliding alongside him.

Dragons in Citeel ranged from the smallest ones that fit into cracks to decent sized ones as big as a pony, for those put to work in places like blacksmith shops and glass blowing studios. They had been domesticated with sugar when they were first captured generations ago. Bane heard of really big ones beyond the city, out in the countryside. He heard tales of a mother dragon as wide as a house who came to collect her stolen egg from the palace in this very city just the summer before, but he had been sleeping off an especially exhausting night of being a werewolf and missed the whole ordeal. They say dragons came in as many varieties as birds, but Bane wasn't too keen on how many types of birds there were, outside of hawks and pigeons. And even those weren't always fully birds. All the pigeons in this city were shifters, descendants of shifters who had been enslaved and bred to only transform into pigeons to deliver mail. Some people assumed shifters could become any animal any time, but that wasn't true. They were capable of one shape beyond their human form, and that depended on the alternate shapes their parents took on. And if, say, a pigeon and a cat shifter fell in love, well it all came down to a gamble in genetics, which strain was stronger. The ability to learn to shift had been lost generations ago.

Unless, of course, you wanted to be a werewolf. Apparently, anyone could be a werewolf. There was no aptitude test, no quest to complete. Just stick yer arm out and bite down on the leather, boy, and you, too, can be as damned as your lover.

Bane didn't like to dwell on the past, but the transformation hadn't taken place that long ago, and he was still overwhelmed at times by his remorse of that decision. He couldn't understand what had made him so stupid, so blind to consequences.

Hormones, his mother had screamed. It had been a whole lot of that, and also what he had considered love. Bane still scratched his head on that one, not sure of the difference. He had been in love, he had been certain. She, obviously, hadn't been.

If Bane could shift into any animal at all, he would be a dragon he decided, looking at the ones beside him, the size of his forearms. In the moonlight, Bane could make out a faint calling rune tattooed on the underside of their wings—a mark that meant they had owners. Bane wondered what they were kept for. Perhaps they were pets, living in the laps of luxury. Or maybe they were kept illegally to fight, which was a dark thought. Bane decided they seemed content enough and chose to give them a happy backstory. He reached out to pet one and it nipped his fingertip. A playful warning. Like a cat that didn't want to be bothered, but hadn't ruled out that you didn't have snacks hiding in your pocket. As it were, they smelled the juices of the grilled meat reeking off him and were trying to coyly decide if he was worth pouncing on.

They didn't get the chance to because in the next moment Bane slowed and descended, then gracefully landed at the end of the street where he lived. He walked the broom to the door on the back of the parchment & quill shop they lived above, Ink Splotch. He climbed the steep stairs to their apartment and let himself inside.

Lusine was asleep on the couch decked in her dragon hunting gear; she volunteered with the new queen to help with dragon entrapping, sterilizing, and rehoming. It really took the energy out of her. He gingerly pulled her rubber boots off, undid the braid in her hair, and used his fingers to gently smooth the strands out as she stirred and incoherently tried to tell him about her day. He waited until she finished, her eyes still closed, to ask, "Are you hungry?"

"I wasn't. But you smell so good."

Bane leaned down and kissed her. It was gentle, at first, but then suddenly her hands were around his neck and she was wolfing him down, mashing her lips against his, pushing her tongue inside of his mouth. "Mmmmh!"

He finally had to tickle her to let go. She erupted in laughter, and he smacked her with one of those frilly, beaded pillows she loved to put on every surface to collect dust. "I'll make you something."

"Not meat."

"Are you certain? You definitely just acted like you wanted some."

"I'll have yours later." She winked and sat up, stretched. "Have a good day?"

Bane nodded to the doorway, which had the Fly-By leaning against the door.

"Look at that!" Lusine jumped up and ran over to inspect it. "Whose beat-up old broomstick is this?"

Bane winced. "Come into the kitchen and I'll tell you all about it."

"I'm tired..."

Bane lifted the glass of wine he had just poured and wiggled it, enticing her in. She grinned and joined him. "Now, if you're ever thinking of getting one yourself, be sure to keep Best Buzzems in mind for all your broomstick needs..."

11

Pickpocket

Bane had gone through enough full moons to recognize the pattern. He didn't need to check the calendar incessantly like Lusine did to know the tides were changing, both in the oceans and within himself.

It started with irritability, about a week before. Little things put him on edge. He usually didn't mind fishing Dutch's crumpled paper out of the bin, but it began to annoy him more and more leading up to the day. Then, the day before transformation day, he was exhausted. All he wanted to do was sleep and at work he was lethargic.

His doctor told him this made sense, that the body was trying to reduce calorie consumption in preparation for the upcoming metabolic exertion.

"Saving energy for the transformation," he translated for Bane.

Bane arrived at Best Buzzems a little tardier than usual, but no one ever minded. Since being bitten, Bane had developed a bit of insomnia and found it hard to fall asleep before midnight. Since the dealership's showrooms didn't open until 10am and most of the customers didn't arrive until noon, this made the job one of the few that was compatible with Bane's sleep cycle. Bane made his way to the New Brooms building to fetch a mug of coffee and the paper that had already been crumpled and deposited into the wastebin.

Bane flattened it on the lounge's table and flipped straight to the finance section. He scanned it to find the new column and was surprised to read:

OCC Value: 8 silvers.

Proof: Horse, though claimed to be lame, was valued at 8 silvers and sold for one OCC.

Future Value Estimate: 10 silvers.

Bane steered his mug into Ezra's office since Aeryn was showing a couple their latest inventory of Precision Pines, which came in bold colors including enchanted forest green and unicorn white. "Oy, you read the paper?"

Erza glanced up from his crisp, fresh copy and gave it a little shake to imply he was.

Bane went around him and started flipping to the page he wanted Ezra to see. Used to this, Ezra let him.

"Here. Look. Eight silvers? How much did Aeryn sell that broomstick for?"

"Go ask Honey, she knows. I saw it was a sack full."

"How big was the sack?"

Ezra threw his hands up. "I don't know! I'm not privy to every deal Aeryn does. If I was, I wouldn't have time to make my own sales, now would I?"

"I'm just wondering why it's not in the paper."

"That's because Aeryn was paid off," Ezra said. "That *Herald* lady came around asking for confirmation from a source. Well, Aeryn is one of the primary sources, and of course Gerwin paid him to keep quiet. When she came, they all denied it."

"Why would they do that?"

"Search me. I think Gerwin doesn't want exciting news before the new owners swoop in."

"Then he shouldn't have taken OCCs as payment. Based on how many were paid and the value of the broom, each OCC could be worth loads more than eight silver! People have a right to know," Bane insisted. "Who tipped Harper Leewood off?"

"I did, of course. Every story has a finder's fee."

Bane gawked at him. "A what? A finder's fee? I never got one!"

"What story did you report?"

"I was there for the original one. At the coffee shop!"

"Oh, that one. It was probably paid to the person at the coffee shop."

"Dante?!" Bane hadn't been back there since the interaction, but he would have never imagined Dante, of all people, gloating for a finder's fee. Bane felt betrayed. Robbed.

Ezra shrugged, unsure who that was. "Perhaps."

Bane stormed out of Ezra's office and back to the lounge. He crumpled up the paper he had so tediously smoothed out and chucked it into the bin. It *was* satisfying. He refilled his coffee, which didn't seem to be making a difference for his drooping eyelids, and went across the lot. He found his work mirror in his desk and dialed Lusine.

"I'm in the library," she whispered. "I can't really talk."

"Did you know that breaking a story to *The Harking Herald* has a finder's fee?"

"No. Why does it matter? What story have you got?"

"I had the original story of purchasing coffee for OCCs."

"I thought that was Dante," she said, which really wasn't the answer Bane anticipated. Had it been Dante? Bane wracked his brain, trying to remember the interaction. "Anyway, why don't you just ask him? Have you visited him since that story printed?"

"No, I haven't—"

Lusine cut him off. "Maybe he has your fee and is waiting for you to go claim it."

"That feels like a bit of a bribe, doesn't it? That I have to go see him to get it?"

"He's not going to chase you down to give it to you, that's beyond absurd. And it's not like he can just ring you on the mirror you don't have. Go see him today."

"This close to...?"

"It's not yet the full moon," she reminded him. It was easy, sometimes, to use the full moon as an excuse not to do things the day before and after it, but Lusine knew him well enough. "You'll be fine."

"I could use all the coffee in the kingdom," Bane grumbled and said goodbye. He looked up to see Terry from F&E doing inventory. The used broomsticks got inspected during the day; they didn't require as much magic juicing as new brooms because they had far fewer test rides. Besides, it wasn't worth breaking in and stealing used broomsticks when new brooms held just as much risk and fetched far more on the obsidian market. Terry looked his way, and Bane gave a little wave and wandered over. "I cleared the shelves out to make your job easier."

"I see that." Terry grinned. "Good on you! It does make my job easier. Especially since I've got to go through and not just juice them all up but unenchant them as well."

"That so?"

"Tomorrow night I'll be doing the same to the new brooms. Then in the morning the new owner's sorcerer is coming in to lock them with their own enchantment."

"Good thing they've got the best security," Bane said with a wink.

Terry gave a good-natured chuckle. "No missing brooms so far! Say, don't sweat this whole new owner business. There's always growing pains, but it will be easier keeping the current crew than replacing you all."

Bane nodded, wanting to believe this. "Say, are you staying on? Once we're bought? Candor's retiring."

Terry shrugged. He was a friendly fellow, middle-aged with a wife and two children, but he didn't talk much about them. He wore a simple blue tunic over trousers, his wand's sheath attached to his belt for easy access. Magic didn't require the use of wands, but it was a handy tool for channeling magic precisely. Like into very specific splits in a broom handle. "Depends. If they have their new sorcerer come in to do the enchanting services, it's their right. But don't worry about me. Lots of lots need extra juicers in their Finance & Enchantment department. I'll always find a job."

Bane wished he had that sort of confidence in his own job security. It apparently showed on his face, because Terry added, "You'll be fine. You know the inventory and you have clients who like you. Best of all, you've got rapport."

"What's that?"

"It means people here like you."

"Do they?"

"Sure. It goes a long way, working with people you like."

Bane couldn't keep the smile off his face. "Thanks for saying that, Terry."

Terry gave him a good-natured pat on the back and resumed his work.

Maybe hearing that made a difference, because Bane sold three broomsticks that day, all to children who weren't pleased with their other winter solstice gifts and their parents finally gave in to buying them a broomstick. It was always fun, asking the children what they wanted in a broom (fast, fast, fast!) and what their parents whispered to him as they made the round around the showroom (cheap, slow, safe).

Candor helped with the financing papers on the one sale that needed it, but Bane could tell he was checked out. While Bane trailed after the customers, he read the Betting & Sports section of the paper, drank from his not-so-secret flask, and looked almost giddy with excitement.

"Tomorrow's my last day," Candor announced as the clock closed in on quitting time. "I'll be here to meet the new owners, walk them through our department, and hand the keys over. Then it's just you and the big boys, Bane."

Somehow, because of Terry's comment, this didn't seem so daunting to hear. "I'll do fine. Thanks for everything, Candor."

"That you will." Candor stuck out his hand and Bane shook it. It felt like a moment of graduation, a shift of power from master to apprentice.

After work, Bane pivoted from his usual route home and instead headed to the familiar Copper University.

The windows were steamed up from the warmth inside. When Bane opened the door, the soft chatter of patrons and the heat of the coffee shop washed over him and made him shiver. He let out a body-wracking yawn.

"Ho! Bane!"

Dante waved from behind the massive espresso machine, which reflected the overhead lights off its buffed, shiny shell and continually hissed steam. It was a magnificent machine, and learning to use it was akin learning a musical instrument. It wasn't enough to know how to turn it on, calibrate the shot, and pull the shot. It was constantly needing to be tuned, like a trumpet, fussy depending on the weather. The massive coffee bean grinder was on the back counter and Bane knew, on a day as chilly as this, it would have to be refilled up to five times throughout the day. The wall behind the bar was a hive of cupboards that held mugs for patrons to use. Then there were the stacks of new, take-away paper cups that Jaymie loathed introducing and using.

Bane dropped into a seat at the bar. "Dante, I believe you owe me something."

"Do I?" Dante winked and called over his shoulder, "Oh no! Not another abandoned vanilla cinnamon latte!"

"No, no, not that." Bane scowled, suddenly uncomfortable with what he was about to ask. He waited until Dante finished fixing his drink, drawing a milk-foam heart in the center. Dante placed the mug in front of him with flourish. "Perfect as ever," Bane praised and took a greedy sip.

Caffeine was caffeine, but it hit differently when it was presented in such a beautiful vessel. There were potions galore for energy, which he knew were just various concoctions of flavored caffeine, but nothing perked Bane up more than coffee crafted so impeccably.

"What, then?" Dante asked.

"Oh, nothing big. It's just...remember that article that Harper from *The Harking Herald* wrote? When she bought the coffee with the OCCs?"

"The fool's gold coins?"

"Yes, those." It irked Bane that Dante wasn't using the official name for those official commemorative coins. Perhaps there were a dozen fake coins on the obsidian market? That he didn't know, but he *did* know that when he said OCC, he spoke of a very specific coin. He wished everyone else would do it the courtesy of calling it by its name.

"I remember."

"Did you receive a finder's fee? For the story?"

Dante frowned. "Was I supposed to?"

"Maybe not. I was just wondering." Bane shrugged, feeling suddenly embarrassed.

Dante froze, looking over Bane's head. "Hey Bane, don't whip around like you do—don't!" Bane froze, half turned in his seat already, because how could he not? "I think someone is picking pockets in my shop."

"It's not your shop," Bane started to argue, but then realized that wasn't the point his friend was trying to make. "Oh. Who?" He gazed into the shiny reflection of the espresso maker, scanning the warped blobs of the patrons.

"You won't see it in that. Have you got a mirror? Pull it out and pretend to ring someone."

"I am literally the last person in this city that doesn't have one," Bane lamented. Dante rectified this by pulling his own out and presenting it to Bane so he could peek over his shoulder.

"Right. Short fellow, brown hair. Green cloak. He came in, stood and looked at the menu pretending to contemplate his order, let people in front of him, and now he's backing away. See him?"

Bane caught sight of the person, who looked hardly older than a boy, in the reflection. His face was smooth, nose sharp, and the green cloak Dante had referred to was so patched and shabby it was hardly any one color, but describing it as green was close enough. "Did you see him? Pick a pocket?"

Dante nodded. "Yes. I see everything in my domain. This"—he traced a circle around the room with a finger—"is my kingdom to reign over and protect. No one steals from my home. Look, he's about to do it again."

They watched as the hand casually slipped into the pocket of a cloak hung on the back of a chair.

"Impressive," Bane confessed, admiring the handiwork.

"Teach him a lesson, will you?"

Bane cringed. "I'm security, but I'm not *your* security."

Dante opened the drawer of the register and pulled out two OCCs, set them on the counter. "Are you now?"

"This is off the books," Bane hissed and swiped them into his pocket. He picked up his drink and chugged it before he calmly stood and made his way to the front door. He passed by the pickpocket and made a show of accidentally bumping into him. "Pardon me," Bane said, catching the young man's shoulders and getting a good look in his face when he turned, startled. Bane saw he was no boy, but in fact a full-grown halfling man.

But Bane wasn't a pickpocket and couldn't use this opportunity to simply retrieve the stolen goods from the thief's pocket without causing a scene. Instead, he opened the door and motioned outside. "Leaving?"

The pickpocket, caught off-guard, said yes and thanked Bane. Bane let him through then followed him out. Why would the man suspect being followed by a patron simply leaving? Bane stayed just enough paces behind the pickpocket so that when the man passed the alley, Bane lunged forward, grabbed him by the cloak, and whipped him in between the two buildings.

The pickpocket flew to the ground. Bane stood over him, a foot planted on either side of the man's hips. "Cough it up, thief."

Bane wasn't expecting the pickpocket to swing his legs up and over Bane's legs, kicking Bane flat on his back. The breath flew out of him. In an instant the pickpocket was over him, a blade in Bane's face.

"Going to rob me next? Go right ahead, I'm flat broke," Bane said, feeling a hand shimmy into his pocket. He watched the man's face closely, saw his eyes go distant with concentration. The moment they did, Bane bent his head forward and grabbed the blade between his teeth. He whipped his head to the side and flung the blade toward his right hand, catching it. Though lethargic, his reflexes were sharp that day. Perhaps to make up for the hazard of being so tired.

The pickpocket stopped his rustling and quickly pulled his hand out of Bane's pocket. Bane shoved a hand against the man's abdomen, rolled the pickpocket off him, and now it was Bane holding the blade in the other's face. Bane had the good sense to point the tip at the throat. He smelled the burst of perspiration and understood that the man was suddenly very afraid.

"What are you, some sort of warrior?"

Bane barked a laugh. "Flattery won't work here. Hand it back." He held his other hand out and the coins dropped in. He stuffed them in his pocket and got up, motioned for the pickpocket to do the same. "What's your name?"

"What's it to you?"

"Way I see it, either I drag you to the authorities, or you tell me your name and we hash out a deal."

The panic left the man's eyes, and he stood. "Name's Balio, Professional Pickpocket." He gave a mocking curtsy. "Does my new master have a name?"

"Bane."

"Is that your real name?"

"Is it yours?"

Balio's eyes narrowed. "Well played. So. What do you want me to do? March back there and put the coins back, perform an apology dance and swear on the gods I won't do it again?"

"Even better. You're going to teach me how to pick pockets."

12

Deal

The request came in the moment, inspired. Bane surprised himself when he said it and wanted to take it back immediately. But the thinking was, in that panicked moment, that maybe he could learn how to steal OCCs. Just those. Harmless, really.

Of course, stealing other coinage and taking it to any vendor worked just the same, but Bane figured they weren't real money, so it wasn't really stealing.

Balio barked a laugh. "Yer jokin' me."

Bane stood a bit straighter. "I'm not. *You* do it. Why not me?"

"Why would I teach my competition?

"That's my business." Bane didn't owe a *pickpocket* an explanation. "Or do you want to get locked in the dungeons?"

"I hear they're not so bad. Could probably get a few square meals there." At this response, Bane bared his teeth, which had already grown a bit longer and sharper throughout the day. That did the job alright. "Fine. What do you want to know? Straight pickpocket?"

"Do you use magic?"

"Not I. Haven't the gift. Wasn't blessed enough to get trained by the fancy people. Simply do it old-fashioned."

Magic was everywhere, to be learned by anyone who put the time and effort into mastering it. It was like learning a new language; there were spells to learn and memorize and practice to make powerful, like perfecting an accent. Plenty in Everdorne knew amateur magic, picked up at home or in school. Some self-taught from spell books available in bookshops. A few practiced medicinal and physical magic regularly to become witches and wizards, and far fewer excelled at advanced and elemental magic to become sorcerers. Bane didn't know any magic beyond lighting a candle in an emergency. He assumed there were spells to pick pockets, illegal as they were, and he wasn't sure he had the patience to learn them. And so he was relieved to hear Balio say this, that there was a way to master thievery without the grunt work of learning and wielding magic.

Bane followed Balio out of the alley into the street, holding onto the dagger as collateral so that Balio wouldn't bolt. "You'll get it back once I've got coin in hand," Bane promised.

Balio led them to a bench in a patch of grass and took a seat, nodded for Bane to join him. "The trick is to be ready to apologize. Act embarrassed to have brushed against them if they notice and confront you. Most people never expect an apology, and it catches 'em right off guard." Balio nodded to two people embracing in the street. "People be so caught up in themselves, they hardly notice the world spin 'round them. Those two? I could pick the gold from their teeth, and they wouldn't even see me."

Bane watched them kiss and immediately thought of Lusine. What was he doing? This was right mad, absolute lunacy. She'd skin him alive if she discovered what he was up to. He dragged a hand over his face.

"Alright, mate?"

"Fine," Bane said quickly. "You look for someone distracted. Then what?"

"Look for a pocket, an open sack, a bulge with easy access. Or drunks with gaudy jewelry stumbling home. Grab 'em under the arm, help 'em home for a bit, deposit them just shy of their front door so the butler don't notice. Never take it all. Too obvious. They'll let you rob 'em blind, but that'll send the hounds right for ye. Take a bit so they think they've left too much at the bar or handed the ring to a pretty gal they just met."

"Does everyone follow those rules?"

"Sure. We've a guild."

"A guild? For pickpockets?" Bane laughed. "You're lying."

Balio crossed a finger over his heart. "If we all robbed everyone blind, there would be hysteria. The Crown would mosey on down, have a look, sweep the streets clean. Don't want that. Would put us out of our profession. That's why there are rules."

"And if you don't uphold them?"

"Then ye meet the Cutthroat Guild." Balio dragged a thumb across his neck and cocked an eyebrow knowingly. Bane howled with laughter.

"You're pulling my leg, thief."

"The underbelly of the city is hidden in plain sight. Those who have this ring on their finger?" He held up a hand, wiggled his index finger to show the red carnelian set in a gold band. "We're the members of the shadow world. Hands for hire. Now that you know, you'll see us everywhere. Welcome to our realm. I thought you knew, seeing as how ye caught me today."

"I didn't, actually," Bane confessed. "My friend did."

"That barista's a demon, ain't he?"

"He is."

Balio let out a string of curses. "Suspected it. Should have followed me instinct on that chap. Where's he from?"

"What do you mean?"

"I mean, where do demons come from?"

Bane blinked at him, utterly confused. "I haven't a clue."

"Ye never asked?"

"No one ever asks me where I'm from. I didn't ask you either. Are you supposed to ask a demon where he's from?"

"Suppose that could be seen as rude." Balio shrugged. "Suppose that might make him feel a bit foreign." He scanned the crowd. "We'll leave the lovebirds. See that man there? Ordering a meat stick?"

Bane nodded.

"I'll take that one. Watch. Then you pick one and come meet me in the alley I go into."

Bane nodded. Balio stood and walked right up to the roasting meats stand, right behind the man he'd pointed out. He pressed up against the man's back as if trying to look around him at the menu. Without thinking, the man shifted, and if Bane hadn't been staring, unblinking, he would have missed the pocket being pulled open, the patchwork cloak swishing, hiding the hand that dove in and out of the pocket. Bane would have clapped it was such a beautifully executed performance. He looked around, expecting someone, anyone else to have also witnessed it, but Balio was right; everyone was completely oblivious to the people orbiting around them, spiraling in their own narratives. Until they collided and, like Bane and Balio, became aware and entangled.

Bane watched Balio shake his head at the shopkeeper and walk off, duck into an alley. Bane scanned the passersby milling around. Who would he pick? He thought of Balio's comment about being part of the invisible underbelly of crime. He decided that if he had stepped through the veil, then he was wearing it and was now totally undetectable. *Be a shadow.* It gave him the confidence he needed to walk up to the woman whose back was turned to him. Her hands were full of shopping bags and her leather purse was draped cross-body, the pouch resting against her back. She stood waiting for the candle to turn green to let her cross the intersection and Bane joined her. *Nothing suspicious*, he thought. *Just crossing the street, same as her.*

He stood directly behind her and reached out, turned the clasp on the purse so that the flap released. He stuck his hand in and then the candle changed green.

The woman lunged forward, and Bane did, too. He grasped the purse with his other hand to keep it from slapping her back, his hand still caught inside, frantic to find something that felt like a coin in the mess in there. How was there so much junk in a purse so tiny?

The purse strap slipped and fell down the woman's shoulder, catching on the shopping bag. Bane got his hand out just in time as she reached to pull it up, glancing over her shoulder as she did. "Oh, hello!"

"Ms. W-walsh," Bane stammered, recognizing the woman as the mother of one of his former classmates.

"Bane!" She immediately recognized him because his mother had taught two of her four children. "Marmie's son, right? Good to see you!"

Bane blushed so hard he half hoped it would keep getting hotter and engulf him completely in flames. He reached out and helped push the strap back into place, because how could he not?

"Happy New Year," she said, finishing crossing the street. She turned to get a good look at him. "My, you're so big!"

Bane gave an embarrassed shrug. "Couldn't help it."

"What is it you do now?"

The terror vanished, replaced by dread. He didn't have time for this, not when there was a pickpocket waiting in an alley for him. Not when daylight was fading, and he was running out of hours before his transformation. But her comment felt a little too perfect not to segue into, "Well, actually, I work for Best Buzzems. If you ever find yourself in need of a broomstick…"

By the time Bane made it to the alley Balio ducked into, he was almost certain the pickpocket had abandoned him. But there he was, chuckling. "Can't help being a good guy, can ye?"

"She needed help loading up her carriage," Bane mumbled, kicking a clump of snow on the ground.

"Ye sure ya want to do this?"

"I'm not," Bane confessed. "But I still have your dagger."

"So you do. Suppose I just steal it back sometime."

Bane bared his teeth and a flicker of something inhuman shone through, stumping Balio, who raised his hands in surrender. "Fine, I won't. But I want it back. It's a bit sentimental."

"You'll get it back," Bane assured. "It'll just cost you."

Balio took an angry step forward. "Naw, yer not blackmailing me to the end of my days."

Bane had about a full head on the other man, but he wasn't in the mood for another fight that day. "No. A simple transaction. I want ten OCCs."

"What are those? The fool's gold coins?"

"Yes," Bane said, deciding it wasn't worth the effort to educate him. "Bring me ten, and the dagger's yours again."

"Right." Balio spit in his hand and extended it.

Bane looked at it, horrified. "Just...thief to thief, I'll take your word."

Balio snorted. "Yer no thief."

Bane wiggled the dagger.

Balio rolled his eyes. "Ye got me there. All right. Ten of ye fool's gold coins. I'll ring when I've got 'em. You've a mirror, haven't ye?"

"Of course." He would by the time Balio had them collected, Bane vowed to himself. Soon as he got the chance, he would go to a pawn shop. Things were getting complicated without one.

13

Full Moon

The day of the full moon, Bane woke up starving and cleared out the ice box. He ate until his stomach hurt and then put the rest in a sack to take to work with him. It was a day Lusine looked forward to, when all the meat that had been hoarded in their ice box was finally consumed, making room for all the things she liked to eat for a few weeks.

Bane was jittery all day. He helped the few customers who came in since Candor decided to spend his last day in the coffee lounge of New Brooms, jollying with the other salesmen and leaving at lunchtime to a flourish of applause from the crew.

It was around then that Bane wondered if he should have stayed home. He felt mopey all alone in Used Brooms, but seeing as all the broomsticks were unenchanted, it was imperative he be there.

Mid-afternoon, Gerwin wandered in and clapped Bane on the shoulder from behind, scaring him half to death.

"Bane!" Gerwin swallowed his chuckle. "How's the new broomstick working out for you?"

Bane gulped. He hid the Fly-by in the broom closet as soon as he arrived, ashamed of the shape it was in. He meant to talk to Son about fixing it up and getting a discount on the repairs, but he figured as long as it still worked there was no rush, especially since he only had fake coins to his name until the next day's pay. He had gone back to the Copper University and given what Balio had stolen from pockets to Dante. "Grand, thanks."

"I was thinking...forget it being a loan. It's yours. As a bonus. You really helped clear out inventory last week. Good job." Gerwin needed the room for the new shipment that was arriving that day, but he wouldn't confide such a thing in someone so low in the chain of command as Bane. Let Bane think his boss was wonderfully generous, at least for the day.

Bane blinked in shock. "You're sure?"

"Dead serious." Gerwin winked and made to turn, but Bane stopped him with, "Our jobs...they'll still be ours tomorrow, won't they?"

Gerwin heaved a sigh. "As of tomorrow, it's the new boss's business. What they decide is up to them. I'm not firing you, and I've put in my recommendation that they keep current staff. But I did make another recommendation. That they move you to New Brooms."

Bane's jaw dropped. "You're joking."

Gerwin grinned. "Keep up the good work. You're all set for tonight?"

"Y-yessir."

"Good. Thanks for your hard work." Gerwin put his hand out as Candor had and Bane shook it. He felt grown up. Working here had given him a sense of inclusion he hadn't felt in years, surrounded by men who mentored him. He knew if he had to leave this lot, he would be devastated.

In the afternoon, a carriage driven by an armed orc arrived. Criss-crossed with swords on his back and knives on his belt, he unloaded the packages. It was new inventory purchased with the OCCs Gerwin received for the Twig. The fact that he was able to write these new broomsticks into the sales contract as part of the final assessment price had Honey's eyebrows raised to her hairline. Those fool's gold coins were paying off surprisingly well. Gerwin hadn't anticipated the broomstick manufacturer to accept the coins, but it was the only one of the big five that did, so he jumped on the deal. All the able bodies—this meant Bane, Aeryn, Ezra, and Son—were rounded up to help unpack as Honey stood with quill and parchment in hand, checking off the order list before paying the driver for completing his job. Watching the orc pull himself back onto his carriage seat, Bane thought, *now* that *job probably pays a lot.*

Finally, closing time came. Bane's stomach had been growling for the last hour. He jumped on his broomstick and flew to Yoni's Grilled Meats. Bane still had a bone to pick with the owner. He jumped off his broomstick and stormed through the door, but Yoni was prepared.

"Nah-ah-ah! I've already been yelled at by your crazy boss."

Bane stopped short. "Mel?"

"Yes! I heard her complaint, I heard what happened, I'm profusely sorry. Meat's on me."

Bane balked. He wasn't much to pick fights, but he would have won this one, he really would have, and he suddenly felt robbed of an opportunity. But free food? "You're still a good man," Bane grumbled, accepting the heaping boxes. He quickly opened each to make sure there weren't any smoldering coals inside.

"Tie them down good," Yoni warned and gave a friendly wave at Bane's parting back.

Usually, Bane had time to go home for a nap between the store closing and when he was due back for security duty, but Terry had flagged him down and asked him to come earlier. He had to disenchant all the brooms, not just juice them up in preparation for the handoff of the store. "It'll just about take all night," Terry lamented.

Bane didn't mind. He still swooped over to his apartment and fetched the overnight sack with his pillow and blanket. Then he headed back to the dealership.

It looked the same as always, but it felt different that day. Everyone had gone out of their ways to say goodbye when they left, as if tomorrow was an uncertainty. Despite what Gerwin told them, and Bane specifically, it still was. Business was business, and Bane knew enough to know he had no idea what decisions had to be made in this situation. He grappled with the thought of losing his position and finally decided that he would ask for his old job back at Copper University if worst came to worst. Or he would keep delivering for Mel, so long as orders came and P.U.K.E. was still on strike.

Bane sat in the center of the lot, on the grass crunchy with frost, and began unpacking his feast. He waved as Terry approached the New Brooms building and went back to setting the platters around him, drooling. But he resisted, knowing it would taste so much better as a wolf.

Bane waited.

His hunger morphed into an anxious knot in his stomach, anticipating the coming transformation. The night was clear. The stars were bright out here so far north, away from the humdrum of the city center. A soft fall of snow began to dust the ground around him. It was nice, the quiet. He didn't always like it—it made him think. With nothing to distract him, his mind flickered through memories, pleasant and equally unpleasant. Often, he remembered the night of his initial transformation, the ritual, the bite. The following rejection by the pack, then by her.

Bane shook his head, trying to clear it and instead focus on happy memories. Remembering celebrations with his mother. Working with Dante. Meeting Lusine in the coffee shop.

Around midnight, Bane's skin began to prickle. He looked up and saw the moon smiling down at him. It didn't matter if it was obscured by clouds; some lore claimed the beams needed to touch his skin, but he felt the magic even through the thickest overcast. He threw his head back and howled. A flash of hot roared through him and his pores opened, releasing a wave of sweat and the new bristles of fur. They came more and more rapidly, coat by coat, until he was covered in fur. His face elongated, his bones broke and reformed into a snout, a tail. His fingers seared with pain as claws emerged, and finally his eyes went blind and then, when his vision returned, he was nocturnal. He could still stand on his two feet if he tried, but it was tiring and made his back ache. Prowling on all fours was the natural way now. The moments immediately after transformation were full of heavy panting. Then, gobbling. Transforming took enormous energy, and he often wondered how shifters did it so often. Maybe they didn't do it so often. Maybe that was why pigeons stayed pigeons; maybe they only transformed on their days off?

The meat gone, Bane laid on his side, eyes fluttering, fighting sleepiness. He watched through the glass as Terry made his way around the shop, zapping little currents of what looked like blue lightning into broomsticks with his wand. The snow came down a bit heavier now, and it felt nice, the flakes sizzling on his nose. The snow blanketed his fur, insulating him, and he grew warm and toasty.

In a bit he would get up and prowl the perimeter of the dealership. Terry knew not to come out until dawn. Bane was in hunting mode, searching for more meat. And everyone was a walking sack of meat. He had yet to come across an intruder; Bane was sure Gerwin made it known far and wide that he had a werewolf protecting his lot. It seemed no one was curious to find out if it was true or not. Bane's eyelids dropped, fluttered, settled shut.

Then, his nose twitched.

Bane lifted his head and sniffed. He opened his eyes and swiveled his head in the direction of the scent to find a perfectly cut juicy steak by the bushes.

Huh, had he forgotten one? Had it gone flying as he tore through the piles, gobbling down his meat?

Bane didn't care how it got there. He just knew he had to go eat it. He pressed up and gave a long, luxurious stretch. He shook the snow off his coat before trotting over to the edge of the lot where the prize was. He was very full from his meal and so decided to take his time and enjoy this cut, savor every bite.

He must have dozed off, because he was suddenly startled awake by shouts. It was morning, so early that the sun was barely peeping over the flat plane of the practice lot. Bane was naked and furless, and Honey stood over him, looking absolutely furious.

14

What Happened?

Bane blinked awake. He sat up and a piece of frozen meat fell from his chest into his lap, a massive bite missing from it. "What? What is it?"

"What happened?" Honey demanded.

"That's what *I'm* asking." Bane rolled over and found that it wasn't his blanket he shrugged off, but rather a layer of snow that had fallen over him in the night. His stomach growled. "What are you shouting about?"

Honey punched her hands onto her hips. "Where were you?"

"When?" Bane's mind spiraled, panicked by her hostility. "Were you robbed?" he asked, trying to guess why she was so upset.

"Terry's passed out inside. He was *obviously* attacked. What happened?"

Bane bolted over to the doors and pulled them open. Gerwin crouched over Terry, gingerly patting him on the face, trying to get him to rouse. He looked up at the sound of approaching steps. "He'll be fine. Something put him to sleep. Where are your clothes?"

Bane looked down and realized he was stark naked. He mumbled an apology, ran right past Honey without daring to look at her, and found his sack half-buried in the fresh snow. He shook it open and pulled out his frigid clothes, which warmed as soon as he wrestled them on. His internal body temperature was astronomically high, which came in handy at that moment. He finished pulling his boots on and trotted back to where Gerwin was pulling Terry to his feet. "What happened?"

Terry put a hand to his head, dizzy. "Let me sit."

Honey was already steering a freshly brewed cup of coffee over. She handed it to Terry, who took it gingerly and sipped. Each gulp seemed to bring him around more until finally he set the mug down. "Thank you. We were attacked last night."

Gerwin and Honey immediately turned to glare at Bane. He threw his hands up to deflect the accusations. "Woah, hold on," he said and scrambled to remember what happened the night before. He didn't have to because Terry said, "It's not his fault. He was bespelled."

Bane put a hand to his head, trying to think even harder. He remembered now the meat he found, the one that had looked perfect, and now that he thought about it, suspiciously perfect. No way he could have afforded that. Yoni didn't even sell meat that well cut in his cases. He felt a fool now. Someone had tossed it in, enchanted with a sleeping spell.

"I was doing inventory when something hit me from behind," Terry continued. "They must have been watching, waiting to strike while my back was turned."

Gerwin went over to a broom lying in the middle of the showroom. He picked up the shiny new Dust Demiser and straddled it. He kicked off and fell back onto both feet. The broom was a dud. He looked around so see all the other brooms that where once suspended by magic now fallen on the floor. "Terry?"

Terry stood shakily and went over, pulled out his wand and aimed it at the handle, and whispered an enchantment. The broom gave a little quiver and stopped. Nothing. "Gods. They came in while they were unenchanted and reenchanted them. They won't accept my magic."

"Who did?" Gerwin demanded, grabbing Terry by the shoulders. "Terry, the new boss will be here *today*. I need these unlocked *now*."

A thud against the window made them all jump. They turned to see a pigeon—probably drunk—on the ground outside a window, shaking its head. There was a note in its carrier. Honey went out, fetched the note, and then the pigeon was off, shaky but gaining altitude.

Honey handed the note to Gerwin. He unrolled it, read, it then made to run after the pigeon, but it was already out of sight. "Gods! We need to get that pigeon!"

"Why?" Honey grabbed the note from his hand and read it. She released a string of expletives. "It's a ransom note."

Bane and Terry glanced at each other and gulped. As security, Bane suddenly got the bad feeling that maybe he was the one who would have to do something about this, but what did he know about dealing with ransoms? He couldn't even pick pockets!

Gerwin interrupted his spiraling thoughts with, "Simple. We pay the ransom. We make it all go away." But even as he said this, Gerwin didn't seem convinced this would be the end of things. "Also, I'm reporting this."

"Just ask the pigeon who sent him," Honey said, as if it was obvious.

"How do we find him? P.U.K.E. is on strike, so it wasn't one of theirs. It's a rogue pigeon," Terry said.

"Surely they have a tab on every pigeon in the city," Honey coaxed. "Just ask."

"Suppose it's that easy?" Gerwin ran a hand through his hair and suddenly remembered he was rich. "A hundred gold for whoever finds the culprit!" Gerwin announced, though it was just the four of them standing there.

Honey let out a low hiss and gave a sharp shake of the head. "Ten," she countered, eyeing Bane. "Ten gold."

Gerwin looked at her incredulously, then seemed to realize what a sum he had declared. "Fine, ten. Either one of you figures it out, I'll hand the coins over myself." Then he stormed into his office, Honey clipping after him in her impossibly high heels.

Bane looked at Terry, who clutched his throbbing head. "You reckon you know who did this?"

"Not a clue," Terry said. "And honestly, ten gold isn't worth the trouble to me. But if you find them and let me sock 'em I'll give you an extra gold."

Bane nodded. Ten gold was nothing to laugh at, and since he had nothing else to do that morning...

He stomped over to Dutch's desk, which Dutch never locked, and pulled out his mirror. He drew the rune for the operator. "Head of P.U.K.E., please."

The woman in the glass snorted and rolled her eyes. "They're on strike, sweetheart."

Right. "What about the next in charge?"

"Them too."

"*All* of them?"

"That's how a strike works."

He fumbled, wondering who to ask for instead. "Surely someone is in charge of the strike?"

"They're not available," she assured. "They're busy with negotiations."

"You won't even check?"

"They have a strict 'do not disturb' rune on their mirror. No going past that."

"Can I...leave a message?"

The woman looked scandalized. "I'm not a secretary," she snapped.

"I just want to talk to someone!"

"For what? Are you a lawyer?"

"No..."

"Then I doubt they want to talk to you. Sorry, toots." And then Bane found himself blinking at his own reflection.

That had been wildly unhelpful. For a moment Bane contemplated calling Lusine, since she was practically a lawyer, but then he'd have to get into what happened in the night and it just seemed like too much hassle. Besides, he remembered someone else just then.

Mel's face appeared in the mirror. Her hair was splayed across the pillow and she let out a tremendous yawn that she didn't even try to hide behind a hand. "Hallo, Bane. I've got more work for whenever you're ready. Did you finally get a mirror?"

"It's a work one," Bane said and hurried into explaining that he needed a letter tracked down. "Maybe your pigeon could ask around?"

"What's in it for him?" Mel asked. "He's not in the network, if that's what you suspect. He's his own master so he doesn't know the happenings of the guild. But I'm sure if you bribe him with enough, he'd look into it for you. Maybe. I honestly don't know what he gets up to these days."

"Can I talk to him?"

"Do you speak pigeon?"

"What do they speak?" Bane asked, blinking in confusion.

"Coos, mostly," Mel said, then gave a snorting laugh. "Look, come over and try to coax him into human form if you like, but I'm not bothering him. He's especially grumpy since they knocked him out of his nest. Say, how do you know the pigeon was even part of P.U.K.E.?"

"I suppose I don't," Bane grumbled, realizing that maybe this was, in fact, worth a hundred gold for the trouble it was. He told Mel he'd keep asking around and she told him in between shouts to her sons to make their own damn breakfast that Bane was welcome to come by if he changed his mind. "We might even have breakfast on the table by then," she said, and then Bane was blinking back at himself.

This went on for about an hour. He called Dante, and then a few acquaintances from school. He was back to contemplating calling Lusine when he noticed figures making their way across the lot toward New Brooms.

He hurried to the front doors and saw it was Mic Void, his hands cuffed in front of him, being dragged in by one of the officers of the Midnight Brigade. Bane gawked and then caught Honey's eyes. She gave a little shrug and leaned over to whisper, "He's the only one who knows the schedule, knows how to enchant brooms, and isn't afraid of a big bad wolf."

"Good sleuthing," Bane grumbled, realizing that he would not be getting the gold now. Not that he was any closer than he was an hour ago.

Gerwin walked over, appearing calm, but trembling with rage underneath the façade. "I should have suspected you would stab me in the back, old friend."

Mic sneered at him. "I give you all my best years, and this is how you repay me? You go and sell it to someone else? You should have taken my offer."

"You shouldn't have put your offer as the ransom amount," Gerwin chided. "Is Aeryn in on this?"

"Leave my son out of it."

"Oh, but I can't. Bad blood and all." He turned to Bane. "Congratulations, your promotion takes effect immediately. Welcome to the New Brooms sales team. Go home, take the day off. Tomorrow you're reporting to this building."

"C-can I get my pay?"

"Right. Honey?"

"Give me a minute." Honey took the sack of coins into her father's office, pulled out the payroll parchment, calculated his pay, and came back out to hand Bane his wage. "Don't spend it all at once," she chided, but it didn't sound as funny as all the other times she said this. She was shaken up, and it showed.

Bane took the sack of coins. "I won't."

He went outside to round up his belongings. The sack sans clothes was where he left it, but it took a bit to find his broomstick, which was hidden under a layer of fresh snow.

When Bane pulled it out, he noticed a fresh crack in the handle and realized Mic must had stepped on it when he trespassed. Bane squeezed his eyes shut and let the wave of fury pass. *At least it's still enchanted*, he told himself as he hopped on and the Fly-By took off. He felt he needed a bath. Or a good cry. Or maybe both, at the same time.

15

Uncle Amos's

Bane arrived home feeling dazed. He walked in just as the sun was high enough that most folks began to rouse from their beds. He approached his bed to find Lusine in it, warm under the mountain of blankets. Just her head and the spray of her hair poked out from under the mound. He leaned down and kissed her. When she didn't respond, he kissed her again, and again, and again until her agitated shifting to escape his prickly pecks turned into pleased giggling. Her eyes finally fluttered open. "Hello there."

"Good morning." Bane pulled himself into the bed, climbed onto the mountain of blankets. Lusine let out a soft "oof" from the weight of him until he got his bearings and hovered over her, and it felt rather nice. "Let me take you out for breakfast."

"You're off today?"

Bane nodded. "It's...been a night."

"Oh? Did something go wrong?"

Bane felt exhausted just thinking about it and didn't feel like explaining before the day's first meal. "Nothing eggs and sausage can't fix."

"And coffee?"

"A bucket of it." He gave her a final kiss and rolled off her, peeling the blankets back with him. She yelped and fought to grab them back. They wrestled like this until Lusine gave in, panting. "Alright. But you're paying," she said and leapt from the bed.

Bane rolled onto his side and watched her dress. Well, undress then dress. He liked that first bit a lot more. He watched her thin shift dress drop from her shoulders to her ankles. She gave a little turn and pretended there wasn't an audience, even as he gave an approving growl.

"I got a promotion today."

"Oh? From the new owners?"

"No..." Suddenly it didn't feel as good, now that she pointed out without meaning to that it would have meant more from the new owners. He decided to tell her about it anyway. "From Gerwin. I'm the new New Brooms Salesman."

"Oh! That's lovely. Who's taking over Used Brooms?"

"I suppose whoever the new owners bring in."

"Will they be in today?"

"Perhaps. They need to disenchant and reenchant all the broomsticks today."

"I thought Terry disenchanted them last night?" She let out a little "oof" as she tightened the strings of her corset.

"Come on, let's get a seat at the Poached Piper before I get into this," he urged.

Lusine floated over and leaned down, gave a loud sniff. "You ought to change, too."

Embarrassed, Bane jumped up and did just that, not putting on a show as Lusine had. Dressed, he grabbed her hand and led her out the door. She tugged away as he tried to pull her onto the broomstick. "Why's it all bent up like that? I thought you knew how to ride?"

"It's...." *A long story.* "Fine! We'll walk!"

Their bellies full of breakfast, Bane and Lusine walked hand-in-hand through the rows of shops in the Commerce District, enjoying the sunny morning, the bitter crisp air nibbling their cheeks. It was magical, the day after a night of snowfall. Everything felt clearer, sharper, more in focus.

"Those all mean the same thing," Lusine teased when Bane said this. "What are we shopping for?"

"A mirror," Bane said with flourish, pulling the door of a pawn shop open.

Uncle Amos's was a labyrinth of just about anything anyone needed, for any price they wanted to spend. There were broomsticks here, too, even quite nice ones, though the shop was known for its jewelry, a vast collection of magic-amplifying crystals, enchanted chamber pots that ate excrement—now that indoor plumbing was getting popular, these were fading in fashion—and carriage parts.

There was a small assortment of cloaks on a rotating display, boots that were in various stages of being chewed up by the cobblestone, and pocket watches set to all sorts of times, occasionally bleating out alarms for who-knows-what.

Bane visited this shop often. He picked up second-hand trinkets as gifts for his mum, and she in turn came right back to exchange them for something else with the hope that her son wouldn't notice.

Lusine had never been inside a pawn shop and kept gawking at price tags, turning them over in shock.

"Yes, I know," Bane kept saying. "You'll never want to pay full price for leather goods again."

She started wandering over to a chest against the wall with a parchment tacked to it that read, "All Yer Dreams & Desires," but Bane grabbed her hand and yanked her back. "Probably some pervert's idea of a joke," he warned. He never opened boxes in pawn shops. *Ever.* Maybe it held an obscene figurine. Or maybe it was a mimic.

"Look at the knives," she marveled, walking up to the glass case, atop which an ancient register sat, battered and exhausted. The wall beyond the counter was covered with swords, daggers, shields, and an assortment of archery paraphernalia. Some still looked bloody from disputes, though Amos swore it was rust and refused any deeper discount.

Looking at them, Bane remembered the dagger he had lifted from the pickpocket. He made a mental note to remember to take it out of the trousers he discarded back at home. He wondered how much it would fetch here, if Balio never returned for it. Probably not a lot. Bane looked down into the case, where magic mirrors crowded the velvet cloth they sat upon, crammed beside glittering rings, bracelets, and amulets.

"I'm looking for a mirror," Bane informed Amos as he lumbered over to them, not used to having customers this early in the morning.

Amos was a grizzly half-giant with a thick black beard and hair tied back from his face. His fingers were heavy with rings, his neck laden with thick glittering chains. "Right-o! I've got a good lot. See one you like?"

"Where did these come from?" Lusine asked, peering down in wonder at all that glittered.

"I've got a man who fishes them out of the river. You won't believe what all people lose in there."

"How about those?" Bane pointed to a few mirrors he liked.

Amos unlocked the case and began pulling them out and setting them on the counter. "I gots a sorcerer who comes in and tinkers with them, makes sure everything works tippity-top."

"Are any of these cursed?" Lusine asked, pointing to the amulets beside the mirrors Amos reached in for.

"Some were. They're safe now."

On hearing this, Lusine reeled a step back, just in case. She looked over at the mirrors Bane was picking up, each nicer than the last. She tried to tell him with her eyes that these were perhaps a little *too* nice, and didn't he have a budget in mind?

"They all work?" Lusine asked, trying to see how this whole haggling business went. Surely it began with insisting that the products weren't as nice as they initially seemed.

"They do. I make sure of it. Wouldn't be in business long if I sold broken junk. Still, people will try to pull a fast one. But I know you, Bane, so I'll do exchanges. No returns." Amos motioned to a parchment tacked to the wall behind him that said just that. Beside the pledge to do good business was the business license stamped with the official royal seal. And beside that was another parchment that Bane squinted at, read, and laughed. "You're joking. You've got the running price of OCCs?"

Amos nodded. "I take those, too. It's nice to meet a man who's not calling them fool's gold coins. It dismisses their worth."

"Why? They're not—" Lusine caught herself before she said "real." If it could be exchanged for goods or services, why, that made any bit of metal a real tender.

Amos gave a sly smile. "There's no tax on OCCs."

Bane and Lusine exchanged a glance. "How so?"

"Law states that taxes are to be paid on all coins exchanged for goods and services. The coins written into the law are the ones printed by the royal mints: copper, nickel, silver, and gold. Aluminum, even, if you're rich enough to pay with that. But there are no sales tax laws written on OCCs. It's no-man's land, completely unregulated. These royal registers?" Amos banged a fist on his and it gave a disgruntled sigh. "It's been enchanted to automatically calculate that tax. Not OCCs. Even if they make a law about these coins, they're undetectable. They're not even real metal! The Crown has no say in its worth; its value comes completely from the people."

Lusine frowned. "How is that fair?"

"What do you mean?" Bane asked her. "Who is it unfair to?"

"I suppose the Crown."

"Oh, so His Highness will enjoy one less feast?" Amos scoffed. "Deregulation is the future. My shop, my rules. No one tells me what anything in here is worth but me. It's not like other businesses that have guilds and oversight on what to price things, and they have to get it into the books at the Chamber of Commerce so the Crown knows what to tax 'em. Imagine, now, if everyone began to pay for everything in OCCs. The power of purchase would go to the people."

Bane's eyes shone with excitement. Hearing this...he finally felt validated. He felt powerful, or at least that he could be, if only he had those coins. He looked to Lusine, hoping she finally understood, but she merely looked confused. "If you say so," she said. "Do you still accept old-fashioned coins? Or do we need to take our business elsewhere?"

"Regular coins are fine, but you'll have less haggle power," Amos said with a shrug.

"Alright. Give me this one for one OCC." Bane picked up not the nicest mirror, but a fairly nice one. It was set in a compact case that closed to prevent scratches. It had a round white opal to press to easily turn the glass from reflecting to scrying. Amos demonstrated how it controlled the channels viewed in the glass by simply rolling the stone left and right or up and down to start and end a call. This enchanted mirror was far more advanced than even the ones introduced a year ago, which required the user to swipe runes on the surface for every command. Bane had no patience to learn them, so this one was perfect. The price tag showed it was worth several silver, which Bane didn't carry on him and if he did, would be loath to part with. He still had his full pay in his pocket (minus the breakfast bill), which he had brought along with every intention of spending. He didn't want to spend the OCC either, but it felt thrilling, partaking in this parallel market. He wanted to see if it worked. Would the transaction go through?

"Sold."

Lusine's eyes went wide, and Bane balked a second, unsure he had heard correctly. He quickly fished the coin out, set it on the counter and said a hurried, "Thank you."

Amos didn't punch anything into the register and simply pocketed the coin. "Thank *you* for your business."

Bane and Lusine hurried out, afraid their good fortune would expire if they lingered too long. Outside, Bane erupted in laughter, and Lusine too had a grin she couldn't shake. "I can't believe you just did that."

Bane pumped a victorious fist in the air. "Watch, I'm going to collect a whole bucket of these. We'll be so rich."

"If you say so," Lusine said. "Try calling me, I want to see how it works. I think it's even nicer than mine."

Bane was proud to confirm that in fact it was. It was now by far the nicest thing he owned, and that included his broomstick.

16

Summoned

Bane got the mirror just in time, because that evening he got a ring from Balio to report he had procured the ten OCCs.

"Meet me at Copper University?" Bane suggested. "The one we met at?" He unloaded his payday coins into a small, perpetually empty chest by his bed. It would be foolish to meet a pickpocket with them on him.

"Fine. But only after it's closed."

Bane decided to leave a little early to visit with Dante and set off on foot. The shop was nearly empty except for a few stragglers, some of whom Bane suspected spiked their cider or hot chocolates with a smuggled-in flask. If he noticed, Dante didn't seem to mind. The demon shouted a jolly, "Ahoy!"

"I'm going to go clean," Jaymie announced. "Hello, Bane."

"Stay for a drink," Bane urged, but she rolled her eyes and headed to the back.

"Tea? Cider? Oh, someone ordered a frothed milk with lavender today, it's..." Dante kissed his fingertips. "Divine. A bit too much of a nod to spring for me, but I found some dried flowers in a jar shoved to the back of a cupboard that came right back to life when they were steeped."

Bane wrinkled his nose. "I think I'll just have a hot chocolate. With pumpkin. And cinnamon."

"I'm going to grate some nutmeg on top, too." The way Dante said this left no room for debate, but with him there never was. Never argue with a bartender, never question a barista.

As Dante steamed the milk, Bane read the menu behind the bar.

Drip coffee~ 1 copper

Espresso shot~ 1 copper

Steamed vanilla or chocolate milk~ 2 copper

Mint-sprig chocolate milk~ 2 copper

(espresso shot + 1 copper)

Cinnamon-Pumpkin chocolate milk~ 3 copper

(espresso shot + 1 copper)

Ask barista for something extra special. Menu subject to change.

"Do they ask you for something special often?"

"Sometimes. Never if it's their first time. Regulars that are chatty will, but they usually go back to their regular orders afterward. They'll almost always try a new seasonal flavor once."

"But they don't like it?"

"It might become their new regular order. It just depends," Dante said with a shrug. "I don't get offended if they don't like something."

"Nothing offends you. Everything just rolls off you," Bane mused. "How do you do it?"

Dante gave a good-natured shrug. "I don't make anything about me. Why, thinking of trying something extra special?"

"I have a different request to ask of you." Bane suddenly felt shy, like he had with asking about the finder's fee.

"This will help coax it out." Dante set the mug in front of Bane. Jaymie walked out from behind the counter to the front door and flipped the sign from 'Open' to 'Closed.' Then she began to politely notify guests that it was time so close shop.

"Oh no, is it too late?" Bane asked, looking around for a clock.

"Help me wipe a few tables after you're done with your drink and you can stay as long as you like," Dante said.

"That's right, you live upstairs."

Dante grinned. "Work perk."

Bane took a sip of his drink and a shiver rolled down his spine. Now that he was a werewolf, he was always hot, sweating, needing little clothing even on a cold winter night like this. But this drink's warmth was the sort that made him want to sink into it, like a cushion worn away by a bottom bigger than his own.

"Dante, how did you come to be?"

"What do you mean?"

"I mean, *I* was born. Most people are born. They're made by their parents and come out of their mothers. But you said you were summoned. Summoned from where? Is that just what your people call being born?"

Dante hadn't been around this dimension as long as Bane, but he had been around long enough to ask around, spend time in the library, and, with the infinite knowledge accessible by mirrors, ask questions directly to specialists. "Where did *you* come from, before you were born?"

Bane blinked, confused. "I don't know. I didn't exist, I suppose."

"So, you were summoned by your parents."

"I suppose?"

"Well, I was summoned by whoever summoned me. That boy playing with the spell book."

"Did the spell summon you specifically? Or did it just open a portal that you fell through?"

"There are theories." Dante paused to clean the milk frothing stick. "That sorcerers of this world found ways to pull people from other worlds into theirs so that they could entrap them and use them as slaves. One day I had a whole life, like this one, and I was just plucked out of it. Others think it's not another world I'm from, but another timeline, either in the future or in the past. Bit of traveling through time. I have no recollection so I can't confirm or deny."

"You told me one day you opened your eyes and saw a boy holding a book and screaming at you. That you ran all the way here, where Jaymie took pity on you and took you in. You were naked, but you could speak our language, and you look human enough, if the tips of your fingers weren't blackened, your eyes weren't crimson, and if your tongue didn't have that bit of a split in it."

"Also this." Dante rolled up his shirtsleeve to reveal the ring of tiny tattoos around his bulging bicep.

"Have you had a sorcerer look at it?"

"No. Not...yet." Dante said it like he was meaning to, but Bane got the impression he wasn't.

"Why?"

"Honest? I like it here. I have a good life. I like my job, I like you, I like the people I exist around. What do I have to go back to? I don't know. It could be worse."

"You could be a Duke or a Prince or a King over there," Bane teased.

"Or maybe I was enlisted in an experiment and volunteered to be summoned here. Maybe I had been trying to escape the other dimension. I don't know. But that there's a chance it could be worse makes me not want to." Dante finished swirling the whipped cream onto the drink and slid it down the bar. "Peppermint mocha for Alex!"

"You're that happy, eh?" Bane marveled.

Dante shrugged. "Dare I say, some people even find me handsome here."

That he was, there was no denying it. Dante flashed a wink at the customer who picked up their drink. They waved a good-natured goodbye, as if they were old friends. Bane was sure that moment would stay with them at least until they went to bed. There were several Copper Universities in this city, but this one was the coziest. It was definitely because of its head barista.

Dante turned back to Bane. "Why ask me this now?"

"I had a crazy idea that if you could be summoned here, people could get summoned elsewhere."

"Where do you want to be summoned?"

"Inside the palace courtyard."

Dante let out a low whistle. "Not the new queen's bedchamber?"

Bane balked. "It's not like that!" Dante pushed the cleaning function on the machine, and Bane watched him laugh behind the screen of steam. When the steam cleared Bane added, "I want to find OCCs. They're worth money. I need money. I want to propose to Lusine, but I can't afford a ring!"

"Here, take mine." Dante reached into the tip mug and pulled out a handful of coins. It was a mix of coppers, nickels, and even three OCCs.

Bane balked even more. "No, I can't!"

"Please. You seem very impassioned. It would make me happy to see you happy."

"You could afford a house with this, maybe, someday," Bane said. But then he reached out and accepted the coins. It was hardly a fortune. He still had to keep his job selling broomsticks. And Lusine was still constantly pulling ahead, getting smarter and closer to her dream career while he had nothing, not even a way to prove his devotion to her. Not that she doubted it or needed something tangible to remind her.

But still...maybe soon this would be enough for a ring?

"Dante, you are the best friend in the world."

"You are kind." Dante handed him a rag, as if this was how Bane could prove it. Bane took it and cleaned with gusto. As he wiped each table he peeked under it, just to be sure. He ran a hand over each chair he passed, sticking his fingers deep into where the cushions met, just in case any coins had been swallowed. When he deposited the waste in the trash, he tried to poke around the bin inconspicuously, in case he caught sight of any fool's gold. No luck. He did see a nickel near the bottom, but that wasn't worth reaching his hand in.

He checked the clock and made sure he had the rag washed, wrung out, and drying in the back before he headed out to his second meeting of the night.

Bane stepped out into the cold that wasn't so cold. He headed to the place he and Balio had agreed to meet and found the pickpocket there already, stomping his feet against the cold. Bane pulled the cloak tighter around him, wearing it as a shield, hoping to hide his image from any passersby.

"Oy, let's make this quick." Balio tossed Bane a pouch. Bane caught it expertly, shook out the coins. "It's all there."

"So it is." Bane pulled the blade from his pocket and turned it over, presenting it hilt first. Balio took it and returned it to the sheath at his belt, patting it as if soothing an old friend.

"Well, so long," Bane said and turned to leave.

"Oy, d'you see the paper this morning?" Balio called, stopping Bane in his tracks.

Bane turned. "No, I was off today."

Balio wasn't sure how the two were related. "Saw an article about some mirror celebrity who used those coins to buy a rare spell book. A first edition of *The Joys of Spell Casting*. Almost didn't bring the coins when I read that. They're worth a lot, eh?"

Bane didn't know what to say besides, "A deal's a deal."

Balio put his hands up to show he meant no trouble. "I understand. All I'm saying is, ye might be onto somethin'."

Uneasiness grew in Bane's belly, but he forced a polite, "Thanks."

"See you 'round." With that, Balio vanished. The shadows swallowed him, or maybe he used magic, Bane wasn't sure. Maybe it was a pickpocket trick. Bane shoved the pouch of coins into his cloak pocket to join the coins Dante had given him. He had never had so much value on him at once, and it made him anxious. He wasn't even sure how much the coins in his pocket were worth, but he knew enough that it made him break into a sweat as he hurried through the streets of his neighborhood.

Bane nearly made it home when a red dragon dropped out of the sky onto his shoulders, wrestled him to the ground, and gobbled the coins out of his pocket, cloth and all.

If Bane hadn't been so tired from transforming, he might have been able to fight it off, but he was simply out of strength. The dragon was no tiny vermin either, but rather a good size, that of a fat alley cat. It had sharp claws and powerful muscles and wings that kept batting him in the face, keeping Bane down as he was robbed. Bane quickly gave in and let the snout sniff and take what it pleased.

When it was off him, taking to the sky and quickly flying out of reach, Bane sat up in the snow and screamed. He pounded his fists on the ground and cursed the gods. No one even noticed; everyone had gone inside their warm, cozy homes. Besides, there were so many voices in a city so big, everyone simply assumed it wasn't their misery to deal with.

Bane picked himself up and dragged his weary bones up the stairs. He supposed he deserved this, trying to learn to pickpocket. He was so embarrassed that he couldn't tell Lusine the truth. When she noticed and asked about his torn cloak, he simply told her he had been pickpocketed and wouldn't say more. He shook his head when she insisted they alert the authorities. "Trust me, there are so many pickpockets in the streets, they'll never catch him."

To be robbed by a professional pickpocket was one thing. To be robbed by a dragon was an embarrassment he dared not mention.

Bane wasn't the sort that prayed, but he did mutter in the bath, "Let this be my clean slate. Tomorrow, I will be a new man. From my lips to the gods' ears, I will it to be."

The next morning Bane woke up none the richer but none the poorer. He still had his full pay in the chest by his bed, and that was something to be thankful for. The coins he lost had been ill-earned anyhow, and he would earn more properly, and they would stay in his pockets for it.

If only that was how fortune worked.

17
Subscription

The promise was short-lived. Bane woke up to pecking on their window and opened it to find a dove with the latest issue of *The Harking Herald*. Baffled, he accepted it, and while Lusine was in the bathroom unfurled it to read the now familiar finance column:

OCC Value: 2 golds.
Proof: First edition of The Joys of Spell Casting *sold for 10 OCCs, or the equivalent of 20 gold, as is fair market value.*
Future Value Estimate: 4 golds.

Bane's eyes just about bulged out of his head. The water shut off in the bathroom and a moment later the door opened. Lusine appeared, wrapped in her bath robe, and she emerged from a cloud of perfumed steam. "Lusine, when did we subscribe to *The Harking Herald*?"

"I just did. I thought you'd enjoy it." It wasn't an especially expensive paper, but it was a frivolous expense, something he simply couldn't afford. There was no polite way to ask how she could afford it, since it seemed they were both scraping by, him a lowly used broomstick salesman and her a full-time student. She supplemented the answer without his asking. "I got the job as the paralegal to the lawyer on the P.U.K.E. case. It's decent pay, and I might have a permanent job at the law office once I graduate this year."

"I didn't know that. When did you mention it?"

"I hadn't. I know you have been stressed about the buy/sell of the dealership."

"But yours is good news. Mine's not."

Lusine shrugged. "It's just work."

But Bane knew it wasn't. It was a big opportunity, monumental. This case, *P.U.K.E. vs the Crown*, it would make history, land in lawyer journals probably, if those were a thing, he wasn't sure. Maybe Lusine had mentioned them, and he had listened, hand to heart, but it was like listening to someone speak another language; it was hard to commit to memory what was said when it was hard to relate to it. "Are you still working at that non-profit, catching and releasing dragons with the queen?"

"I've got one last day planned. I need to train the girl taking over. I'm sort of relieved to be done with it. It's a lot of work. I know it looks great on a resumé, though."

Resumé. "Should I make one of those? A resumé?" Bane asked. "In case the New Brooms post doesn't work out?"

"You'll do fine there," Lusine assured.

It was kind to say. Bane worried he only got the job because Aeryn got fired but then remembered that Gerwin had offered it before that happened. He looked Lusine over and found himself envying her. She would never be given a job because of lack of personnel to fill it. The jobs Lusine would have, Bane knew there would be dozens of candidates vying for those positions, all equally brilliant and just as motivated as the next to be the shining star at a firm. And she would beat them all out. The envy morphed into ferocious admiration. He didn't feel worthy in that moment, being the baggage she dragged after herself from one great accomplishment to the next.

Lusine saw the smile fall from his face. She grasped his prickly cheeks in her perfectly manicured hands. "You're good enough," she whispered, and kissed him. "You'll get there."

"Where? Where am I going? I want to be your husband, Lusine, but I can't even afford a ring."

Lusine melted against him, pressing her mouth to his fiercely, trying to convey in that kiss all he was to her. He was the greatest supporter she had ever had. No one cheered for her louder than him, no one celebrated successes harder than he did. He went out of his way to sweep aside any and all obstacles that might trip her on her way to fulfill her dreams. She had told him this before, but he needed to know, and so she told him again between planting breathless kisses on his face, his neck, his shoulders, and finally in a place that made him think perhaps they would be alright after all.

"Are you excited to meet the new owners?" Lusine asked, steering the cup of coffee into the nest of clothes and blankets they had tousled around in the bed. The salesmen had been instructed to show up after lunch, since there was still owner-to-owner business to finish before they arrived and opened for the day. Gerwin already channeled a message through the mirror to all their prospects and customers. The story of the sale was also printed there in black and white in the business section of *The Herald*.

"I suppose I'm nervous," Bane said, taking the mug from Lusine and catching her in his lap.

She ran a hand through his dark, thick locks and kissed him on the crown of his head. "You'll be fine. We'll be fine. I promise."

They sipped their coffee in silence, holding each other, mentally preparing for the day. Then they got dressed, stepped out their front door, and made their way down the stairs that led like a spine to the door in the back of Ink Splotch. Lusine felt sure she was their number one customer. She ripped through quills at an astounding rate, the shopkeeper once noted. They stepped out into the cold and kissed each other goodbye before parting ways, Lusine to her fancy new job that smelled of expensive wood and leather furniture and much fancier ink, and Bane to what was formerly called Best Buzzems. He straddled his wonky broom and kicked off into the cold.

18

Black Staff

Bane pivoted in the center of the practice lot when he remembered he was no longer on the Used Brooms side. It sat dark and was probably locked, and he didn't have a key. Bane set his broom in the broomstick rack in front of New Brooms and pushed through the front doors into a scene of absolute chaos. Four sorcerers scrambled around, trying their best to disenchant the enchanted brooms so they could reenchant them with the new owner's spell. It seemed the louder they shouted, the more potent the spell was. Or perhaps that was just their frustration elevating. Gerwin was in his office, frantically gesticulating to the mirror he was facing. The meeting was clearly not going well.

Bane poured himself a cup of coffee. "I see it's going well."

Ezra, sitting at the lounge table trying to appear inconspicuous as he attempted to eavesdrop, heaved a sigh. "The door's too thick."

"Is Honey here?"

"No, she's a bit bent out of shape over what Mic did."

"Why didn't Gerwin just get Mic to bring that sorcerer back and un-spell all this?" Bane waved a hand around the showroom.

Ezra snorted. "Bane, you don't summon the same black staff sorcerer twice."

Bane frowned. "Black staff?"

"You know, black magic. *Illegal* magic. There's also grey staff. Those usually work for the Crown so technically all their magic is legal but still sometimes on the shady side of ethical." He nodded toward the ones barking orders at deaf brooms. "And then there's your everyday, easy-to-hire white staff sorcerers."

Bane blinked, confused. "They don't carry staffs."

"Not anymore. Now it's metaphorical staffs."

"Have they got their physical staffs at home? How do they advertise what they are?"

Ezra shrugged. "I've never hired a sorcerer. That's for rich people."

"Why would anyone choose to be a black staff?"

Ezra gestured around them. "Look at this mess. Mic paid him a pretty penny to do this. So long as there's work, there will be criminals in the underbelly."

There was that word again, the one Balio used. *Underbelly.* "How could Mic afford it?"

"That's just it. Gerwin finished the audit this morning and turns out, Mic has been scraping off the top and funneling profits into his own, private little nest egg for years."

"Isn't Honey our accountant? How did she not catch this?"

Ezra gave a dismissive wave. "She booked appointments and made bank runs. Mic was Gerwin's right hand, the real money man. That's why he was so livid that Gerwin up and decided to sell the place without consulting him. Mic didn't have time to clean up his mess. That's what the black staff was for, a distraction. It was never about getting a ransom. In all this scrambling, he was going to come in, say he was closing the books, and cook 'em until they crowed."

Bane wasn't sure what the last bit meant, but he got the idea. Mic was a *criminal.*

"Did Aeryn have anything to do with it?"

Ezra gave another wave. "Nah. He just wanted to sell broomsticks and make his pa proud. Well, he did one of those real well."

"It's a shame. Will anyone hire him?"

"Won't matter. Him and Honey are getting hitched, and she's as rich as the duke now after this sale, assuming it still goes through. They'll be set."

"Honey and Aeryn? Really?"

"Oh yeah. Well, I guess you weren't around here to see it all, being in Used all the time. Gods, we finally had to sit them down and make Honey swear on a Cosmic Swoosh that she wouldn't play favorites with appointment bookings. It was getting out of hand."

Bane nodded, taking it all in. "I take it we're still employed?"

"Me, you, the Turners, and Dutch, if he decides to show up."

"He ought to retire like Candor did."

"Can't. Bet it all away."

"On dragon racing?"

"Allegedly." Ezra slurped his coffee. "Want some?"

Bane raised his mug, confused.

"No." Ezra pulled his cloak open to flash the top of a flask peeping out of the pocket.

"*Oh*. N-no." When Ezra shrugged, Bane wondered if maybe he should have accepted it—maybe the offer was a sort of initiation? "What's going to happen to Used?"

"They'll probably hire people or bring someone over from one of their other stores. They own three more lots."

Bane let out a low whistle. "Must be nice. Bet they're as rich as the duke."

"Richer." Ezra cocked an eyebrow as if he could see their books firsthand. He looked over at Aeryn's desk. "I suppose you better go claim it while you can."

"What do I do? Pee on it?"

Ezra laughed, slapping a hand to his chest. "Gods! That's funny. Put something on it that's yours."

Bane patted himself down, trying to see if he even had anything. He had his new mirror—which he was terrified to part with—and a few coins he grabbed blindly out of his coin chest. He could have fetched his work mirror from the other building, but it was cold, and the trek wasn't worth it if he was only going to find the doors locked. The only thing he had of value, but also maybe didn't, was an OCC coin. He plucked it out of the pile in his palm. As he did, he looked up to see Ezra's eyes trailing it. Ezra glanced up and met Bane's eyes. There was an understanding there.

Bane hesitated but then asked, "You...have some?"

Ezra's brows furrowed. "The first rule of OCCs is you don't talk about OCCs. Never disclose what you have. People will think you're fishy, or they'll want what you have."

"Do you think I'm fishy or rich?"

Ezra smiled. "Let's just say I've been keeping a keen eye on the finance section."

Bane understood. It was that coin he decided to place into the drawer of the desk. Leaving it there meant he trusted Ezra, who understood the gesture. Ezra nodded, pleased. "May we have so many we don't know what to do with them."

Bane raised his mug as if to toast that, and it felt like things would be alright, after all.

Then Gerwin burst out of his office, red in the face, and screamed, "Why aren't you selling broomsticks?!" before storming off to screech profanities in the center of the lot. Bane and Ezra craned their necks, trying to get a peek at the new owner. The door swung shut before they could catch a glance. They walked over to the glass wall and watched, sipping languidly from their mugs as the steam rose off Gerwin, who looked just about ready to combust.

A few minutes later, Toby arrived with his box of turkey legs, straining to be heard over the noise of the sorcerers still shouting. He was nearly sold out when Mel came in, who beelined straight for the meat seller.

"You nearly missed Toby," Bane chided, strolling over to Mel, who was huffing and puffing.

"Sometimes I hate it when he's early."

"He's not. Why are you so late? You're never late on Mondays."

"This blubbering business—thank you, Toby, just one today. The boys are fending for themselves now that they're back in class." Mel counted out her coins before continuing her vent. "Do you know how many employees I've got? Thirty. Thirty!"

"Is that including me?"

"Thirty-one!" Mel let herself get steered to the lounge and Toby went to try his luck with the frazzled sorcerers. Bane sat in a chair that gave him a view of what was about to unfold. Maybe he would pick up some sales tactics. "Speaking of you..." Mel raised her eyebrows and Bane remembered the delivery fees he owed her. He pulled the coins out of his pocket and handed them over. He had placed them in a separate place on his shelf so he wouldn't accidentally spend them. Mel pocketed them without looking and pulled coins out of her purse. She placed three OCCs in his empty palm.

"This is too much," Bane protested.

Mel looked at him, puzzled. "It's what you wanted, so take it."

"Absolutely," Bane said, realizing this was no time to argue. He stuffed them into the lone pocket he had left on his cloak. He would have to take his cloak to the tailor, he thought, since his mum was gone. He didn't realize how much he took her sewing for granted until he found himself in need of a new pocket. Maybe Lusine sewed?

Hold on...

Bane's brain rewound. Something about what he just thought pricked him, suggesting there was an importance there. He thought it over again, slowly. He wished his mum were still there to sew—

His mum!

The coins!

That cursed ugly teapot on the mantle!

"What? Are you choking?" Mel leaned forward and looked into Bane's gaping mouth, trying to see if there was something lodged in the back of his throat.

He closed his mouth and said, "No, you just gave me an idea."

"A good one, I hope. Then you can think up another one for me. Everything is so disorganized..." Mel vented until Bane's turkey leg was gone and barely a bite of hers was missing. Bane hadn't heard a word; he was too busy formulating a plot. But the solution came quickly, and he found one for her trouble as well.

"You should all meet up. Get together. Organize a meeting. Maybe not all thirty, maybe the ten most senior members. Create a system, a solution for how to divvy up the deliveries and such. You need to organize."

"Not like a union, I can't afford that," Mel insisted. "I'll be honest, I've been praying to the gods that this whole strike with P.U.K.E. blows over and they win their negotiations."

"Why? Wouldn't that put you out of business?" Bane asked.

"Aye. I've got more coins than I know what to do with and if I didn't have my husband as an accountant, I would be writhing in panic over what to do with taxes. When you work for someone, they take care of all that. When you work for yourself, suddenly it's up to you to know which ones to pay and when. It's a bold nightmare, I tell ya. I know those union negotiations take time, but I'm ready to disband."

"You're talking crazy. You're just overwhelmed," Bane insisted, unable to believe that Mel was ready to terminate such a good business so soon. He nearly offered to take it over if she was so unwilling to become rich, but that didn't feel like the right thing to offer right then. He didn't feel she really meant it. She was just wanting a bit of advice. "Go to the Copper University on Swan Dive Drive. I used to work there, and my friend Dante still works there. There will be plenty of room, and if you're not too loud I'm sure you can hold a meeting there."

Mel rubbed her chin. "That's a good idea. Alright!" She took a bite from her cold turkey leg. "What's new with you?"

Bane pulled out his mirror. "You can call me now."

"Ooh! That's a nice one! Where'd you get it? It looks new!"

Bane huffed. "As if! Amos's."

"The pawn shop? Oh, love that place. I get all my boys their gifts from there. Homer's, too..."

19

Spare Key

Asking Lusine to help him break into his mother's house would have sounded a bit alarming. Instead he approached her with, "I need your help letting myself into my mum's house for my spare cloak."

Lusine surprised him by asking, "Don't you have a key to your mum's place?"

Bane snorted, as if this were a preposterous thing, to have a key to the home you grew up in. "Do *you* have a key to your parents'?"

"Of course! Why didn't your mum give you a key while she's in Bambrough? Don't you look in on the house while she's gone?"

"She hasn't got houseplants to water," Bane faltered, confused. What was there to look after?

"Anything could happen. She might have forgotten fruit on the counter that could spoil. Or maybe someone tried to pick the lock and it needs replacing. Or a dragon got in through the chimney she forgot to close and is eating the pantry bare, soiling the carpets and bed."

Since he wasn't the homeowner, Bane had never worried about the house. It was his mum's house, hers to worry over. Now that Lusine pointed these predicaments out, he was starting to feel offended that he was never tasked with watching the house, even before the incident that got him banned from being in it alone.

Lusine added, "Or like now that you've got a spare cloak in the house you need to get. It would be nice to have that spare key."

"Right," Bane said. He wanted to seem agreeable because this made him seem far less guilty than he felt. Had his mother really never trusted him? "Do you go into your parents' house while they're gone?"

"I don't..." Lusine stopped before she could finish, *because my parents have servants*. "I don't need to because their neighbors do it for them. And they in turn check in for their neighbors."

"Huh. So then maybe my mum's neighbor has a key?"

The neighbors did not have a spare key. They did however have big feelings about his mum selling the place "after all these years."

"Don't you want to inherit it?" one neighbor asked, which seemed an odd question.

"She's selling it to move to the seaside," Bane explained while feeling this wasn't his information to tell. Rather than continue asking all the neighbors on the street, Bane pulled out his mirror, rang his mum's realtor, and asked her to meet in front of the house.

"I can't do that," Joan said. "Your mother gave strict instructions that no one was to be let in."

"I'm her *son*."

"*No one*." Joan gave him a sympathetic look through the glass. "Look, I'm doing an open house in a few weeks. If you wander in you wander in, I can't stop you."

"It...will be warm by then, I won't need my cloak," Bane said, unsure how to navigate this lie he was trying to weave. Lusine was listening and so he was really trying to sell the bit.

"I'll just mend it," Lusine offered, pulling her own cloak tighter, growing weary of standing outside the locked house.

"You don't sew."

"Everyone knows how to sew. There's nothing to it, really. You could do it, if you really tried."

"I want it fixed a bit more professionally than that, thank you."

"Honest, you'll have a new pocket by the end of the day, let me just have at it. I'll take it to the tailor if you're really all that concerned," Lusine insisted, starting to shiver.

Bane grit his teeth. "You...don't have the right thread, and I don't need you going out and buying more. Mum had the exact right thread. It would be a waste to get a new spool."

"No, it won't. You'll rip your cloaks plenty. I'll have it on hand for when you do."

Bane let out a groan and grabbed two fistfuls of his hair in frustration. He squeezed his eyes shut before he confessed, "There's no other cloak. Or thread. Remember the coronation? And that hideous teapot Mum gave us? There's a matching one on the mantle, into which she dumped the OCCs she collected."

Lusine let out an equally frustrated sound. "Are you seriously trying to break into your mum's house for coins made of *fool's gold*? What is your obsession with these?!" And as she gesticulated angrily, a rolled parchment slipped out of her pocket. She didn't notice until Bane scooped it up and peeled back the already broken wax seal, which he recognized as their landlord's emblem.

"What's this?"

"Nothing!" Lusine jumped and tried to snatch it, but didn't quite make the leap. Bane put one hand on the top of her head to keep her in place and with the other unfurled the parchment. Lusine sunk into the snow and tried a new tactic, toppling him over, but she wasn't able to before he read the line she knew would upset him.

"Gods, that's thievery!"

Lusine cringed. "It's an annual raise in rent. It happens."

"Ten percent? For what! For the crime of wanting to be sheltered? Hold on, when does this go into effect?" His eyes resumed scanning the page. "Today!"

"It's not that bad." Lusine ducked out from under his palm and swiped the parchment back, stuffed it into her pocket. Their landlord wasn't the Ink Splotch owner, but rather a lord somewhere who owned the whole building and leased it to all of them. Collecting a pretty penny to pay for his lavish hobbies, Bane imagined. Once, Bane got asked in a job interview what his dream job was, and he got so irked at the idea that one would dream of working that he said, "Either a landlord or a philanthropist, but the latter would perhaps be too much work."

"I have this new job, and you have that new position. We'll make out just fine," Lusine insisted.

"It puts us back to where we started. We'll never get ahead like this, if costs keep climbing faster than our pay raises. Look, inside this house there are coins that could actually change our lives. I could pay the whole year's rent up front and maybe even negotiate a lower future rate. Money holds power, and for once I'd really like to have it."

Lusine stood there, her eyes stinging with angry tears of frustration before she shouted, "Do what you like!" Then she whirled around and stormed home.

If Bane were a smart man, he would have gone after her, forgotten this whole business. But he was determined to fix this all on his own. *This is all for her*, he thought, and if he were any less noble, he would have called her ungrateful. But he knew Lusine wasn't. She just didn't seem as concerned with money as he was, which astounded him. He knew how much her school tuition cost. And now the rent was going up. Bane felt as if he was in a hole and the walls around him kept rising. If he didn't leap now, catch the ledge, he was afraid they would never make it over the poverty line.

He turned his attention to the lock, tried to jimmy it open. He threw himself at the door and earned a bruised shoulder. He even braved climbing up onto the roof but saw that him mum had the good sense to shut the chimney before she left. No dragon and no son would be trespassing through there.

For a manic moment he considered breaking the window, but it would cost money to repair it. Perhaps more than the coins were worth. Besides, if he hung around any longer the neighbors would get suspicious. He looked around in despair, trying to wrack his brain, when something glittered on a man as he walked by. Bane squinted, but it was only his wedding band.

Bane remembered the pickpocket's ring. Of course!

But how would he find Balio?

Bane remembered their meeting, Balio saying something about seeing the underbelly now, or was it the shadow world? What did that mean?

Bane strolled towards the little park just yonder. He sat on the frozen bench, trying to look inconspicuous, and simply watched the people go by.

What he saw amazed him. He saw *everything*.

He noticed the tips of snake tattoos poking out from the tops of collars, out of coat sleeves; worshipers of the god Kigyo. Then there were those with a porcelain brooch pinned at their collars, painted with flowers in honor of their goddess Primavera.

Bane noticed, too, the red stone rings, flashing so obviously. Bane spotted a man wearing one and got up, followed him until he vanished through a door Bane had never seen before.

As the door swung shut in front of him, Bane startled back a step. He looked up to read the sign that was not there. He looked to the left and saw the barbershop's red and blue twisted pole, and then to the right, at the liquor store he'd been to many times before. But this door? He had never seen it. Had it always been there?

Bane half expected it to be conjured by his imagination, but when he turned the handle the door creaked open. Eyes inside swiveled to look at him as he stepped through, unable to back out now that he had entered the shadow world.

20

Shadow Pub

Bane beelined to the bar and fell onto a red leather stool. He tried his very best not to look around, but he couldn't help himself. His eyes swept the room, surveying the hunched figures seated in matching read leather booths whispering or laughing. With each bellow, the hoops in their ears and the metal caps on their teeth twinkled in the candlelight from the wax stumps at the center of the tables. Bane had never seen so many sword and dagger hilts peeking out from under cloaks and coats. Why, if there were a pickpocket for pointy objects, this would be the place to rob!

The room would have been dim if not for the enormous mirror behind the bar, framed by bottles of booze. It was scryed into a mirror that faced a quaint room holding a harpsicord and its very animated player. The lively melody flowed through the mirrors and into the bar. The volume was perfectly comfortable to be heard over or to hide secrets under.

Peering closer, Bane could see a billboard behind him by the door through which he entered, torn pieces of parchments tacked to it with dinner knives. Each had a calling rune drawn on it with a message beneath. Bane read a few of the notices.

Call for a proper arsonist.

Best exterminator in town. Bane had a feeling this wasn't for exterminating vermin.

Ready for a raid?

Potions, poisons, and explosives. Cheap!

Need sugar?

The bartender shuffled over. Bane hid his hands inside his cloak, just in case. Did he need to show proof? He began to tremble. What lair did he just walk into?

"What's yer poison?"

"I don't work in poison!" Bane blinked rapidly at the bartender who frowned, confused. "Oh, you mean—" Bane cleared his throat. "What have you got?"

The bartender jabbed a finger over his shoulder, eyeing Bane suspiciously. "Are you old enough to drink?"

Bane suddenly remembered he was a werewolf. Was he not also part of the underbelly? Or some underbelly? Surely, he could fit in here. He unclasped his cloak and tugged the top of his shirt down, exposing the burly hairs on his chest.

"Good enough," the bartender muttered, satisfied. He didn't have that much hair on his entire body combined. "Beer? Wine? Spirits?"

Bane kept scanning the menu, not actually able to read it in his momentary panic. "Red," he blurted. "Wine."

The bartender nodded. He figured Bane was a new induction. He learned from his predecessor that he was there to serve drinks, not ask questions. Liability by association, he had been warned. Best not to know what you don't know.

While he reached around for a bottle, Bane read the parchments tacked to the mirror, stuck there by Endless Putty. *Break my mirror I break your neck.* The one under it read, *No fighting inside.* The final one read, *Jon makes the rules. Don't like it don't come here.*

"Are you Jon?"

"Yeah, why? You got a suggestion?"

"For what?"

Jon narrowed his eyes. "Anything."

Bane gulped. "Nope. Not a single one. Haven't a thought in my head."

Jon stared hard for a moment, then shrugged. He raised the bottle he selected.

"This one's a—" The bartender squinted at the label, then pulled the glasses at the end of the beaded chain around his neck up to his face. "Ooh, a merlot by

Blood of the Vine. *From the volcanic soil of Superstitious Mountain,*" he read off the label. He poured a generous glassful and lavishly set it on a napkin in front of Bane. "Have you been there? To the mountain?"

"*I* have," said a familiar voice. "Make it two, Jon."

Balio took the seat beside Bane. He didn't look at Bane as he accepted the drink with, "Put it on my friend's tab."

Jon looked at Bane expectantly, who pulled out two nickels. This seemed to cover the bill, and Jon went back to reading his worn paperback romance in the dark corner, the cover torn off.

"I'm impressed you found me."

Bane kept staring at Balio, who kept staring straight ahead, taking slow, savoring sips from his glass. Finally, Bane said, "You didn't exactly leave a calling card."

"I thought our business was concluded."

"New business."

Balio smiled and finally turned to face Bane. "Murder? Arson? Arsenic?"

Bane looked horrified. "You do all those? I just need you to break into my mum's house."

Balio's grin widened. "Good. I was makin' sure ye came in here lookin' for the right shadow man." He cocked his head to the rest of the small, stuffy bar. "Anything else, you'll need to go make new friends."

Bane dropped his voice. "What is this place?"

"Refuge. From the cold." Balio sipped his wine. "Bit of a co-workspace. A safe place to meet clients, take yer mirror meetings, catch up with ye fellow guild members."

"But what is it called?"

"Hasn't got a name."

Bane narrowed his eyes and tried again. "Suppose you're meeting a, ah, a client, right? Where do you tell him to meet you?"

"Ah. I tells him to meet me in the shadow."

"So it's the Shadow Pub?"

"It is if ye call it that. *I* call it 'The Shadow.' Some call it 'Next Door.' I've heard it be 'My Place.' It's got no name and every name."

Bane smirked, rolled his eyes. "I suppose that's clever." He took a sip and looked around. "I can't believe they let anyone in here."

Balio frowned. "What do you mean?"

"I mean, I'm not—" Bane motioned around vaguely. He wasn't sure if certain words were offensive, so he landed on, "a guild member."

Balio smiled. "Ye don't need be. Trust me, you've enough dirt on yer hands to grease the handle like the rest of us."

Not sure how to take this, Bane didn't say anything and instead took a swig of his drink. His stomach growled, and he wondered if there was a secret menu somewhere with snacks.

As if on cue, the door opened and a jolly, "Hallo! Turkey legs! Get ya turkey legs!" boomed through the small space. Every patron flew out of their seats and scrambled over to Toby.

Bane gawked at the meatman, who, once the crowd thinned enough, noticed the broom salesman. Toby got so excited he whipped his hat off and waved it at Bane, who could clearly already see him. "Hallo! My friend!"

Bane burned with embarrassment. "Hello, Toby."

"Turkey leg?"

"N-no, thank you. Just Mondays."

Toby made his way over and clapped Bane on the shoulder, offered one to Balio, who politely turned it down, then went back out into the cold, on to solicit at the next business.

"Just Mondays?" Balio asked.

"He..." Bane took a gulp of his wine, bristled at the dryness. "He sells them for half-off on Mondays at the broomstick dealership I work at."

Balio let out a hoot of laughter and slapped Bane on the shoulder as if he had just told a splendid joke. "Yer a scoundrel yet! Ah, I knew there was a reason you saw me, and it wasn't just because yer friend pointed me out."

"Hey, there's nothing wrong with being a salesman."

"But a broom salesman? Oy, yer the worst o' the lot." Balio motioned for another round of drinks. Panic climbed in Bane's throat as he had to fork over two more nickels he frankly couldn't afford to part with. "All right then, so yer mum's house, eh? Don't have a key?"

"Apparently I'm the only one who doesn't."

"What's in there?"

"That's my business."

"That'll cost extra."

"No, it won't," Bane growled.

"Fine." Balio shrugged. "Just curious."

"Then you'll do it?"

"It'll be the easiest job I've done in a while, so yeh, why not." Balio finished his wine and motioned for Bane to do the same, but wine wasn't exactly a thing to drink quickly. Watching Bane's face screw up in pain, Balio rolled his eyes and assured Bane he didn't have to drink it in a hurry.

Their glasses empty, Bane put an extra copper on the bar as tip and led Balio out the door and back to his mum's house.

Balio crouched down to inspect the lock and let out a laugh. "Easy enough. This is what ye called me out for?"

Bane rolled his eyes. "Can you do it without damaging the lock?"

"Course I can. I'm no amateur," Balio huffed. He reached into a pocket in his cloak and pulled out a roll of leather, in which were the tools of his trade. Bane tried to watch him work, see which tools he used, but he was too anxious and instead played the lookout, unsure what to do or say if anyone actually approached and confronted them.

Lucky for him, Balio was a professional, and it was done within moments. The lock clicked and Balio turned the knob, pushed the door open. "Don't tell me there's a guard dragon in there."

"No need to worry," Bane assured and pushed past him. He went straight for the mantle but saw within the first few steps of entering the room that the teapot was missing. With it, the OCCs.

Bane went around the room anyway, pushing aside plush animals, lifting pillows, peeking under plates just in case, but he knew as soon as he saw the teapot gone that the coins had gone with it. He couldn't wallow then, not with Balio outside, and he choked down his disappointment.

"Back already? Got what yar lookin' for?"

"Yup. Lock it back up, will you?" Balio reached inside and turned the lock, then pulled the door closed. It gave a definite click. "Oh."

Balio winked. "Won't charge ye for that."

Their business concluded, Bane reached back into the coin purse that was quickly dwindling of coins and pulled out what he thought was fair payment. He presented the three nickels to Balio, who shook his head. "I don't much know the going rate of breaking and entering," Bane apologized.

"That's not what I want."

Bane frowned. "A gold?"

Balio cocked an eyebrow. As soon as he did, Ezra's words came to Bane. *The first rule of OCCs is you don't talk about OCCs.* "How do you know I have any?"

"Because I've already picked yer pocket, checked ya coins, and put them back without ye noticing."

"It's not worth half!" Bane protested, but Balio put up a hand to quiet him.

"It's worth what I say it's worth, and I say they're worth one breakin' an enterin'."

Bane could hardly argue with this. He pulled out his OCCs and begrudgingly pressed them into Balio's open palm. It included the one he had put in his new work desk, having replaced it with his work mirror. While he trusted Ezra not to steal, he didn't know any of the new hires wouldn't. He loathed parting with them. "That was low, even for a thief."

Balio gave a little bow. "Welcome to the underbelly, friend."

Bane watched him go, bothered by the comment. He felt dirty, the way he had felt his first transformation after being shunned from the pack he was just initiated into.

He didn't think he had done anything wrong, going into his mum's house; the coins would have sold at an immense profit, and he would have shared the wealth with Lusine and his mum. He wanted to fix up this house so his mum could sell it for more and retire like a royal instead of just comfortable. He wanted to buy Lusine the ring she deserved, throw a wedding she surely dreamed of—his mother had assured him every little girl dreamt of her wedding from the moment she could dress her dolls—and move her into a proper home. He was sick of their leaking, crumbling, overpriced rental.

Bane had tried for better jobs without any luck, since he had the same basic education as everyone else competing for positions—and no magical skills to set him apart. Sometimes the irritability and fatigue leading up to the full moon made it hard to concentrate or get anything done, making him a lousy employee. Those days he moped around the dealership and hoped the person wandering in already knew what broomstick they wanted and were ready to pay the price on the tag without question. His insomnia ruled out any job that required an early wake-up. His current job was flexible and paid the most of all the ones he'd had in the past. Plus, he felt like he was finally gaining some recognition.

He just needed a little help, that was all. He wanted to provide and be on equal footing to Lusine, who seemed to be brimming with an optimism—and opportunities—Bane never had.

On the way home, he decided not to mention to Lusine what he had done; confessing to hiring a pickpocket hardly seemed like an easy conversation to have, and she needn't find out. Especially since he didn't get anything he needed out of the house.

Bane found Lusine in bed, nearly swallowed by a pile of pillows, watching a program in the large mirror hanging above the dresser across the room. Her hair was already swept up in curlers, and her face mask was applied. The room smelled of the sticky-sweet lotion she slathered all over herself. Bane only ever found her like this if he was out late because it made her completely untouchable. The message was loud and clear; he was in the doghouse that night.

She glanced at him in the doorway and turned her eyes back to the mirror. "You don't like this channel."

Bane came in anyway and dropped onto the end of the bed. He reached under the covers and found a foot and began to rub it, trying to get her to warm up a bit.

Lusine let out a huff that wasn't so irked but almost dared him to speak, interrupt her watching. He didn't. He simply rubbed her feet and focused his eyes on her splay of perfectly painted toes and wondered when she had the time to do them, in between running around from classes, studying, catching and releasing dragons, and now working as a paralegal. He felt wholly lazy beside such a whirlwind of a woman.

Finally, she said, "How many teapots did you steal?"

"I went...to a pub," Bane said, not lying.

Lusine sat up and leaned over, sniffed his breath. "Wine? You?"

"It...was the house special."

"Was it good?"

"It wasn't bad," he admitted. "Want a taste?"

Lusine rolled her eyes and leaned back, but not quickly enough. Bane pounced on her and wrapped his arms and legs around her as she shrieked. They wrestled until Bane let himself get thrown off onto the other side of the bed. Lusine patted her hair, making sure the curlers hadn't budged. "I'll forgive you in the morning," she promised.

Bane leaned over and kissed the one spot on her temple her cream mask had missed. "You hold grudges so well. Ooh, the Midnight Brigade is on patrol now, can't we watch them? They always run into some bad guy or apprehend a criminal." Bane wondered if he might recognize someone he spotted in the mysterious pub that day.

"No," Lusine snapped. She settled back down under the covers but found his hand and held it. When she fell asleep, Bane eased out of bed and tiptoed across the room. He swiped across the mirror's glass until his favorite channel appeared—projecting from a mirror mounted on a Midnight Brigade officer's armor—and drifted off to sleep to the pursuit of a delinquent.

21

Reluctant Meet-Up

It was a last-minute round up, which Mel had done on purpose to ensure not too many women showed up. But there they were, the independent contractors of Mel's Deliveries, summoned to the Copper University on Swan Dive Drive.

It felt like the beginning of a new era, and it terrified Mel.

She arrived as early as she could, assuring the household before she left that everything was prepared for dinner, they would have to find plates and spoons and scoop the stew themselves, but *they were big lads, eh?* and that bedtime was still bedtime, and finally she told Homer after a wet kiss on the lips not to wait up. All the way Mel shifted this way, then that way on her broomstick as her baby kicked inside her, not loving the bouncy ride. With each sudden gust of wind or a puff of hot air out of the top of a chimney, Mel felt an altitude change. She adjusted her grip and held onto her broom for dear life.

Since most folks were cozy in their homes preparing or already enjoying dinner, the coffee shop was in a lull, the slow period before the after-meal espresso enjoyers and sleepy time tea orderers arrived to curl up with a book before getting home to bed. Mel arrived to find there were plenty of tiny tables available. She geared up to start pushing them together when the little bell above the door rang and a familiar figure walked in, beaming with excitement. "Mel!"

Mel accepted the hug, a bit awkward around her belly, but it felt nice, less formal and more familiar. Less employee and more co-worker. "I'm glad you're here. I'm trying to decide if I should ask to push these tables together or just do it."

"Just do it, they won't fuss if we do it quietly. Let me help."

By the time they got three together, the bell began to chime in one long, continuous song as eight more women streamed in. It took about a moment each for them to realize what was going on before they started picking up edges and shifting tables. It wasn't until the chairs started scraping that they seemed to be noticed, and Jaymie ran around the counter.

"What is this, another Pretty Potions party? No, I won't have it in here. If you want to swear in new cult members take it somewhere else, like the one on Mad Raven Road."

Dante hurried out from behind the bar as Mel argued, "This isn't one of those businesses. I assure you, businesswoman to businesswoman, that this is a legit one where I pay my employees and they are absolutely, definitely not their own bosses."

"If everyone orders a drink, I suppose there's no harm in letting them stay until their mugs are drained," Dante offered, setting a placating hand on Jaymie's trembling shoulder. "You'll find you can write the expense off as a business meeting," he added to Mel, who quickly jotted this down in her little leather notebook. Dante gently turned Jaymie by the shoulders and gave her a soft shove in the direction of the espresso maker, tacitly assuring her he would take care of this.

"Alright then," Mel said, looking around as everyone settled into chairs. "I suppose I'll round up the orders..."

"I'll be out to take them in a bit," Dante countered. "That way I can be sure I get them just right." He flashed that dazzling smile that distracted people from noticing his blackened fingertips or his eyes that looked just a little bit unusual.

Back behind the bar, orders tacked to the little clothing line that slid them from register to espresso machine, Dante and Jaymie stood shoulder-to-shoulder preparing the drinks.

Dante pulled the espresso shots while Jaymie frothed the milk to the perfect consistency.

"You ought to be kinder," Dante offered gently. "I know you have been stressed of late, but she's right. Businesswoman to businesswoman, give her the benefit of the doubt."

"Give a breath and they'll steal your lungs," Jaymie muttered.

"I know how you keep loiterers away," Dante confessed. "I know you use me to scare them." He tisk-tisked. "Telling them that if you could pull me from another dimension, you can send them there. Naughty, naughty."

Jaymie blushed. "What are you saying?"

"I'm saying, they're not loitering. We're making their drinks, aren't we? And we're not even crowded for space. A coin's a coin, Jaymie."

When the drinks were delivered, Mel motioned to Dante and whispered she would be the one paying the bill. He whispered back the total, and she pulled out the coins. "I'd like a receipt please. It's an expense, after all."

"Of course."

Dante had never written a receipt in his life, so he asked Jaymie to help. She assured him she would take care of it and nodded to the new pair of customers that had walked up to the register.

The man at the counter held up OCCs. "I still have a few of these from the coronation, any chance you'll accept them?"

"No—"

"Absolutely. It's our honor to serve the Crown," Jaymie interrupted. "One per drink." She wrote Mel's receipt, delivered it, and came back to measure the herbal teas into the mugs as Dante heated the water. He cupped the bottom of the kettle in his palms and channeled the infernal fire within him to his fingers. Within moments, the kettle whistled happily, and he poured the boiling water over the leaves. It was a handy skill—especially since certain teas required precise temperatures—and he could heat the water just right for each one. It was the trick he showed Jaymie that convinced her to hire him, and a skill he quickly perfected. It was also useful on busy days when the milk frothing wand couldn't keep up with the pace of orders or for a quick re-heat when someone didn't sip their drink quickly enough.

Dante sent the mugs down to the end of the bar. "Two herbal teas at the bar!"

The man came to claim his drinks and steered them to the seats they selected. Halfway there he stopped, pivoted, and returned to the bar. "Sorry, I don't see the honey?"

"Those are out by the..." Dante craned his neck to spot the condiment station. He saw then that the long end table by the window that usually displayed jugs of milk, cream, stirring sticks, a jar of honey, and individual packets of sugar was cleared of everything except napkins. "Honey, was it?" Dante looked behind him and saw Jaymie presenting the jar. Dante accepted it and handed it to the customer. "Just leave it there when you're done."

"Thanks."

Once the customer steered his mugs over to his companion, Dante turned to Jaymie and asked, "Are we closing up early?"

She furrowed her brows, unsure why he was asking. "No?"

"The condiment station is missing everything."

"Oh, that. I've confiscated everything behind the bar now."

"Why?"

"Cost of materials is going up, and with the looming threat of a sugar tax I've been catching people stuffing fistfuls of sugar packets into their pockets. It's getting mighty expensive and cutting into my margins."

"How many sugars can I give people when they ask?"

"Two per drink."

"That's going to upset old Mr. Murry. He takes four with his. In fact, I fill his mug half with coffee, the rest is sugar, and he tops it off with cream."

"No wonder he's got no teeth left," Jaymie muttered. "Maybe we're actually doing him a favor."

"Or he'll go down to the one on Mad Raven Road," Dante shot back.

"Fine. Regulars get their usual amounts of sugar. And offer the honey here. I'm sick of the mess people make. It's like they're painting the countertop with it. Out of control."

"And what's with these?" Dante asked, holding up the OCCs. "I don't have a slot on my register to put these." He motioned to the drawer, which sure enough only had places for coppers, nickels, silvers, and golds.

Jaymie swiped them out of his hand. "The value of these is skyrocketing. So long as people don't know better, they can trade one per drink. Soon these will be worth an aluminum coin each, if the gods have any mercy on me."

When Mel and her troupe finally cleared out, a little after closing but Jaymie didn't seem to mind, Dante went to clean up. He cleared the mugs from the tables, which he dragged back to their places and paired with their original chairs. Then he assured Jaymie he would lock up. She finished counting the register and putting the excess coins into her bank pouch to take with her.

"Make sure you clock overtime," she insisted, and gave a massive yawn. "Goodnight."

"Goodnight," Dante echoed and walked her out so he could lock the door behind her. He fell into his closing chores, relishing the silence it came with, the peaceful time he got to relax and have his thoughts without the hum of chatter in the background. He wiped the tables, washed the dishes, cleaned the espresso maker. He swept, mopped, and tossed the wilted flowers from the vases on the tables into the trash. He took the trash out to the back, where he held it over a heap of ash and incinerated the bag and everything inside it. Tiny dragons scurried out from the shadows and dove into the embers while they still glowed. Dante squatted and watched them, smiling. He knew of the attempts by the new king to rid the city—perhaps the whole kingdom—of dragons, but he felt they were an integral part of this world, the way he had begun to feel as well. As if he, too, melded into the natural order of the stone buildings, the cobblestone, the static of magic in the air, and the medley of smells that permeated the city and cloaked everyone who roamed through it and called it home.

Dante liked it here, this world, this coffee shop. This coin business made him nervous, and he finally understood why.

If Jaymie collected a whole lot of them, and they became worth a fortune, would she sell the business? Retire? Leave him there with a new boss who wouldn't let him live in the loft upstairs or practice the unusual otherworldly magic he possessed inside himself?

Back upstairs, Dante tossed and turned in his cot. He kept thinking of those stupid coins, wondered about their value going up. To what? To the value of aluminum? Was it really possible? That was an outrageous amount of money. No one even carried aluminum coins around. That was the currency businesses paid to each other and to banks. They probably didn't even exist except as a concept. He certainly had never seen one. Perhaps he'd ask Jaymie, her banker husband surely knew. Despite his nagging curiosity, Dante resolved not to check his mirror until the morning, or he would never catch a wink of sleep.

Sleep did come, ushering in an uncertain morning. Dante rolled over and grabbed his mirror, flicked through it until he found a finance guru speaking prophesies of fortune into the mirror. Lo and behold, the price of OCCs had indeed gone up.

22

The Mints

The new King of Everdorne, Eadwine Norsdorf, grew up as any first son of a king did; he learned politics early, trained in swordfight all his life, and once he hit puberty was matched for marriage with a princess whose kingdom's power rivaled his own. He was ambitious, though a slight limp and a lisp he overcame in youth waivered his confidence some. He hadn't run around with the other more strapping young boys, was left out of a lot of inside jokes, and finally decided to get back at them all by being the most cunning prince of them all.

He learned tactful charm.

He read poetry and traveled into the woods to seek inner peace.

He ate any and all cuisine, which he once heard built character. It also gave him a whole host of parasites he had to routinely flush.

He focused on skin care, keeping his hair tidy, and used artificial means to straighten his teeth. His smile was brilliant and terrifying; his new wife had spent a whole day of their honeymoon raking her fingernails across his teeth, marveling at them. *As perfect as winter's first frozen lake*, she whispered. It didn't do anything for her like getting her in the mood, but it was touching, her appreciation for something that had been painstaking and painful for so many months.

Their courtship had been swift, their engagement short, and their wedding grand. If it hadn't been for a surprise dragon attack that nearly burnt them all to a crisp, it would have been as mundanely perfect as any other royal's nuptials. But the scandal of it secretly thrilled Eadwine. No one else in any of the other twelve kingdoms had had a wedding nearly as exciting, and the wedding night that followed was passionate beyond belief, both husband and wife in awe that they made it through alive.

Now that Prince Eadwine was King Eadwine, he focused on what he thought a kingdom really needed and implemented laws his father had scoffed at.

Sanitation was of utmost importance. He implemented sewage projects, offered credits from the Crown for anyone who wanted to replace their old chamber pots with a new self-flushing toilet. The elderly population refused to convert, convinced they would plunge down the pipe along with their excrement, but it was catching on with newlyweds, who were putting them at the top of their gift registry.

Then there was the dragon business. They were filthy, foul creatures, the likes of which he had first been exposed to when he came to court Princess Damora. She insisted they were cute and helpful. She showed him around the palace to see their different duties, but all he saw were ways that magical advancements could replace such rudimentary beastly toil. And the waste they left! The whole city of Citeel smelled like the inside of a dragon's arse. After a brief stint of bickering, he finally relinquished the task of driving off the dragons to his wife, who insisted on curbing the population humanely, to his disgruntlement.

King Eadwine was also determined to cut the sugar import in the city; it was bad for the health of the citizens, and it was what attracted dragons, who went mad for it. Domesticating dragons with sugar had been brilliant, but the downside was that the feral ones sought it out anywhere and everywhere, making them a nuisance. Still, citizens' demand for sugar far outweighed their annoyance of dragons. When Eadwine proposed the sugar slash there was plenty of pushback from his advisors, Mosley especially, who pointed out that diplomacy was this kingdom's top source of income. Everdorne hosted festivals and conferences for royals of kingdoms all across the continent, and feasts that included sugar were essential. The tourism influx that came with these events, thrown nearly monthly, was what kept the economy churning through the city. King Eadwine pointed out that there was always booze to make money, and brothels of course. A bit of exercise was good for the population, was it not? It didn't seem to sway any of the advisors, but the king didn't push the sugar ban proposal far from his mind.

And now there was this coin business getting in the way of those other big projects he was so eager to campaign. What came as an innocent incentive to get the public to participate in the coronation, to get some coinage circulating and to sell officially licensed Crown paraphernalia, had turned into a currency with a mind of its own. It was getting enough traction that Mosley insisted King Eadwine call on the Heads of the Royal Mints immediately and try to put a stop to it.

"It's completely washed currency," Mosley explained. He blubbered in his panic to explain it with the gravity it deserved. He was flummoxed by the columns that appeared in *The Harking Herald* stating its current and future worth, and the paper refused to comment when reached out to. *Who oversees this? Who controls the price? Who is putting the words on paper? Who is literally at the quill, writing this out?* Mosley had demanded, but the Editor-in-Chief of *The Harking Herald* answered to no one and had certainly *never* been on the side of an institution, especially not the Crown.

"We can't tax it, so we can't take a profit. If citizens stop using the other coins, then we won't be able to control inflation," Mosley explained, rubbing a hand nervously over the dome of his shiny, shaved head.

"What even is inflation?" Eadwine asked. "Does anyone even know?"

"I certainly know what taxes are," Mosley shot back. "I know it's what fills your coffers and keeps me employed. It's what you're going to want to keep your eyes on closest during your reign."

Mosley had never spoken so openly, especially not with the last king. But King Varundil granted Mosley tenure before he left the palace to join his estranged wife in the woods to pick magic mushrooms and smoke questionable plants while wearing scarce amounts of clothing.

King Eadwine took a seat at the desk of his apothecary. He was working on vitamin tablets to give to the masses, something that could cure scurvy and whiten the teeth in the same dose. This was what he was passionate about. Improvements. Money, he didn't care for, because he always had so much of it. It felt like being reminded to breathe when his lungs had been working all along. It seemed absurd that he would ever find himself in a shortage of money. "Alright, then advise me. What should I do?"

"Each of the Heads of the Royal Mints has asked for an audience with you. Some have made several requests, each getting more frantic. It seems nickel's use has dipped considerably."

"Fine. Arrange it. But during breakfast so I can be done with it early in the day," Eadwine agreed and turned to ask the royal pharmacists what the benefits of consuming charcoal were, dismissing Mosley with a wave.

That was how King Eadwine found himself torn from his feathery bed far too early to meet with four of the wealthiest people in all the kingdom:

Lord Nigel Copperton, Head of the Copper Mint.

Sir Conrey Nilman, Head of the Nickel Mint.

Lady Salora Silversmith, Head of the Silver Mint.

Count Jeanburg Goldstem, Head of the Gold Mint.

The three men and woman sat at the formal dining table, their lavish fur coats held by their attendants standing at attention behind them, sweating under the weight of the outerwear. The nobles were speaking cordially to one another. They met like this occasionally and it was understood that there was a hierarchy, one that simply couldn't be broken because of the inherent value of the coins they dealt in. Despite this tacit rule, there was a bit of rivalry currently ongoing between the copper baron and the earl of gold.

"You can't tell who baked these," Count Goldstem insisted, motioning to the massive pile of pastries before them. "It could have easily been either your son or mine."

"Such perfection is rare talent. We're honored to be treated by my Noal's pastries this morning." Lord Copperton's plate was piled high with the golden, flaky goodies. Though both of their children worked as royal pastry chefs in the kitchen below, there was of course no way for either Head to know whose son made what pastries. Lord Copperton figured if he ate one of everything then he would surely taste one his son made.

"They graduated together! Equal rank, equal talent," Count Goldstem huffed. "You know they worked on the wedding cake together."

"Head Pastry Chef Gregor Brimstone hired your son Elis out of either pity or politics, and you know it. To think, the son of an earl bumping elbows with the lowly son of a baron!" Lord Copperton nearly burst with pride. Their rivalry hadn't been his idea, and he, an artist, had spent most of his professional career actively trying to avoid arrogant aristocrats exactly like the earl. But since he took over the running of the copper mint, it was proving to be unavoidable. That he was sitting here sharing pastries with the earl...why, that tickled him fuchsia.

"You're not even the most powerful mint," Lady Silversmith muttered, aiming the jab at the arrogant earl.

"Lady Silversmith, what a pleasure. Let me get that for you," Count Goldstem offered, reaching for the carafe of coffee to pour her a cup.

"How's your wife?" she asked brightly.

"Well, she-she's well."

"Then I take it she's still alive," Lady Silversmith huffed, giving him a pointed look. This was always her way of greeting him.

Count Goldstem resumed his seat. "Who's your tailor? That dress is exquisite. Perhaps I'll get one made for her."

"She won't wear it as well," Lady Silversmith scoffed.

These two had grown up in the same aristocratic circle, the one with the fanciest balls, the most lavish vacations, and the most scandalous affairs. Their parents were close friends and had been hopeful for a someday marriage, but Lady Silversmith had always found Count Goldstem arrogant and vulgar, traits she heard his son inherited. The earl often reminded her she could have married into the gold mint, and she fired back that he hadn't the courtesy to die early like her husband had. She loved being a widow—the genuflecting she received from her suitors, and especially the looks the earl now gave her.

The door opened to reveal the king, fluffy blue robe flying open behind him, silk pajamas on full display. "Morning, mints!"

They all rolled their eyes, used to this, but forced polite laughter like applause at the king's tardy entrance.

"Thank you for joining me today." King Eadwine dropped into the massive chair at the head of the table. It was deliberately elevated quite a bit higher than the other chairs and tilted forward ever so slightly. It was a chair designed by the last king, and was assured by the craftsman that it would deliver optimal intimidation. Eadwine noticed the platter of sugary pastries and wrinkled his nose in disgust. He asked if everyone had enough coffee before plunging into business. "Well, this whole meeting wasn't my idea. Who would like to go first?"

As if on cue, the doors burst open and Mosley scurried in, running as calmly as he could under his beautifully tailored robe. His sleeves nearly touched the floor, and his purple royal broach was pinned prominently to his chest. His head was freshly shaven, his eyeliner fiercely applied, and he came prepared with notes. "Sir, if I may, I have a few notes of business."

"Mosley, won't you join us?" King Eadwine gestured to the chair across from him, but Mosley turned up his nose. "I already ate."

"Shame, these are the best pastries in the kingdom," the baron said, waving a griffin claw, flaky and packed with sweet cream and raspberry jam. "My son makes these."

"*Some* of these," the earl added through gritted teeth.

"I'm sorry, are we in the business of pastries?" Mosley chirped. Lady Silversmith stifled a snort. "Marvelous. Back to the business of the official commemorative coins." He snapped his fingers, and a quill and parchment floated over from a nearby desk and stood poised at the ready beside him. "Who would like to complain first?"

He meant it as the dare he made it sound, and so all the lords and lady looked at one another, trying to decide which of them was bravest.

It was to no one's surprise when Count Goldstem spoke first. "What are you doing to curb the usage of these false currencies?"

"Why don't we begin by you telling me how it's affecting the kingdom?" King Eadwine countered. "Apparently you're all seeing enough of an impact to your coffers that it begs interrupting my breakfast."

"It's putting nickels completely out of circulation, for one," Sir Nilman jumped in. "It's coppers for the poor and silver for the middle class and gold for all the fancy folk. No one's bothering with nickels anymore."

"That's hardly news," Lady Silversmith drawled. "These fool's gold coins are being adopted by the hopeful middle class. They're using them to buy goods, and businesses are accepting them at whatever value they fancy that day. These coins are turning into a rogue money system because they are completely unregulated."

"*My* businesses," Count Goldstem huffed. "My employees are accepting them and then writing merchandise as losses."

"Why do you allow them to accept the coins?" Lord Copperton asked, confused.

"I don't! They just do it because they know they can pocket the fool's gold then turn around and buy a few pints at the pub with them."

"Sounds like a management issue," Sir Nilman scoffed. They all watched the earl's face grow pink, then red. Before the steam could whistle from his ears, the king asked, "How does this affect the mints? Frankly, I'm minimally concerned about your profit margins."

Lady Silversmith steered the conversation back on course. "Each year the Crown decides, based on its economy, how many coins should be in circulation to reflect the riches of the kingdom. Too many coins and there's an inflation, a devaluation of the coins. That's what's happening. There are coins circulating around pushing up the price of goods, devaluing the official coins minted by us. Furthermore, OCCs, as they're being called, are being used on the obsidian market because they are untraceable, and also to avoid taxes."

Avoid taxes was what perked the king up in his seat. Mosley had warned him about this! *No one would be stealing from his coffers.* "Elaborate on tax evasion."

"Each coin that passes hands in an official business registered in the Everdorne Business Bureau gets tracked by the register based on its enchanted serial number. Every quarter when it comes time to pay taxes, official registers tally up the correct total to be paid to the Crown. If someone were to use a different tender that wasn't legal, like say an apple, or in this case an OCC, the registers are not calibrated to detect it. Taxes will not be pulled from that sale. And if everyone adopts it, unless we can collect the coins and reissue them with enchanted serial numbers, they're simply unofficial, untaxable, untraceable tenders."

Mosley cleared his throat. "Has anyone come with a proposal to put a stop to their use?"

"I suppose we could send a team out to collect all the coins. I know a few guild members who would take the job," Count Goldstem suggested with a look that implied the hired help wouldn't be asking for those coins politely.

"What will they need for that? Sorcerer magic? Weapons?" the king asked.

"Dragons," Lady Silversmith said, staring at Count Goldstem, knowing exactly who was in possession of the largest pack of gold-sniffing dragons. "They'll need their noses recalibrated to sniff out fool's gold, but I'm sure the trainers of those impeccable creatures are more than capable of doing that on short notice?"

Count Goldstem narrowed his eyes at her. But before he could say anything, the king cut in with, "No, absolutely not. How would that look if the Crown employs dragons when I'm in the middle of ridding them from the palace and the kingdom as a whole?"

"That's an agenda only you seem to be keen on," Count Goldstem muttered under his breath. So that everyone would hear he said, "We're eager to know what the Crown has at its disposal for such a venture."

King Eadwine finished the last of his coffee. "I will put a pin in this project. Excellent work. Really well done."

"If it weren't for us bringing it to your attention, this new tender wouldn't have raised alarms until businesses start trying to pay banks with them, and when banks pay the Crown in them. It's trickling up," Lord Copperton said.

"Odd, I haven't a complaint from the top mint," the king said, looking around pointedly for the missing Head. "No bells are ringing for me."

It was beginning to dawn on the others that until the Crown's purse strings were being pried open, little change was to happen.

"Your Majesty, without meaning to sound insistent, the sooner we squash this, the better," Sir Nilman said. "Before the craze takes over. One OCC is now worth four gold coins."

"It sounds like I should issue more and pay off all the debts we owe!" King Eadwine stood, a sign of dismissal. "I'll have Mosley open an investigation on this. Please do update him with any new developments."

"A proposal, in the meantime," Lady Silversmith hurried to interject before they could adjourn. "What if the Crown sets the price? What if Your Majesty posted the official price of OCCs to the Chamber of Commerce? You could control the price while we figure out how to control it completely."

King Eadwine side-glanced at Mosley, who shrugged. "It's an idea."

"Alright, make it so. Who decides how much it's worth?" the king asked.

They all looked around, blinking at one another.

"That's just it," Lady Silversmith said. "It's completely rogue. It's worth whatever someone will give for it."

"Ridiculous. Alright, Mosley. Let the Chamber know that one OCC is worth...one gold." The king cocked an eyebrow and was given slow nods. This seemed acceptable.

As they filed out, not entirely placated that the situation was being given the attention it deserved, Lady Silversmith whispered to Count Goldstem, "I believe it's time to alert the Aluminum Mint."

23

Fraun

Fraun the Fire Stoker was an expert hunter. This was because the cravings gland in his brain had been bred through the generations to be easily triggered and in constant need of a fix. As the dragon breeder explained, Fraun was treat-motivated and very obedient because of it.

First it was the palace that tried to ban dragons, then it was the businesses surrounding it, which included Badger & Bard, the pub where Fraun was employed to light the evening torches and keep the peace, rouse the drunks in the morning, and make sure they paid their dues in housekeeping chores before he chased them out. Though the dragon ban was not entirely enforced, businesses that employed dragons were already beginning to be frowned upon. Lucky for Fraun, the owner of the pub loved him and decided to get ahead of the matter and made sure his dragon went to a good home. Somewhere he could be trained a task and be rewarded generously for it. The mysterious man who offered to purchase the "Sweet dragon, highly motivated, low-maintenance. Must be loved and well-fed," ensured all of these, but would not disclose what, exactly, he would be retraining the dragon to do. Of course he didn't disclose it would be pickpocketing.

Fraun proved to be perfect for the job—there were plenty of pockets to be picked in this city, and dragons could easily be trained to sniff out any treasure their master wanted hunting down. And Fraun was determined to make his new owner proud.

Fraun wasn't a tiny dragon, and his shiny red scales weren't easy to hide, so he employed a more direct approach in stealing—brute force rather than stealth. More of a robber than a pickpocket. Few put up a fight, deciding to let the thirty-pound dragon take what it was sniffing after rather than risk wrestling off the fire-breathing beast. Still, Fraun had scorched off a mustache here, a toupee there, the hem of a cloak on multiple occasions. It was never the women who fought, but they were rarely the ones that carried the coins he was after. The men liked to try to land a kick here and there, but Fraun loved snapping at a well-crafted leather boot. Most didn't want to be left with only one of the pair and quickly gave up that game, to the dragon's dismay.

Fraun's master had a simple request—coins, any sort, any amount. A treat for each, regardless of what metal it was made of.

But Fraun had noticed there were new coins in rotation, funny tasting ones, not metallic like the others. He couldn't place it on his palate because he had never tasted anything like it before. What he knew for certain was it garnered him *twice* as many treats, and so he was now on the hunt for those especially.

He already cleared the festival grounds in the palace courtyard of those coins. They had earned him so many treats it took him days to recover from the tummy ache he got from gobbling them all down. Then he found those strange coins discarded in gutters and in trash bins around the city. But those sources quickly dried up, secured in pockets and purses by those who also caught on to their value. Lucky for Fraun, those coins were always out and about, never hidden in banks. Though he suspected there was a finite amount, they were out there, calling him, taunting him.

He had just ripped a mighty good stash out of the pocket of someone who wasn't human, and that had earned him treats galore as well as generous scratches from his master.

His master was young, well-off, and had a very nice fire constantly roaring in his loft, and Fraun wasn't even expected to keep it lit. Once, Fraun climbed into the fireplace and rolled in the ashes, like he had enjoyed doing at the pub, and he got scolded in earnest for it. But if he pulled in an extra good haul, his master would light a fire in his beautiful yard, bring the embers down to smolder, and let Fraun play in it to his heart's content, the butler standing at the ready with an enchanted bucket of endless water.

Aside from masters, dragons were solitary creatures, even the domesticated ones. He had siblings in the world, that he knew, but dragons weren't raised with siblings due to the rivalry, the litter envy got so bad. But Fraun, in wandering the city, would frequently bump into dragons, despite the attempted dragon ban he, as a dragon, knew nothing about. He knew enough of the other dragons to know he was most likely the only one trained for pickpocketing these coins, and that was information enough.

This knowledge relaxed him a bit, because being in competition with another dragon was far more threatening than any threat from a person.

This was true until he wandered right into a trap.

24
Caught

It was Lusine's last day on the job as volunteer dragon catcher. It was messy business; fixing broken traps, setting new ones, hauling them onto the carriage that would send the trapped dragons to the countryside, and releasing them into the wild all while attempting to go unscathed by bites and burns. The job paid in experience, and many volunteers went on as pest control apprentices, a formidable trade that was growing quickly as the call from the Crown came down to drive the pests from the city.

Queen Damora loved animals; she had a menagerie of critters in her palace, where from a young age she mended and tended to wounded animals she found around the palace grounds. Squirrels with broken legs, possums abandoned by mothers, cats that got their tails nipped by dragons, dogs left behind by dignitaries once they discovered their prized pets were expecting after a tryst with an impure mutt that wandered in through the scullery door, and a whole host of birds and reptiles. Not dragons. Those were left in the care of Andrus, the palace's official dragon wrangler and trainer, who put dragons that wandered across the moat to use or out of existence.

Queen Damora harbored the hope that a city rid of dragons would make other creatures flourish. Maybe even bring back the elusive otters that once swam in the river that wound through the city's center. It was why she supported her husband's new agenda of humanely rehoming dragons. It was also out of fear that if she didn't comply, Andrus would be ordered to clear them out using a more direct approach.

First was the attempt to outlaw pet dragons, to the dismay of those at court who loved their pets. It was agreed upon that they would be kept until death, but no new ones would be allowed into the palace. Then there was the business of removing the kitchen dragons, but those too proved to be a bit too useful, and so a law was passed that absolutely no new dragons would enter the palace or the city. Already the palace's light fixtures were getting replaced by the new stardust lights, jars of captured stardust that needed just a bit of shaking to get glowing. It was a new phenomenon, very expensive, but apparently cheaper in the long term than constant dragon care.

Thanks to backlash, it was finally decided that perhaps the dragon banishment would happen in phases, starting with passing an ordinance to have all kept dragons fixed and vaccinated. Now there was the catching and relocating of feral dragons, those that many found filthy and pestilent. These dragons wormed their way into stonework to make nests in the bellies of attics and basements. They gummed up chimneys by making nests in them. They invaded fireplaces and ran amuck in deserted buildings, breeding to impressive-sized families.

The traps the queen and her volunteers used were easy enough to set—a box with a trip latch and a heap of sugar inside. This was what Lusine was showing her replacement how to use, explaining how the door would close and trap the unsuspecting dragon inside.

"In the city, space is the constraint. In the countryside, food scarcity is what keeps them in check. Give them enough food and pasture, and they'll grow as big as a mountain," Lusine explained. "But they're also very territorial, and a large dragon claims large swarths of land to prowl. Eventually, fewer and fewer dragons will exist, even if they do become massive."

"Even those small ones? They'll grow that large?" the newbie asked.

"Allegedly. We don't follow up with the dragons once we release them. Bit of an out-of-sight, out-of-mind tactic."

"What of the farmers whose sheep they eat?"

"I suppose they get compensated."

The newbie looked over at the queen as if she would ask, then thought better of it.

"I'm going to go inspect the traps I laid the other day and collect any that have a catch. Keep filling these with sugar, you're doing just fine," Lusine encouraged and got up from the temple stairs they had been working on. Dragons loved temples best of all, gobbling up offerings and getting mistaken for miracles. They kept the rodent population, also enticed by the bowls of wine and fruit left out all day, in check. But eventually the dragons found themselves too at home in the rafters, starting to believe they, too, were being worshipped.

Lusine picked up her staff; it stood as tall as her chin, thin, with pretty carved vines curling up the pole, embracing a fist-size stone of amethyst at the top. It was given to her by her parents for protection, though she hardly used it unless she was out dragon hunting. It was the only lavish item on her. Lusine didn't want to be flashy when she was out and about and so dressed in a simple dress and stockings and a cloak that was understated even if expensive. She had long replaced the jewel-encrusted clasps of the cloak with simple brass wire ones and removed the luxurious fur trim from the edges, thinking perhaps it would offend Bane. She blended in with this uniform of a middle-class Citeelian, same as the other volunteers who dressed in muted garb even as everyone knew it wasn't the poor who had all that time on their hands to volunteer.

Lusine walked the path she knew the traps had been laid. When she came across one, she crept carefully until she saw it was empty, not wanting to startle anything caught inside. She crouched to inspect it, making sure nothing had gotten in and escaped, damaging the wires. The first three were obviously empty, minus the ants that had made their way in and were greedily devouring the crystals, but the fourth one she heard from quite a way away. The traps were checked every twelve hours, so while the dragon inside was furious, he wasn't starving or, she saw as she approached, hurt in any way. Its wings were tucked in tight against its body, so she couldn't see if it had ownership tattoos.

"Come on, big boy," she coaxed, pointing the amethyst at the cage. The box levitated on command, and she began walking with it, poised in the air right behind her. The dragon inside began to fuss, which was expected. But while some dragons huddled scared in a corner, this one began to throw its weight around ferociously, so much so that the cage lurched forward and bumped

Lusine on the shoulder. Startled, she tripped on a crooked cobblestone and toppled forward. Her staff went down, and the cage along with it.

There was quite a commotion, the crashing of the metal cage on cobblestone, the caws of distress from the dragon. Lusine rolled out of the way as a spray of fire shot through the cage where a crack appeared, which was otherwise fire-proof. Unfortunately, she was not. She patted the edge of her cloak where it was singed and pointed her staff at the dragon. "Behave, or you'll be taking a nap."

That was when she noticed it scooping coins back into the pouch in its armpit, which must have shaken out in the tumble. One was wedged in the door of the cage, and she picked it out before he could get to it. She could tell immediately it wasn't an official mint issued coin, but rather an OCC like the ones Bane had become obsessed with.

The dragon hurried to stuff the rest back into their hiding place and curled up in a tight ball, glaring at her, huffing as if daring her to come for his treasure.

"He'll defend his hoard with his life."

At the sound of the voice, Lusine startled back and fell onto her bum in surprise. She looked up to see a hooded man, his cloak black, the clasp at his throat shimmering with black diamonds. This man was very wealthy. Before she could say anything, he added, "Keep it. In exchange for releasing my dragon."

"Th-there are rules. Once caught, a dragon must be checked against the records to confirm it is fixed and up to date on its shots."

"Ah, but what if I assured you that he is, in fact, perfectly in compliance?"

"Do you have proof?" Lusine asked, not sure she was even qualified to confirm such a thing. No one had claimed a dragon that was caught, at least none she had caught. She felt annoyed that her very first confrontation should happen on her last day of volunteer work. She decided it wasn't worth the argument and had already made up her mind to let the dragon go when he said, "In exchange, I'll give you another one of those coins of mine you stole."

This bothered her so much that she narrowed her eyes at him and said, "That *I* stole? Where did your dragon get them from if he didn't steal them himself?"

"Ah, so we're equally criminal. I won't tattle if you don't either." The stranger pulled his hood back and attempted to dazzle her with a smile. It was bold of him, to reveal his face, but if he didn't give away any other proof of his identity it didn't do her much good.

Much good for what? She wasn't about to fight over taking away someone's pet dragon. Without a word, she pressed the stone of her staff to the lock and the door sprung open. Fraun leapt out and crawled up his master's shoulder, snuggled into the warm spot against his neck. The man was her age, younger even, perhaps. Handsome, clean-shaven, his hair impeccably trimmed. It was odd, she always figured criminals who stalked the streets would be ugly, disheveled, and haggard. At least, that's what all the fables assured her. His appearance suddenly made her question who was in the right, in fact. Surely *he* was, looking so impeccably put together.

"See? We have missed each other so very much." He reached back and under Fraun's arm. The dragon allowed him to pluck a coin but watched intensely as it was tossed to the woman. Fraun let out a hiss of disapproval—dragons didn't like to share. His master reached down and offered Lusine a hand. She looked at it, adorned with rings, the fingernails clean and trim, and accepted it, allowed herself to be pulled to her feet. She noticed him eye the clasp at her throat, also sizing her up, trying to decide if money would, in fact, intimidate her. It didn't, but his cleanliness did. She decided he had no business learning that fact.

"I'm so glad I could reunite you two." Lusine pocketed the coins before she reached for the cage, warped and warm, and picked it up. "Please do keep a closer watch on him," she instructed and made to walk past the pair back to the other volunteers. But as she did, the man stepped out in front of her, and she fell back against the stone wall of the alley they were in. With her pressed against the wall, he whispered, "I do appreciate discretion for my dragon's hobby."

"Seems like this was just about to wrap up, and it had better," came a voice from above.

Two heads looked up to find a man crouched on the roof, leering over the edge like a gargoyle. He shifted so that the sun could catch its light on the polished blade of the dagger he had pointed at the man in black. "I think ye best let the nice lady go."

"Balio, this isn't your territory," the man snapped.

"No? Can't see a red ring on yer plump, pretty finger. Alls the better to wash yer hands of yer dragon's business?"

Lusine looked between the two and cleared her throat. "It seems...you two have much to discuss," she said and scooted sideways, back still pressed against the stone, trying to get by. Her eyes were locked on the dragon's yellow ones, which trailed her intensely.

"Leave her, Vito," Balio ordered. "Yer dragon might be the one pickin' pockets, but I've been stalking *ye* fer a while. I've got stories on ye, and know where to tell 'em, Yer Grace."

"Shut it," Vito snapped. He rocked back on his heels and motioned for Lusine to go. "You saw nothing," he hissed as she hurried by.

The interaction felt so strange she didn't dare tell anyone about it. She planned to take it to the grave, forget it altogether, assuring herself she had played it up more in her mind than it deserved credit for. That was until Bane confronted her that evening with the coins he found on the counter, where she had set and forgotten them.

"Where did you get these?" he asked, trying to sound nonchalant.

"Oh, I caught a dragon today. One of those red Fire Stokers. He had a whole bunch of them on him. I think he's been trained to steal them."

Bane's eyes grew wide. "Where is it now?"

"The dragon? Back with its owner."

"Where are the other coins? Did you confiscate them?"

"Why would I? I'm not the Midnight Brigade."

"You just told me they were stolen!"

"I *suspect* they were stolen, but I wasn't about to wrestle them away from a fire-breathing dragon now, was I?"

"So now the queen has them?"

"No, the dragon's master showed up and claimed him. He gave me those coins to let his dragon go, took the dragon and the rest of the coins with him."

"You should have asked for more."

Lusine rolled her eyes. "I hardly felt in the position to negotiate." She turned back to the mirror but then looked back at Bane. "Don't do anything, alright?"

"Huh? What?" Bane had in fact immediately started plotting to do something alright.

"I wasn't about to get caught up in the criminal world, and I'd like you to stay clear of it, too."

"Some would argue being a broom salesman is pretty criminal," Bane said, joining her under the covers. "But that's why you're with me, isn't it? You like a bad boy."

Lusine let out a shriek of laughter as his fingers began tickling her. She forgot all about the matter in a few minutes.

Bane, on the other hand, laid there naked and spent after, panting and plotting.

25

To Catch A Dragon

Now that Lusine had subscribed them to *The Harking Herald*, the paper whacked against their window every morning at exactly the same time, not too early but early enough to read it before heading out to work. Sometimes it even made it through a window when they remembered to leave one open, and then Lusine lamented over the flutter of feathers that accompanied it. Other times the bird that arrived didn't wait to be let in and dropped the paper, and Bane had to lean out and pluck it off the awning over the door below.

It became their new alarm system, and when the paper arrived Lusine shot to the bathroom while Bane shuffled to their kitchenette to put a pot of water on to boil. He ground the coffee beans fresh, at Lusine's insistence; this was part of a not-so-short list of *must-haves* for when they agreed to move in together. By the time Lusine emerged, hair curlers removed, face washed, creams and lotions and perfumes and deodorant applied, the coffee aroma was ready to battle the cloud of scent haloing her.

That morning Bane looked Lusine over and saw similarities in her that he had begun to notice in the clientele he now served in New Brooms. Subtle clues of luxury that Used Brooms clients didn't have.

First, her impeccably lacquered nails. Hers were a light pink, so subtle it almost looked natural if it hadn't been for the perfect shape of them. They had been worked on by an expert.

Then there were her eyebrows, much thinner than his caterpillar ones, clearly sculpted and artificially darkened.

Her clothes were cut carefully to her frame, and there was not a single snag, stain, or fade.

Her ears held small, tasteful diamond studs. Not tiny ones. Not glass ones. She *smelled* expensive, when before he thought she just smelled nice.

Numbers began to whirl in Bane's head as he stared at her, as if seeing her for the first time. Lusine looked up from the gossip page she'd pulled from the newspaper and caught him gawking. "What? Have I something on my face?"

That perfectly manicured hand flew to her lips, which had been painted a subtle, cheery plum, making the blues of her eyes even bluer.

Bane narrowed his own brown eyes. "What did you do with those OCCs?"

"The coins? They're in the key dish." Lusine nodded in its direction. She took another sip of her coffee and went back to reading about the will-he-won't-he proposal of some foreign royal.

Bane peeked under the table to see her legs crossed, the ankle of the foot closest to him encircled with a gold chain, delicate and sexy, each little link perfectly set. He thought maybe she had spent those coins on this upkeeping, but when he casually meandered over to inspect the dish, he found both coins still in there. "Huh."

"Told you." Lusine looked back up at him. "What am I to do with them? Exchange them for rent? What are they worth now, anyway?" She reached for his page and read aloud, "Six gold. Huh. Technically we could pawn them to pay rent, this place is only ten gold a month." She peered up at him. "Why don't we?"

"If we can get a few more and hold onto them for a few more weeks, maybe even a few months, who knows how much they'll be worth. Maybe a hundred gold apiece! And if we have a hundred of them..." Bane made a motion with his hands as if his brain were exploding like a supernova.

"You're saying if we just crawl around on our hands and knees searching for them in the rubbish around the city, we'll have enough to buy the palace?"

"Don't sound dismissive." He couldn't admit to her that he had, in fact, crawled around nearly every park and open space in the kingdom looking for them, so much so that he had rubbed the knees of his old pair of trousers threadbare from the effort.

"How else are we going to acquire them? It's in the *Herald*, for gods' sake, therefore now everyone knows they're gaining value. Either folks don't trust it and don't bother with them, or they believe in them as much as you do, and they have the same plan of holding onto them until this price jumps to the moon. And looking at you now, we'd have to pry the coins from their corpses it looks like."

"Or they sell them to us. They find some and they don't think it's going to go up in value any more and they want to get out with a tidy profit."

"So *you* sell them. *You* make the tidy profit."

"Not while there are dragons out stealing them. That lets me know they're still valuable." As soon as Bane said this, the solution flew to him.

Of course! The dragon! Bane stooped and kissed Lusine full on the lips, heart pounding with excitement.

"You're not finishing your coffee?" she protested, but he was already tugging on his shoes and hurrying through the door, pausing only to scoop out the contents of the key dish on his way out.

Bane flew to Uncle Amos's. As he did, he noticed a crowd gathered around an official building. He dropped altitude, thinking this was maybe another demonstration by P.U.K.E., but there weren't enough people, just a handful. Bane casually landed and peeked over their heads to find a notice nailed to the door of the Chamber of Commerce:

OCC Value: 1 gold.
Proof: His Majesty King Eadwine has declared it so.
Future Value Estimate: 1 gold, indefinitely.

Bane huffed. *We'll see about that,* he thought as he kicked back off the ground. When he made it to the pawn shop, he walked in with his broomstick; this wasn't the sort of neighborhood where it was safe to leave it outside.

"Oy, Amos, have you been to the Chamber of Commerce?" Bane asked by greeting, too riled up for formalities.

"I'm looking at now," Amos said and flashed his mirror around to face Bane. "The Crown really thinks it has a say in this? Hah!" Amos got a fierce look on his face and pointed to the parchment tacked to the wall behind him. It had the *Herald*'s value written boldly on it. "It's the people who dictate the price, not the Crown. *I* decide. Same as I decide what everything's worth in my own shop. And if people think it's too high, we can adjust accordingly. But so long as I can take these coins and turn around and pay for more expensive things with them, I'll keep accepting them. Power to the people."

"Power to the people," Bane echoed, feeling a lump in his throat.

"I'm turning this off, it's riling me up." Amos stuffed the mirror into his breast pocket. "Whatcha looking for?"

Bane felt the coins in his pocket, the two OCCs mixed in there with the others. He was loathe to part with any of them, but he had to for what he anticipated would be a massive payoff. "Got any traps?"

"What are you catching?"

"A..." Bane paused, unsure how discreet the place was.

Amos sensed the hesitation and added, "So that I know what dimensions you're looking for."

"Something the size of a dragon."

"Oh, I've got loads of those," Amos said with a wave, as if this was such a common request. He led Bane to the back where they hung from the ceiling. He used levers on the wall to lower the ones Bane wanted to take a closer look at. He needed one simple in operation, fireproof, and not too chewed or clawed up.

"I've got this new shipment of channeling crystals coming in tomorrow, they're all the new craze," Amos chatted while Bane inspected. "Know how you have to draw on a mirror to change the channel? Well, if it's in your hand no biggie, but I've got one of them big wall-mounted mirrors in my den, and I hate getting up to change the channel. These crystals? You do a simple enchantment to connect them to your mirror and you can change the channel from across the room. What a time to be alive!"

"This one will do," Bane said, not ignoring Amos but deciding that something that fantastic was positively out of his price range. "How much?"

"What have you got?"

"Coppers and nickels, I'm afraid." He decided two cages ago he wasn't going past a nickel for it.

"Three coppers. Anything for the miss?"

Bane was already peering through the glass case at the jewelry, eyeing the rings. He decided gold was best. Traditional. The diamonds were pricy even in a place like this, but Bane thought maybe a sapphire would be nice. "Would she know the difference, if it was a precious or semi-precious stone?"

"I've seen her walking with that staff of hers. She knows her crystals. So, then you've got to wonder, does she care?"

Bane blew out a breath, making the rogue curl hanging low on his forehead flutter. He pushed it back into the mass that was growing bushier by the day. He didn't even like to spend money on a haircut until Lusine finally sent him. They tried cutting it themselves in the kitchenette once—the first and last time they did that. He didn't make a sale all that week and she swore it probably had nothing to do with it. *Probably.* "I'll wait. I want to save up for something nice."

"You're ready then, eh?"

"Are we ever?" Bane pulled out the coppers and handed them over, not waiting for the magic quill to write him a receipt.

"I'll buy it back when you're done with it!" Amos called as a parting, and Bane realized that was a very good idea. If the cage survived.

Bane knew from Lusine's stories where the usual traps were laid, which temples were most frequented by dragons. In hindsight, he probably should have asked her where the incident took place. But he had a trick up his sleeve, something to entice this dragon specifically but not the others.

It wasn't sugar he set into the cage when he found a spot he liked, but rather one of the OCCs. Then he thought better and put the other one in as well. Just to ensure the beast was definitely tempted to wander inside. Big risk, big reward. Then Bane slid into the shadows and waited.

26
Gilded Bridge

It didn't take long to catch the dragon.

It was a fat one, too. Clearly owned, clearly trained with treats, and clearly performing to expectation. He waddled right into the trap as if he hadn't been saved from a very similar one just the other day.

Bane sighed with relief when the trap closed, since with all the rust it hadn't been a given that it would. The dragon whipped around at the sound of the metal door crashing down, startled. It flailed in panic, scratched at the walls with its sharp claws, the coins he had just shoved under his armpit shaking out around him as he fought to escape. When Bane stepped out of his hiding spot, the dragon immediately noticed him and stopped his attempt to escape long enough to scoop the coins back under his arms. Fraun hissed and thumped his tail threateningly.

Bane crouched down a safe distance away. No one was immune to dragon fire, no matter how many burn marks they boasted. He grew up in the city and knew dragons, knew that their blast radius varied with their size and kept just outside it. He didn't have complete faith in second-hand fire retardant. "Hello."

Fraun hissed.

"Old boy, the way I see it, you can either drop your treasure and I release you, gentle as can be. Or you're coming home and getting roasted over a fire, and I pluck those coins out with a fork before I eat you for dinner."

"Dragons are too tough to be tasty," came a familiar voice. A moment later Balio dropped from the roof.

"Balio!"

Balio pressed a finger to his lips to shush Bane. "Master ain't far. See the collar? Gots a tiny mirror on it. He's bein' tracked. Ye better let him go before we get company."

"What are you doing here?"

"Whatcha think?" Balio nodded at Fraun. "Was hopin' to scare him to drop 'em coins, but he had to go wander into yer trap, didn't he?"

"You've been following him?"

"Aye. He was caught the other day by some gal. I happened to see 'em and saw what he was trackin'. Determined, that one."

"Was she the owner?" Bane asked, confused. Was he referring to Lusine? Had she met Balio? Talked to him? It felt bizarre to think they exchanged words.

"Nay, but I know the owner and he ain't too friendly a chap, so we best hurry. I can help wrestle his treasure away if ye split it with me."

Relief flooded Bane, seeing how the dragon was dragging those sharp claws down the cage walls. "Yeah alright. I'm not much with dragons anyhow."

"That won't be necessary," came the voice they had been hoping to avoid. Vito stepped out of the shadows. "But I would appreciate you letting my dragon go. *Again.*"

"Wasn't me either time," Balio insisted, raising his hands in innocence. "But we'll release him in exchange for yer payin' ransom."

A rapier appeared in Vito's hand. It was immediately blocked and pinned to the brick wall by Balio's dagger. "Those swords sure look pretty on the hip, but ain't got much use," Balio chided. "Have yer dragon shed his treasure and he's yers."

For a full minute they all stood stark still, calculating.

"Fine." Vito released the tension, and the dagger released the sword tip. Vito sheathed his sword slowly, still thinking. An idea came to him. "I'll make you a deal. I'll give you the coins," he nodded to Balio, then turned to Bane. "And I'll buy you anything you want."

"What's the catch?" Bane asked.

"It must be absurdly expensive. Then I want you to contact Harper Leewood of *The Harking Herald* and inform her that you purchased it with a single OCC."

Bane balked at the request. "That's a lie. That would jeopardize journalism."

"She jeopardized the whole economic system of this kingdom when she wrote that puff piece. Let her see the ramifications of her words."

"That'll make the price..." Balio let out a low whistle that climbed in pitch, mimicking the sounds of an old, loud broom taking off and vanishing into the clouds.

Vito ignored Balio. "A new broom perhaps?" Vito nodded to the one not well hidden where Bane had been lying in wait. "A new mirror? Cloak? Jewelry?"

At the last suggestion, Bane's eyebrows shot up. *A ring.* "Alright," Bane said and stuck out a hand to shake. "Be a man of your word, and I'll be one of mine." He looked at Balio, pleading, but Balio had already pulled his glove off like a gentleman and was also extending his hand.

Vito shook them in turn, sealing the deal.

"Please tell your dragon not to burn me," Bane instructed. He and Vito crouched down and Bane fiddled with the stuck door while Vito coaxed Fraun to be calm. At last the beast was free. Fraun scurried up Vito's shoulder and hissed at the other two, but let his armpits get picked clean. Balio accepted the coins, eyes shining with excitement. "Always a pleasure," he said to Bane, winked at Vito, and in the next moment had scaled the wall and disappeared on the roofs.

"Do you have a place in mind?" Vito asked. He whispered to Fraun, who jumped onto the wall, scrambled to the top, and also vanished into the rooftops.

"Um, maybe," Bane lied. The only shop he had ever been to that sold jewelry was Amos's, but he felt embarrassed to go there. He also felt uncomfortable, unsure what, exactly, the budget was.

"I know a place," Vito offered, turning on his heels. Bane followed.

Vito took them to Gilded Bridge, which was the oldest and sturdiest bridge in the city. It crossed the river that ran through the city, which once fed water into the palace's moat but was now not much more than a creek. The bridge was lined shoulder-to-shoulder with fine jewelry shops. The windows glittered with the faint winter sun, sparkling the ropes of gold and silver chains in the windows. In the summer, it was nearly intolerable to walk across the bridge without smoky quartz spectacles, so blinding was the shimmering of all the precious metal.

Vito seemed perfectly at ease on the bridge that Bane had only ever been on a few times, when his mother felt like dressing up in her finest dress and pretend to be a lot richer than she was, but only ever to window shop. Anxiety squeezed in Bane's chest as they passed the guards stationed at the end of the bridge, a clear warning to thieves. His heart hammered as they entered a shop, and Vito addressed the shopkeeper by his first name. "Something nice, but not vulgar," Vito instructed, and the jeweler beckoned Bane over to a counter that held extraordinarily crafted pieces. Bane knew they were expensive because unlike in Amos's shop, there weren't little price tags sprinkled throughout the case.

"Any preferences?"

"Gold. Absolutely no silver."

Bane was presented half a dozen choices, and he took his time inspecting each. He had made up his mind that he would pick the diamond, if there was one, no matter the size. Sure enough, one was presented to him, the stone about the size of a rice grain. Before he could stop himself, he asked, "How much?"

"Fifty gold, sir."

Bane gulped so hard Vito heard it across the shop, where he was inspecting a platinum collar for Fraun. He strolled over to the pair and peered over Bane's shoulder. His eyes flicked up to the salesman. "Is that all? Your puniest cut?"

"So sorry sir, my mistake." The man hurriedly swiped the ring away and replaced it with one set with a diamond the size of a pea.

Once more, Bane couldn't keep the question back. "How much?"

"One hundred and five gold, sir."

Bane froze.

Vito nodded. "We'll take it."

Leaving the shop, the ring burning a hole in his pocket, Bane remembered his part of the bargain. "I'm happy to contact Ms. Leewood, but I don't know how.

I could possibly reach her by pigeon, but I don't know how long that would take, with the strike."

"I have her direct line." Vito pulled out a piece of parchment and handed it to Bane, the symbol to scry her personal mirror drawn on it. "This afternoon would be best, so that it can make it into tomorrow's paper. Let her know when and where the ring was purchased."

"This...is huge," Bane whispered, gratitude swelling in his chest. "Thank you."

Vito clapped a friendly hand on Bane's shoulder. "I hope she likes it." And then he was gone, strolling away as if he had merely passed Bane in the throng shuffling around on that stone bridge. Bane's instinct was to run home, but Lusine was out anyway, and besides, he ought to show up to work at some point.

Bane imagined the fallout of disclosing this purchase. Why, if one OCC was worth *one hundred and five gold*, then the two he had at home...Bane's heart began to hammer. *He was rich*!

In the next instant Bane remembered that he, in fact, actually had none. He had put both coins Lusine obtained into that cage to lure the dragon, and both had been given to Balio. All Bane had was a ring. A beautiful ring, but...a fierce sense of urgency burned suddenly in him. It was his one shot to be wealthy.

He *had* to get more of those coins.

27

Brooms of Van De Besens

Best Buzzems was now, according to the new sign that was finally hung that morning, called Brooms of Van De Besens. The sign was handsomely made and hung a little higher than the former sign had been hung, Bane noticed as he walked into the dealership. He wore his new uniform shirt, trousers, boots and a belt. In fact, the only things he wore that hadn't been issued new were his socks and underwear. But those were new too, because Lusine had taken one look at his new clothes and insisted that he couldn't keep wearing the cobwebs he called undergarments any longer and immediately went out shopping. He burned red with shame when he found the socks and underwear on their bed, but then he showed her his appreciation by modeling them and nothing else. Now Bane felt a few inches taller as he walked, as tall as all the other salesmen in fact. Maybe even a hint taller.

The dealership was renovated, and as someone who went there every day, the changes were obvious. But to someone like Mel who didn't spend all day every day inside the dealership, they would have been subtle differences:

The worn brown seats in the customer lounge were replaced with real, expensive leather ones. *Bull leather*, Ezra whispered, *because unlike cows, the skin doesn't have stretch marks.* The manually operated coffee maker in the lounge was replaced by a highly enchanted sleek box. With a mug placed beneath it, a single button press brewed the coffee instantly and dispensed it at the perfect temperature. The steam that wafted from the brew was extra fragrant, Bane noticed. He fixed it with the usual cream and sugar, now in porcelain carafes instead of dinged-up metal ones. He steered the mug over to Ezra, who was staring out the floor-to-ceiling window.

"Ready for the all-hands meeting?" Ezra asked, not looking away.

"What is there to be ready for? The pledge of allegiance to our new overlord? The scolding that it's all about sales, sales, sales, and that unproductivity should be churned into productivity?"

They snickered, remembering the animated monthly meetings Gerwin held.

"You boys ready?" Dutch asked, walking by them on his way to the conference room. They followed him in, nodding at the new salesmen that had been hired on. They were very handsome, very broad-shouldered, and looked as if the new uniform shirts had been cut specifically for their frames. It was a flattering top, but clearly a little too tight for some, especially poor Dutch, who was constantly tugging the material away from his collar and protruding tummy. Glittering nametags were pinned to everyone's chest, and new, top-of-the-line hand mirrors had been issued as well. Money dripped from the Van De Besens, or at least they wanted to give that impression.

The meeting began as they all did, with updates on sales so far, goals, and the individual quotas for each salesman which, for a newbie, would have been humiliating but was just routine for the veterans. Bane was still getting used to the horrifying spotlight it cast on him. Ezra always gave his shoulder an encouraging pat after they moved on to the next victim. Whenever it got to Dutch, he made a show of rolling his eyes, and they were quick to move on.

New to this meeting was the new Finance & Enchantment Manager, Marvin, who listed new products he would be selling to customers and, to Bane's surprise, mentioned the new business's acceptance of OCCs. *Encouragement*, in fact.

"They're out there, and we want them," Marvin said. He was an imposing figure, unlike the previous F&E Manager Mic. Marvin inspired. Mic lectured. Bane wanted those insurances, those anti-theft charms installed, though he knew he realistically couldn't afford any and they would be a waste anyhow on his busted broom. Mostly, he wanted to *be* Marvin. "Folks don't want to spend their gold. They want to use gold for safe purchases. A practical broom. And that's fine! Something for everyone, we say. But OCCs, that's play money. That's uncertainty. They don't know what they can buy with them, and that's your way into that sale. Let them know everything is negotiable. Let them know we'll take them seriously where other businesses might not. Overcome those objections, lads. Let's show this city who's new in town."

Bane found himself clapping his hands together, applauding Marvin with the rest of the team. He looked at Ezra, who was enraptured, then at the new owners, Virgil and Jr., father and son, with heads full of shiny hair slicked back with expensive product. Bane was wrong about who the new shirts were modeled after; seeing the pair, it was clear the cloth had been cut to *their* dimensions. And they both looked like they ate a dozen eggs each for breakfast and scaled walls and lifted boulders in their free time. Their arms were crossed, intensely watching the meeting unfold, and their biceps bulged under the short-cut sleeves. Bane ran a hand through his bushy hair self-consciously, eyeing their impeccable cuts, and vowed to get a haircut after work. Something new. Something clean. His eyes turned back to Marvin as he cleared his throat for the applause to cease.

"We're so certain of this new tender that we're offering your pay in OCCs, at the conversion rate of ten gold each."

"Not mine!" Dutch shouted, cutting off the applause Marvin expected to receive.

Marvin forced himself not to roll his eyes. "For *anyone who'd like,*" he corrected, giving Dutch a knowing nod. Everyone else, including Bane, would be signing up for the program later. Then Marvin said something strange.

"Remember, boys, we're not in the business of selling broomsticks. We're in the business of selling loans."

Bane frowned. That didn't sound right. He glanced beside him at Ezra, who was still staring forward, enraptured, seeming completely unbothered by this statement. Bane turned back to watch Marvin. The more he spoke, the more he seemed to contradict himself. First, he said the dealership acknowledged OCCs and accepted them as payment—or did he say collateral?—and now he was saying not to accept money at all. Insist buyers take out a loan on the full amount of the broomstick. The words began to buzz without meaning as Marvin went on, and Bane's head kept rolling the same sentence around over and over again: What did that mean, *business of selling loans?*

Bane was too embarrassed to speak up and ask then, during the meeting. Instead, he found Ezra after they were adjourned. "I'm confused. Are we accepting OCCs or not? Because at first it sounded like we are, but then I think Marvin said not to take them?"

"Not to let them *pay*," Ezra clarified. "If we take their money in full, the transaction is over. We get what the price tag on the broomstick says. But if we tell them to take out a loan and finance the purchase, we also collect interest on the loan. See, some broomstick dealerships are just giant banks. Customers take out loans, the broomsticks being the collateral, and we get them to pay for as long as possible."

"How does that work?"

"Like this. Say a broomstick is worth, I don't know, a hundred gold coins."

Bane let out a low whistle, but Ezra gave a dismissive wave. "Use your imagination. If they pay coin, we get a hundred gold. But if they take a loan at five percent interest, over the course of, say, five years, compounded annually, they'll pay..." Ezra dropped into his desk and motioned for the enchanted quill to start scribbling. When it finished tallying, Bane leaned over to see as Ezra read off the total. "One hundred and thirteen gold coins. Give or take, depending on taxes and fees and don't forget post-sale add-ons like insurance."

An extra 13 gold coins? For what? Bane's head was swimming. "What if they stop paying?"

"Then we take back the collateral. In this case, their broomstick."

Bane considered this. "What if they almost finish paying it, but then stop? Is it theirs? Say they've paid 90 gold coins of 100?"

"Of *113*," Ezra corrected. "Nope. Broom comes back. Then we chuck it over to Used and they sell it for say, 50 gold. Now we have 90 gold, plus the interest, plus the 50 when it's sold again."

Bane's eyes nearly popped out of his head. "That's criminal!"

Ezra shrugged. "It's just good business."

It was in that moment that Bane understood why Balio thought he could see the Shadow Pub—not because he was a werewolf, but because he assumed Bane made shady deals like this. It wasn't about *who* he was, but rather *what* he did.

And for a second, Bane actually felt relieved. Then it dawned on him that it was his job now to sell loans, not broomsticks.

"Gerwin didn't make us do it like this."

"No. And the commissions weren't half as good, either," Ezra said, cocking an eyebrow. It was very much a *Get on our side* look.

And because Bane very much wanted to make lots of money, he decided he would get on that side, starting with his appearance. "Say, where do you get your hair cut?"

"You don't have a barber?" Ezra asked politely, because it was obvious that if Bane did have one, he clearly didn't visit him often.

Bane faltered and said, "He died," rather than admit it was an old lady down the street who cut hair in the back of her shop and served fish soup out the front.

"Louie's. On Beauty Lane. I'll give him a ring, let him know you're coming by."

"Do you think he can fit me in today?"

Ezra looked Bane over and said, "I'll convey how dire the situation is."

Bane playfully smacked him on the shoulder. Then he went off to greet the gaggle of customers that had just walked in before Ezra could jump out of his seat, trying to beat everyone else to them.

Bane found himself trailing after customers, hoping that somehow, one of them would happen to drop an OCC for him to find. He thought maybe he would run to Amos's after work and try to buy a few coins off him; surely Amos had some and would be willing to part with just a few? Maybe Bane would trade the ring for more coins before he called and broke the news. Five, maybe. Two, even! And then he could go back to the jeweler and use one to buy a new ring and still have another that was worth a fortune.

Bane's mind whirled like this as he sat with Marvin and signed the new contract to be paid in OCCs, all the way until closing. He sprung onto his broomstick the moment the doors of the dealership were locked.

Alas, Uncle Amos's was closed.

Bane banged his forehead to the cage around the thick wooden door, frustrated. He gave it a few good thwaps, hoping Amos was still inside, dusting maybe, but the sign on the door said he had closed more than an hour ago, so probably not.

Disheartened, Bane kicked off and made it to his hair appointment, even though he was in no mood now. That changed almost instantly as he stepped through the barbershop door and was whisked into a chair. He was so properly pampered that by the time he stumbled out in a daze, he couldn't remember why he had been so intimidated to go to one for so long. The price would have shocked him if the scalp massage hadn't been so incredibly relaxing. Catching one last glance at his reflection, he thought he looked like a completely new man. He pushed a hand through his locks, now cropped short around his head, tastefully shaped around his ears, and rubbed his chin that hadn't been so smooth since before he hit puberty. *Mighty fine.*

Wanting to show off the look, he headed next to Copper University. He found himself in such a good mood he insisted on paying for his own drink. It felt so wrong to Dante that he merely charged Bane for a simple, black coffee and then dressed it up as a chestnut latte. Irked, Bane dropped the difference in price into the tip mug. "Aha! You can't touch that until the end of your shift!"

Jaymie walked out of the storage room to peek into the tip mug and gawked. "Bane, have you won a dragon race bet?"

"He must have, his spending's out of control!" Dante motioned to the two coppers in the tip mug. Then he squinted. "Did you get a haircut?" When Bane merely grinned, Dante slapped a hand to his forehead. "Look at him! We've a prince in our midst!"

The first rule of OCCs is you don't talk about OCCs.

Bane rolled his eyes. "Business is good at the dealership. It got bought out and we all got raises. Oh, and I'm in the New Brooms department!"

"Charge him double," Jaymie only half joked. "Congratulations. The further you are from returning to work here, the better."

"You'd take me back?" Bane batted his lashes.

"Desperate times might call for desperate measures." Jaymie shrugged and went back to stocking the shelves.

Dante presented Bane his drink with a flourish. "Enjoy." When Bane stood from the stool and made to steer away with the drink, Dante's face fell. "I thought you'd sit and chat."

"Ah, um, got some business. After," Bane promised. He steered his mug to a quiet corner of the shop and settled into a comfortable chair. It enveloped him, like a hug from an old friend, but Bane knew from experience that it always seemed to grow hard right after he finished his drink. It made him suspicious that the furniture was custom crafted by more than just elves. A dust of magic was surely woven into the fabric's fibers. He brought the drink to his lips and shuddered with pleasure as the liquid touched his tongue. Maybe the ambiance elevated the experience, but there was definitely something different about the coffee in here. It just tasted better, Bane couldn't explain it. He made coffee at home using the skills he had obtained here, but it just never tasted the same.

When he had drunk enough that his courage found him, Bane pulled Vito's clip of parchment from his pocket along with his hand mirror. He inspected the rune, took a breath, and drew it on the glass. A moment later his reflection rippled, and Harper Leewood's angular face replaced it. "Hello?"

"Hello, Miss Leewood. I don't know if you remember me, but my name is Bane Woods and I have an OCC story I think you might be interested in…"

28

Surprise

Bane pushed the front door of his loft open, head swimming with thoughts. He felt the finality of what was coming; a lot of people were about to get really, really rich. And he wasn't one of those people.

Still, he forced himself to remember the ring he had. It was *not nothing*, and so he tried to focus on that, on the positive of the day's events. He was eager to stow the ring somewhere safe and begin planning the date where he would propose to Lusine. He wasn't sure what they would do, though he had spent the ride home brainstorming all the things they enjoyed. None of them seemed Grand Gesture enough. Dinner, but where? A walk after, but where? Where was the most magical?

Anywhere with her, his brain had offered, but that sounded sappy and stupid and wasn't helpful, even if true.

Bane poked his head into the bedroom, hoping somehow Lusine had been caught up at work late so he could hide the ring in peace, but no luck. Lusine was already in bed, but he noted that her hair was loose around her and no creams were slathered over her face. The strap of her nightdress was slipping off one shoulder. The sight activated him, and he prowled into the room.

Lusine glanced over and giggled at his attempt to seductively move in on her. He dropped onto the bed and made to wrap his arms around her, but she stopped him with a, "Wait!"

He sat up and looked around in time to see the mirror go blank, the glass reflecting them. Bane's surprise was caught clearly in it. He looked back at Lusine. "How did you do that?"

"Turn it off? Oh, this little thing." Lusine pulled her hand out from under the covers to reveal an obelisk-shaped rose quartz crystal. "Makes it so much easier. Now when I fall asleep you can just change the channel to whatever you want, like Midnight Brigade. Sort of works like a wand."

Bane nearly imploded. Here he was worrying about the rise in rent, in finding dropped coins in the gutters, and she was frivolously spending on a mirror channel changer. "That's new," he stated, trying to keep his voice even.

"Isn't it wonderful?" She did another demonstration, turning the mirror back on and increasing the volume. Bane snatched it out of her hand and squeezed it. He wanted to destroy it. He wanted to smash it against the mirror to make her understand how furiously trapped he felt. Why didn't she feel as stuck as he did? How could she spend money without thinking of the ramifications? How much did this crystal cost? Her lotions and perfumes?

"Bane? Bane!" Lusine drew up to her knees and caught his face in her hands. His furious tears flowed freely. "What is it? What happened?"

And because it was all too much to put into words, he reached into his pocket and pulled out the blue velvet case, popped it open, and presented the engagement ring.

"Ooh!" Lusine gasped. Her hands flew from his face to her mouth and her eyes widened to twice their usual size. She gaped at the ring. Finally, she looked up at him. "But why are you crying?"

He had no money. This ring, and her, and his mother, were all he had in the world. And he was terrified it wasn't enough for Lusine. "Will you marry me?" he choked out, terrified of what she would say.

"Yes. Yes!" She caught the velvet box, which had begun to tremble in his hand. "Of course I will."

Bane collapsed onto the bed, relieved, but still seized by terror. She laid down beside him and ran a hand through his hair. "Is that why you got a haircut? You look very handsome," she whispered, thinking that because of the haircut the proposal had been planned all along. "Are you alright?"

"You'll be my wife? Really?"

"Hurry up and put this ring on my finger, you fool."

Bane sat up, pulled the ring out of the box, and slipped it onto her finger. It was a little loose, but she insisted she didn't mind. She stared at it, held it up to inspect it in the dim light of their ancient loft, and smiled. "I had actually planned on proposing to you."

Bane's jaw dropped. "That's ridiculous."

Lusine reached over and pulled open the bedside dresser, tugged out a law encyclopedia, and opened it to reveal a ring set with a diamond the size of a quail egg. Bane gawked at it.

"It was my grandmother's," she explained. "It was given to me on my last birthday by Nana. She told me to give it to a man I found worthy to give back to me. I wanted to wait until I finished my degree." She watched him inspect the stone, mesmerized by the size of the diamond, and realized maybe she had offended him. "I don't mean to insult the one you got me. I love it, I really do. I just want to assure you that I have been thinking of marrying you for a while now."

Bane was no gemstone expert, but he had spent enough time recently browsing the jewelry counters of pawn shops and fancier shops to know that this specimen would never have been shown to him without an appointment and still wouldn't have been shown to him when he disclosed his budget. He had seen rings like this only in the windows of the shops on Gilded Bridge, shops even his mother hadn't had the courage to go into, they were so intimidatingly expensive. He knew, turning the ring over in his hand, that even those he had seen in the windows dulled compared to this one.

"This has got to be stolen," he joked. "What kingdom did they barter to get this?"

When she didn't say anything, Bane looked up, concerned. "Is it stolen?"

"No, of course not," she snapped. "She just liked nice things. Let's celebrate." Lusine jumped up, realizing she wasn't ready to overshadow the news of the engagement with a confession of her family line. She snatched the heirloom ring out of his hand and dropped it back into the dresser. "I'll grab the wine."

Before he could say anything else, she was out of the room. Thrilled, he pulled his hand mirror out and called his mum to share the good news.

"Darling, that's wonderful!" Marmie cheered, clapping her hands excitedly. "I *knew* she was the one!"

Bane grinned and thanked her. Then, before Lusine returned, he quickly dropped his voice. "Quick question, Mum. Those commemorative coins you had, do you still have them? The OCCs?"

"Yes, we're using them to play cards. Well, we were supposed to, but no one has the time to just sit around and play cards. They're all hiking or swimming or getting mud facials or eating at restaurants! Sometimes I feel as if I'm the slowest person here."

"Great, so you haven't lost them playing Seven Spread?"

"Not yet."

"Mum, don't. Listen, hold on to them for just one more day, will you? And please, *please* read *The Harking Herald* tomorrow. You can get a copy out there, can't you?"

"I'm reading *Seaside Chronicles*. It's got all the best restaurant reviews. What do I care what's happening in the capital?"

Bane felt frantic. He wanted to tell her everything, but also only enough that she understood the urgency before Lusine came back. He didn't feel he could talk to her about the coins anymore. "Just please, is there anywhere you can get a copy?"

"There's the café here, they sell all sorts of papers—"

"Great. First thing tomorrow, get a copy and read the finance section, got it? *Finance*, Mum."

Marmie sensed the tone in her son's voice and nodded solemnly. "Alright, I will."

"And then...do what you think is best."

Lusine appeared in the doorway holding up a half-full bottle of sad, vinegar-flavored red liquid that was once wine but had been left open and forgotten for too long. By the pinched look on her face, she had already tasted it. "Maybe we go out for a drink to celebrate?"

"Let's! Bye, Mum."

"Bye Marmie! Mum! Hah!"

Bane tossed the mirror aside and accepted the glassful of the putrid liquid. He couldn't get himself to drink it. "No. Not even to pre-game."

Lusine took the glass back and sniffed, just in case she might change her mind, and stumbled back a step. "We won't be able to walk after if we do. Alright, I'll get rid of this, you get dressed."

After one too many fruity, fizzy cocktails at a pub around the block that was rather affordable and which turned especially lively this time of night, Lusine tugged Bane out the door and in the direction of the city center. "It's not so cold out. Let's take a nice long walk."

Bane was in no mood to object to anything. He let her lead the way as they wandered deeper into the city to see the palace lit up at night. As they got closer, they saw the shadowy figures of the stardust sweepers flinting across the roofs, collecting the magical dust that illuminated the new lights in the palace.

Lusine steered them past Everdorne University, past its imposing, gothic Royal Academy of Engineering and Design, and into the Artists' District. The streets were suddenly smooth under their soles, the houses stood a little straighter, as if going to attention for them, and the streetlights glowed brighter from starlight instead of the flames the other lamps around the city were lit by. Each shrub was impeccably pruned, even those bare in the winter's cold, and the air itself seemed to go sweeter.

It was a romantic place to stroll through, with the evergreen wreaths hung on the doors of the homes, the garlands of ornaments tinseling the roofs, which were all sleek and uniform, not a hole in one. Everyone they passed was impeccably dressed, and they nodded jovially at the couple basking in the thrill of their new engagement.

Bane felt Lusine tugging now, where before it felt like they were meandering. When she abruptly halted in front of one of the imposing, impossibly pretty houses, he understood why when she said, "This is where I grew up."

It was basically a mini palace, frilled up like all the others around it, not one to be outshone. Bane gaped at it. "Here? What are you, some sort of long-lost princess?"

"A baroness," Lusine admitted, staring at the toes of her pointed leather shoes.

Bane let out a bark of laughter. He gave a comical courtesy. "Lady Lusine!"

Lusine blushed deep red and swatted him. "Come on, let's get out of here."

"Why? In case the servants run out to present you your misplaced coronet? Wait, did you have servants growing up? Do your parents *still* have servants? Lusine!"

"What does it matter?" Lusine grabbed his arm and dragged him along, at least until they were out of sight should anyone peek out a window.

"It matters because it says a lot about a person, if they have to bend down and tie their own shoes or not."

"I tied my own shoes," she confirmed and raised her runny pink nose. She gave a ferocious sniffle. "Always have, always will. Because I'm not one to conform."

The laughter fell from Bane's lips. "What do you mean? Something happened? You don't go home anymore, do you?" He had wondered, of course, why he hadn't met her parents yet.

She shook her head, wiped the snot on her dress sleeve. "They didn't like the direction my life was going. There are acceptable careers for a noble and there are those that bring shame upon a family," Lusine tried to explain, but Bane cut her off, sensing where this was going.

"You're a lawyer! You know the laws of the land! Are you saying they're disappointed in you?"

"Yes. I know the laws for protecting the pigeons, for creating sanctions for stray animals. I represent shifters and changelings, and I guess werewolves, too. I help write city ordinances against rats and other pests. I represent those who cannot defend themselves. The ones seen as the lowest of the low in this city, perhaps in the whole kingdom. That I'm not my family's lackey to call when they need to bend the laws in their favor is what upsets them."

Bane narrowed his eyes. "Your parents want you to learn laws that benefit them?"

"Divorce law for their friends or estate law for their many summer homes or merger law for combining businesses when their children marry."

"Aren't there enough lawyers for that?"

"Not one that's under their thumb. That's why they refused to pay for my schooling, so I had to scrape the tuition together on my own."

Bane set his hands on her shoulders, forced her to look into his eyes. "You are brilliant, Lusine Glowry, and you will be dearly loved by the citizens—and vermin—you serve."

Lusine buried her face in his chest, and he held her fiercely. Then he whispered, "Are you sure we can't drop in? I bet the pantry is stuffed."

Lusine laughed and pulled his face down for a kiss. "You can meet them, if you really want to. But you won't ask for my hand from them, because I am my own person, not a thing to be given."

"What I wanted from you, you already gave," he teased and braced for the punch that sailed into his arm.

Bane slid his arms around Lusine and pulled her into him, kissed the top of her head. He smelled her hair, now a familiar scent, and felt, finally, like this was real. She was his, and she would be his wife. He felt, looking around them in that pretty neighborhood where they didn't stick out at all, that someday, maybe soon, they would get to this point. *Luck must be on my side*, he thought, and began to believe that he did deserve such joy in his life.

29

Breaking News

T he office of *The Harking Herald* was a warzone, working overtime to put out an emergency issue. Eldron Mooris, the Editor-in-Chief, was raging behind his office's closed door, ready to strangle the subordinate who had caused them all to be called back into the office after-hours. The subordinate was Harper Leewood, who simply sat on the lounge chaise, filing her nails, eyebrows raised at the tantrum her boss was throwing around the room like a rubber ball that she simply refused to catch and play with.

"Why couldn't you have sat on this until the morning?" he demanded.

"You know as well as the best that news waits for no one," Harper replied haughtily. "I've already confirmed with the jeweler. He was about to explode with excitement. He wouldn't have waited, either."

"But *you* could have waited. Gone home, had a drink. Come into work fresh as a daisy like the rest of us. Now I've got my wife calling because she has dinner guests she has to entertain alone and they're *my* friends." Eldron rolled his eyes to express just what he thought of the Monrels being *his* friends. "And I have a printer that's running out of ink and an issue that needs to be padded with as many advertisements as we can muster for this novelette that needs to come out first thing in the morning."

"So *you* delay," Harper snapped. She tossed the nail file onto the desk hidden under towering stacks of parchments and teetering jars of ink. "You're the boss!"

Eldron slammed his hands on his desk, sending two stacks of parchments toppling over. He was always the demurest in the office, until he wasn't. His fuse was long and his outbursts far between, but gods were they glorious when they popped off. Harper was *loving* this. "I can't. Because my work mirror is compromised. Someone scryed into it as you were breaking the news to me and the mysterious stranger is threatening to leak the news if we don't, and then we'll lose out on ad revenue. And that'll really bring down The Boss."

The Boss was Atticus Alry, who as Head of the Aluminum Mint essentially controlled Everdorne's Treasury—and, with it, the kingdom. He was also a vampire and the one who started *The Harking Herald* newspaper as a project when he was mortal and full of ambition. Now he was ancient, bored, and so powerful and rich that the only amusement he had was his vineyard, Blood of the Vine, and this newspaper. *The Harking Herald* was the sword he wielded against the Crown, the permanent power struggle nearly palpable.

"Is that so?" Harper pulled out her mirror and dropped it on the floor, as if a slug she had just discovered in her pocket. "That's nasty news. Did it compromise mine as well?"

"Possibly. I'm not entirely sure how this new mirror magic works. Better get a new one just in case."

It gave Harper the *ick*, to think that someone was peeking in at her when she wasn't aware. "Wait, why did you tell The Boss?"

"*I* didn't. His stepson did. Our dear darling new finance intern somehow found out."

"Vito Alry?" Harper frowned. "But he's what, twelve? What does he know about mirrors? Or, for that matter, finance?"

"He's twenty-two and an heir. I know he's got money, and that you and I"—Eldron wagged a finger between them—"do not. Therefore, if you would like to keep taking home your meager paycheck, you will solemnly swear in this office before all the gods and critics peeking through my blasted mirror that you will not be dropping earthquake-sized news in the middle of the night ever again."

Harper leaned in and whispered, "I'll be a double agent if you force my hand, dear Eldron. I'll sell it to the next highest bidder."

"The highest bidder?" Eldron laughed. "We're hardly paying you at all."

Harper cracked a smile and stood to shake out the signature purple cloak she wore like a cocoon around herself. "That part is true. Be sure to send me a thank-you card for your ad bonus, won't you?" With that, she stepped out of the office and headed straight for the thorn in her side.

Vito Alry was a beautiful man, and he knew it. It was tainted only by his arrogance, brought on by his very high status in Everdorne society. He wasn't a vampire like his stepfather, and neither was his mother, but he seemed to harbor a cold heart in his chest nonetheless. What did he know about finance? That he had money, and everyone else had less of it.

"You're on my shit list," Harper hissed, tossing her tainted mirror on his desk.

"Oh? Because of this?" Vito plucked it up, tossed it into the air, and caught it playfully. "Or because...the economy is about to implode?"

Harper narrowed her eyes. Vito had a finger in this. She wasn't sure how, but he wasn't just keeping a feel on the pulse. He was definitely stirring the pot. He might even be orchestrating the whole mess. "Stay out of my mirror," she hissed and stormed down to the Supply Closet to request a new one.

The extra issue printed in time, of course, a leaflet inserted into the already printed issue for the next day. It included an extra juicy gossip column that was completely biased and unsupported by any evidence, and nearly a dozen advertisements including one for the newly acquired Brooms of Van De Besens, which had been hounding the paper for ad space since before it even bought the location. And of course, there was the full-page notice:

OCC Value: 105 golds.
Proof: Purchase of a diamond ring from Franklin's Fine Jewelry on Gilded Bridge, worth 105 golds, for 1 OCC.
Future Value Estimate: ?

Eldron and Harper had argued over the future value. They pulled in Roland Baines, the Head of Finance & Accounting for the newspaper as well as Heathrow Montry, the Head Finance Writer, who simply shrugged at the evaluation. "We always knew it was possible."

"'We?'" Harper asked.

Heathrow jabbed a finger at Roland. "We've had a bet going since the first column you put out. He's got over a hundred of them, I have eighty-three."

Harper's jaw dropped. "Isn't that a conflict of interest?"

"Isn't everything?" Eldron grumbled, rolling his eyes.

"Hardly," Roland insisted. "It's like reading an article about a new business that opens and reading up on the investors then going out and purchasing a share of it. If it happens to go up, that's not insider trading, and if it goes down, we're not liable for causing any financial loss. We're not fortune tellers, but if you read close enough and study trends, you make your own luck."

"That means when this publishes..." Harper's eyes went wide at the thought. "Are you allowed to sell the coins?" she asked, but she was glaring at Eldron, who was silently pleading with the gods that his mirror wouldn't suddenly flicker alive with Atticus Alry's face in it.

"Sure. We didn't sign any agreements," Heathrow said. "Of course, their true value depends on who will buy it."

"It's only worth what someone will give for it," Roland supplied. "Sure, the paper prints a fact that someone traded one coin for something valued at 105 golds. But if no one will accept that again, then it's not actually worth 105 golds. Maybe someone will offer me 100 gold instead for it, hoping to turn it around and sell it for 105. Or maybe only 50 and then hope someone else will give them 90 gold for it, who will then try to sell it for 105. Or I hold out and hope someone out there will give me 200 gold for it in a week or so. See how it works?"

"It's just gambling," Harper insisted. She pinched the bridge of her nose, suddenly remembering something. "Hold on, didn't the Crown decree that an OCC is only worth one gold? Is that the true value?"

"Depends on who's enforcing that. The seller or the buyer," Heathrow said.

"Or no one at all," Roland added. "No one's obligated to take the coins at all. Not for one gold, not for a hundred gold."

"Then what if the jeweler who took that coin for the ring can't buy anything at all with it tomorrow?"

"What if he can give it to his bank and pay off every single debt he owes?" Heathrow countered. His hands fell open, palms up as if in silent prayer. "*Anything* can happen tomorrow."

"Should we get legal in on this?" Harper asked.

"No. Never," Eldron snapped. "Not on my watch."

Eldron now sat in the newspaper's cafeteria, drinking a bitter black coffee to shock his system awake, bracing for the onslaught of mirror calls, messages by mail, and more than a few carriages pulling up with investors, outraged by what they read. He had instructed his staff to go home and return after lunch, if they felt like it, if they still needed a job. He wondered about Heathrow and Roland, wondered if they were brilliant and, if they were, if he was the biggest fool of all, having watched this incredible thing unfold and not pounced on the chance.

Eldron Mooris lived a comfortable life. He had traveled all the kingdoms as a young man fresh out of Everdorne University's School of Journalism, seen the continent there and back. He had worked in every tiny newspaper that would gamble on a wanderlust young man who sought the thrill of adventure.

He had seen it all. And not every kingdom was as peaceful as Everdorne.

But in a lot of ways, they had also been much the same. He met people and met them again in different cities; different faces, but the same personalities, the same temperament, as if the gods only made a handful of molds and recycled them. Eldron met himself over and over again, those he felt instantly drawn to, as if they were made of the same stardust and were magnetized to seek out and find one another, then get blind drunk while gambling on dragon races.

Then there was his wife, his daughter, and the recent need for stability. He was offered this newspaper, where he assembled his dream team. For the most part, that was exactly what it was. And like any fruitful kingdom, it was always waging war, defending itself from enemies, trading and dealing with even the unruly types to keep peace and stay afloat. Despite his immortality and power, Atticus Alry, like every other citizen in this kingdom, served the Crown; even he genuflected to whoever wore the crown. But Eldron knew from experience that a Crown could be challenged, and crowns fell when the heads below them were severed.

Eldron shivered, flashing back to scenes of gore he had witnessed in his youth. He hadn't seen violence in so long, but he had learned to recognize the warnings of a coup. And this reeked of one.

30

Raining Riches

Before the news broke that morning, before the papers even hit the stands, a man and his dragon went for a walk. Vito Alry had been up all night at the office in preparation for distributing the supplementary insert with the Big News printed in it. But that was only the beginning of his plan.

Vito was born into a wealthy family, made especially wealthy when his mother, widowed with a toddler, became the sixteenth wife of Atticus Alry, immortal Head of the Aluminum Mint. Vito grew up knowing he was a rich boy, and an *especially* rich boy the moment the wedding fused his family with the immortal bastion of power. Atticus commanded the most powerful tender in the kingdom, and as such, was one of the most powerful people on the entire continent. He had banks everywhere, owned businesses under aliases, and had a direct input in what the Crown spent money on. The mints were the checks and balances of the Crown; the king had the purse, but mints held the coins he could draw from it. It was in their best interest to advise His Majesty on how to use their money; where to lend it, and to deter things like war and expansion where there was a poor chance of return. They didn't mind their money leaving, so long as it landed back in their coffers, with interest of course.

Some took over such positions by force or matrimony, but Atticus took his over by simply outliving everyone. No one knew how he got the position originally; no history on the matter existed anywhere and all the witnesses were long dead. Frankly it didn't matter; it was his until someone drove a silver stake through his heart and set his decapitated head on fire.

Allegedly.

There were a lot of rumors about how to kill vampires. And werewolves. And ghosts. But the truth was, they coexisted same as elves, orcs, dwarves, and other foreigners in the kingdom. They were given a second glance, but rarely more. No one asked *what* someone was, that was quite rude, though sometimes it was evident. Looking at Atticus, it was hard to tell since he took so much care with upkeep, but he was legendary, and everyone knew who he was. It was only in the last century that he finally stopped pretending it was avoiding direct sunlight and applying moisturizer that kept his skin looking so firm and young. He even started to coyly flash his fangs at parties.

And the thing with vampires was, if they went around making everyone else vampires, why, they would have competition for resources. For the fresh blood at the butcher's, the money in circulation, the power all around. Vampires were like dragons—territorial, and rather protective of their homes. That was why they didn't just go around biting everyone's neck. As for mortals in power, Atticus didn't mind them too much. He got along with the current Mint Heads just fine. And the new king, well, he would die soon enough. As would the next, and the next, their lives lasting the length of a blink of an eye to Atticus. His opinion of them hardly mattered, they'd be gone before he could form one.

But a son? Atticus would never suspect that his wife's child was the culprit behind all this excitement. The one who had asked, rather loudly in the conference room at the newspaper one day, "If these coins can be used at the festival, will other businesses accept them?" giving Harper the idea to offer it as payment at the coffee shop.

Vito made sure her article ran in the finance section, where just the right audience would read it. A puff piece anywhere else, a spark of curiosity there.

After the coronation, Vito scoured the festival grounds, sweeping up and collecting the discarded coins, though there hadn't been many. Most were spent quickly, returned to the Crown by vendors wanting their credit. Plenty had been taken back with citizens as souvenir trinkets.

Initially, Fraun the dragon was tasked with finding the fool's gold coins discarded in trash bins, gutters, and park benches where coins liked to escape pockets. Fraun was instructed not to steal coins directly from anyone, but sometimes he got a little carried away, the downside of teaching a highly motivated dragon a new trick. He didn't start jumping victims until the coins really became scarce.

Then there was Balio, the pickpocket he met years ago in the Shadow Pub and had the misfortune of always running into. Balio and the whole Pickpocket Guild could have wreaked havoc on this plan, but since they all caught on too late, they neither hindered nor helped it along.

Luckily, because Balio would have been very surprised at this next move.

Vito walked the mostly deserted streets, quiet but for a few pubs open late, a massive sack of coins hidden under his cloak. It was so heavy that he carried it in both arms, and the dragon perched on his shoulder didn't help. Vito's arms and shoulders burned from the effort of carrying the sack from its hiding place all the way to the university. The guards on duty nodded him through the door, though they could have been nodding in their sleep standing up, it was too dark to tell. Vito followed the signs and headed to the Astronomer's Tower. It wasn't the tallest tower in the city, but it was the tallest public one. On a night like this, overcast with snow clouds, there would be no one there, at least no one looking at stars. Just in case, he knocked before entering, pausing for ample time to give anyone inside time to pull their clothes back on. When he pushed the door open and turned the stardust lights on, Vito saw that he was alone. He immediately set to work.

Vito lifted Fraun onto a work desk, pulled his *Quick Guide to Spells* from his pocket, and opened it to the dog-eared page. He read the line he found earlier and cast the spell to lighten the load of the sack. He could have done this sooner, but he was no wizard and only knew amateur magic that lasted a short while and burned a lot of energy, and so he didn't want to waste it.

Vito pulled out a dagger and sliced a gash in the levitating sack, held the lips together to keep the coins inside. He pulled out a needle and a spool of nearly translucently thin thread and sewed the cut together in loose loops. When he let go, the OCC coins inside threatened to burst through. A few good shakes and they would snap the thread and sprinkle out. *Perfect.* He made a few more gashes all around the sack and haphazardly stitched each one back together.

He tied the sack to Fraun, aimed him at the window, and commanded, "Fly home!"

Nothing happened, of course, because that was an awfully big trick for very little payoff, and flying was such a drag. Fraun began pawing at Vito, trying to climb back onto his shoulders to be taken home, the shoddy sewing job threatening to burst prematurely.

Vito grabbed Fraun by the scaly red arms and with some effort pulled the dragon off. He held the wriggling beast close and carried him to the ledge of the open window. Again he commanded, a bit more firmly, "Go *home*."

And then he tossed the dragon out the window.

Fraun should have expected this, but no one had ever thrown him, a dragon, out of a window before. He scrambled, spinning head over tail a few feet before remembering he was a *dragon*. His wings, which had been folded sleek against his body, burst open and caught wind. He gave a few flaps to gain altitude and recalled his mission. And because he was a good boy and there might be treats, he did as he was told, gliding over the roofs to the semi-remote community across the city studded with lavish mansions and ample roaming yards for pet dragons and prized ponies.

It didn't take long for the stitches to burst open and for the fool's gold coins to shower down. They pelted like hail onto rooftops, startling citizens awake. They clanked onto the cobblestone streets below, waiting to be found. They hit the heads of a few drunks, who immediately turned tail and went back to spend their found prize on another pint. They peppered carriage hoods and bounced off into bushes and down gutters. But most of them stayed where they fell, sprinkled in plain sight, waiting to be found in the morning by the luckiest people in the kingdom.

Fraun didn't even notice his load getting lighter, he was so frantic to get home, the fantasy of what prize was awaiting him growing grander by the mile.

It was a whole roast chicken, and his belly nearly burst from fullness after he devoured it. He slept the best he had in months, not realizing he was now officially retired, doomed to grow fat and lazy and into one of the happiest dragons in all of Everdorne.

31

Trickle-Down

It was rotten luck that at Van De Besens the sales team recently made a schedule change, assigning new employees morning shifts and veterans the busier afternoon shifts.

Thanks to his insomnia, Bane happily accepted the new schedule. By the time he woke up, Lusine had left for work and the streets were picked clean of OCCs.

It wasn't until Bane landed by the dealership entrance, having dodged half a dozen wayward broomsticks being test ridden on the lot, that he suspected the news had broken.

He just wasn't prepared for the *other* news.

"Oy, suddenly everyone's found their coffers?" Bane joked, walking past Ezra to deposit his broom in the closet.

"It rained coins, didn't you hear?"

Bane frowned, put his broom away, and went back into the lounge. "What did you say?"

"The coins that fell from the sky last night."

This was a strange way to say that the price of OCCs shot up. "Are you referring to the price of the coins going astronomical?"

"No, he's referring to this," Dutch snapped, turning his mirror to Bane. He pressed a finger to the corner of the glass to rewind the clip and then let go to play.

"At approximately 3am this morning, official commemorative coins, also widely referred to as OCCs, showered all across a specific section of the kingdom. This made many citizens extraordinarily wealthy overnight, thanks to the news that broke in this morning's The Harking Herald *that the latest valuation of*

a single OCC is one hundred and five gold coins. More on this story—" Dutch flipped his mirror shut and threw it into the bin. It clamored loudly, turning a few heads. Dutch knew he would have to fetch it in a moment to save it from being drowned in deposited coffee, but in that moment, doing that felt very, very good. If only he had miraculously known that on that morning, of all mornings, he should have woken up at the crack of dawn.

"Wh-who-what-who did that?" Bane sputtered, finally landing on a question, one of a million that exploded in his brain.

"Some good-for-nothing rich bastard," Dutch spat.

Marvin poked his head out of his office, looking frantic. "You three," he hissed, locking eyes on his salesmen. "Round up some coffee. I'm stuck in a deal and have three more waiting to be sold insurance. I need them kept patient. Virgil's already ordered a spread for dinner. It looks like we're all staying late, boys."

This was at least some consolation prize. The three salesmen did as told then eyed the front door, waiting for fresh blood to enter. They all harbored secret resentment, sure that every customer that day was a lucky bastard who had no business being more fortunate than them. And to splurge it on a new broom? Monsters, the lot of them.

Mel walked in, and Bane grabbed Ezra by the collar to catch him. "She's with me, you know that." It wasn't turkey day, so he was a bit surprised to see her. "More practice flying gone wrong?"

"Actually..." The door opened right behind her and in walked her son. "This is Joyce, the rascal that nearly scared our pigeon to death. We're here to buy him a new broom."

Bane looked at the young man that followed her in and realized he was her *son*. It shocked Bane to see Mel's son grown, because that was a bit strange, wasn't it? Having a friend who has a son close to your age? He never really thought of Mel as old, or as a mother, despite all her stories and even with her stomach protruding so obviously now. And she wasn't old; she was 36. Bane, a professional at this point, fixed his face and stuck out a hand. "Bane. A pleasure to meet you, Joyce."

When Joyce was on the lot test riding the latest Wizby, Bane looked at Mel and cocked an eyebrow. "Business going well?"

"Like you can't imagine," she said, and nodded for them to head inside for a coffee. "Are you going to make any more deliveries for me? Or are you too busy now that you're in the fancy building?"

Bane chuckled. "Here and there, sure. Especially if it's going this well!"

"Oh this? No, that's all Joyce. He found a few of those OCCs this morning. The first time he remembers to take out the trash, of all the days to do it!"

Bane saw red. Rage erupted in his belly and raced up his throat and he nearly gagged with the heat of it. He stuck a finger in his collar, which had suddenly grown quite tight, and tugged, finding it hard to breathe.

"Are you alright?" Mel asked.

"I just...haven't had my morning coffee. Bit of a headache is all," Bane panted. He grabbed two mugs from the shelf, pushed the button twice, and concentrated on his breath. He calmed down before he presented her with one of the mugs. "Rotten good luck. For him."

"And for *you*." Mel winked. "That commission money must be good. It's so busy today!"

It *was* busy. Bane tried to force himself to feel grateful, to realize it was trickling down to him, for once. He was reaping benefits, even if second-hand. He forced a smile, remembering where he was and who he was with. "If I make more deliveries, will you still pay me in OCCs?"

Mel chuckled. "When you asked that I pay you with them, I thought you were a fool. Now I think I overpaid you." She shook her head. "No. If I ever get my hands on any more, I won't tell a soul. But there would be signs!"

"How about finally upgrading your broom?"

"Now there's a thought..." Mel took a gulp of coffee and sighed. They turned to watch the practice lot through the window, basking in the cozy warmth radiating off the cleverly hidden enchanted heaters. She watched her son land and hop off the broom, his legs trembling with adrenaline, both terrified and thrilled. He looked around, spotted his mum through the glass, and ran inside. "Mum! You've got to try this!"

"Not in my condition," she said, patting her belly. She turned to Bane. "I think he's found the one."

Bane rolled his shoulders back and mustered his most genuine smile. He was determined to ensure Joyce had a fantastic experience buying his very first broomstick.

"Now, you need to remember, going into F&E, it's a bit different than on the Used side," Bane said, dropping his voice conspiratorially. "Marvin's going to try to sell you everything, all of it. He's going to make you feel paranoid and in need of protection, and he's going to want to add all the flashy lacquer and blinkers and light-up twigs. Keep in mind your budget."

Mel shrugged, unbothered. "I figured he can spend it all however he wants, it's his money. Besides, who knows how much it'll be worth tomorrow?"

"I'm not even sure how much it's worth today," Bane confessed.

"My husband's an accountant, and Homer said they're worth thirty, conservatively."

"I'll ask what we're accepting them for," Bane assured. The Wizby wasn't worth as much as a Twig, but it was a sturdy, reliable model, built to last. Unless, of course, you'd like to trade it in in 2-3 years for something top of the line?

Bane knocked on the door next to Marvin's. It was Gerwin's old office, and the upgrades to the lounge were nothing compared to the upgrades in this room. It even had its own fancy new coffee box all to itself, which was currently working overtime and being tested to its limit. "Oy, Big Boss, got a moment? I need to know what those coins are worth so I can gauge my customers' price range."

Virgil Van De Besen looked up and grinned. "Bane! Come in, please. Of course I'm happy to help. How's Marvin doing?"

"If he had a moment I would ask him, but he's up to his ears in deals and looking a bit stressed."

Virgil nodded, pleased. "I've already called Jr. to come in and help, he'll be here shortly. That will help ease Marvin's load. Take a seat."

Bane did just that, and his back sang from the lumbar support of the chair. He rubbed his hands on the armrests, momentarily forgetting why he was in the office. Virgil pointed an obelisk crystal to the mirror on the wall to his left, which flickered through surveillance channels set around the dealership for security. "Can never be too careful, eh?" Virgil winked. He waved the crystal until the image he was searching for appeared. "I assume you know about OCCs, yes? Gods know we've talked about them enough in our meetings."

Bane nodded. "Yes."

"Well, the news broke that someone used a single coin to purchase a ring valued at one hundred and five gold coins. This, by street law, means that the new asking price for an OCC is 105 golds. But we can't value them as such, because then who would buy them from us? We need to value them low enough so that we can turn them around and make a profit, but high enough that people will accept the price. I've discussed this with Marvin, and we've decided to set the value at fifty gold coins. Any lower and customers won't part with their new treasure, or they will take it to a dealership that offers more."

"Is everyone accepting the fifty gold valuation for them?"

"The Chamber of Commerce put out a new sign this morning that insists it's worth only five gold, up from their declared one gold. Naturally no one's paying that any heed. It's the pawn shops that have the best forecast, and they're saying forty-five. For now. It was forty when I woke up this morning." Virgil nodded to the mirror, which was trailing on a parchment in some credible pawn shop somewhere. Not Amos's, Bane decided, leaning in for a closer inspection. But one just as nice.

"What will it be worth tomorrow? Sixty, maybe?"

Virgil broke into that dazzling grin. "From your lips to the gods' ears, Bane, let's hope so."

Bane left the office in a daze to deliver the good news to Mel, who grabbed him by the shoulders to steady herself from the blow of it. "I thought, like, ten!"

"How many does he have?"

"Six."

"Get him the light-up twigs," Bane joked, but not really. They might as well spend that here, where he would benefit as well. "The dealership offered to pay us in OCCs."

"That's a good move. It's to avoid taxes," she added, and then explained to him how the official registers all worked.

"Is your business registered?" Bane asked.

Mel looked guilty. "I don't have an official seal, if that's what you're asking."

"Isn't that illegal?"

"Technically, if it's a business run out of your home and you make less than a certain amount of profit annually, you don't need one. That's how all those Pretty Potions 'business women' run their 'businesses.'" Mel used aggressive air quotes as she spoke, and Bane wasn't entirely sure why but didn't feel like asking for an explanation. He didn't care what Pretty Potions and other businesses-in-a-box did. He knew of them, of course. His mum had been a Healthy Herb gal herself back in the day, touting the weight-loss remedies. Bane always suspected they were just laxatives and mild poisons that caused nausea, but they claimed to "suppress appetites" in the pitch, which his mother had practiced in every mirror of the house a dozen times a day.

Toby with his turkey legs showed up then, making extra rounds because he, too, read the news. They were *not* half off, like they were on Mondays. Virgil came out of his office and insisted every customer have one and paid Toby with his own coins. Gold coins, Bane noted. Turkey legs in hand—two for Joyce, as he was still a growing boy—Bane ushered them into Marvin's office and turned to greet the new customers that had just walked through the front door.

32

To The Moon

In the two weeks since the all-time high OCC price broke and the coin shower happened, the price of OCCs steadily climbed. It went from 105 to 40, then 50, and up and up and was now hovering at 200 gold coins apiece. It terrified everyone who had them. Most refused to spend them, stowing the coins away in enchanted, locked chests in hiding places around their homes, too terrified to admit to their families that they possessed such wealth. For some, that was an entire years' wages. For others, a retirement egg they had never dreamed would materialize.

Now that they were getting paid in OCCs, Bane grew anxious. His pay was based on the price of OCCs being 10 gold, so by his calculations Bane expected 12 OCCs, maybe a little extra with the added commission. At the rate of 200 gold each, why, that month's pay came out to *almost double what he made in an entire year*. At their meeting the day before payday, they were informed that while this was the first time they were getting paid in OCCs, it would also be the last. "But," Virgil said, pausing for the groans to subside, "commission percentages are going up by 10 percent."

The groans morphed into cheers, and everyone dispersed to make calls to prospects. By now Bane's client list had grown, but it was only a month old. He decided to take a peek at the list of Used Brooms clients he had in the past—maybe they would be game? He wiped the back of his hand across his forehead, sweating despite it still being winter. It was that time of the month again.

Bane and Lusine had prepared for that evening; it was the first full moon that Bane would not be spending gorging himself on the lot and prowling the dealership premises. It apparently hadn't been discussed in the deal with Gerwin, because Bane wasn't approached about it, and he was too intimidated by Virgil to bring it up. It wasn't easy, confessing to an employer that he was a werewolf. Though it became immediately apparent that the Van De Besens could afford good, reliable enchanted locks on their doors. Plus, there were the magical mirrors that played surveillance on loop in both Virgil's office and his personal pocket mirror. Virgil was always monitoring, this dealership and the three others he owned.

Bane ordered the meats ahead of time, and they were ready to be picked up on his way home. He also had the place in the woods picked out where Lusine would tie him to a tree by a collar. She would spend the night with him, reading to him, and sleeping beside him—a safe distance away—under the stars. Lusine had insisted on this, that if she was going to be his wife, she needed to see him at his worst, as a transformed werewolf.

They ended up not needing the collar.

Bane realized that with Lusine there, he could channel his hunger into a different need. Filled with meat and still ravenous, he turned his eyes on her and found he wanted her. Not to eat her, but to...

Before long they were both naked, sweating, and howling in unison at the moon.

Curled up against Bane's furry body, her back pressed to his still very full belly, Lusine admired her engagement ring and dreamed aloud of what she hoped their future would bring. She wasn't sure if he understood her, in this state, and so she was brave, speaking of children and a house that maybe had a little yard for them to toddle around in. A bed big enough that he could sleep beside her in wolf form. Would their children be werewolves? Maybe Marmie would like to move in, or have a spare room decorated to her liking to visit whenever she wanted. Maybe Lusine and her parents would make up, and they would get the grandchildren into the finest schools in the kingdom, purchase them the crisp, tidy uniforms she had worn as a schoolgirl. She wondered if her mother still had them somewhere, perhaps in a trunk in the attic...

Lusine yawned, rubbed her face against her fiancé's fur, and tucked her cloak under her head like a pillow. Winter was fading and though it was still cold, there was no snow, and the heat they created with their lovemaking glowed like a tangible bubble around them. Lusine almost felt too hot. She fell into a deep, peaceful sleep and awoke to a man beside her, snoring loudly, clumps of fur shed all around him.

"Morning," she sang, pressing her lips to his.

Bane twitched his nose, as if still beast, and awoke. He looked around the forest, surprised, and then found Lusine, right in front of him, wrapped in his arms. "Gods, were we really so stupid to do that?"

Lusine nodded to the staff leaned against the tree. "I was never in any real danger. Not until you tried that one move...We should try that in your human form," she giggled. And then they did, but quickly, because it was payday and Bane was eager to get to the dealership and collect his coins.

Bane hadn't told Lusine he agreed to be paid in OCCs, because she still seemed highly skeptical, even as it was an open secret anyone could look up and see charting up into the stratosphere. He figured he would sell one immediately to Amos so they could pay rent and afford their usual bills and groceries, but he would squirrel the rest away. He had been fully alert last night, listening to Lusine describe the life they were destined to live. And while he hadn't been able to respond in anything besides barks and growls and howls, he understood every word and had taken each to heart. Those coins would go towards building that life for her.

For *them*.

33

Another Reluctant Meeting

Mosley put off this meeting as long as he could. He had been explicitly told by his employer not to bother him unless the Head of the Aluminum Mint himself rang the mirrors demanding an audience. That was why Mosley said nothing when the price of OCCs skyrocketed overnight with the purchase of a ring. Why he made no mention of the coins showering mysteriously from the skies.

But now, banks were being asked to keep OCCs as collateral, and the Heads of the Mints were nowhere to be found. Banks were calling *him*, Mosley, and demanding to know if they should accept or not. What did he know about collaterals and loans? He was barely keeping above his own debts; dressing the part of the king's right hand was expensive. Why, his shoes alone, worn thin within months from all the running around the place, were costing a small fortune. He was on the brink of accepting an offer from a patron, to be kept comfortable in exchange for always being able to gain an audience with the king, day or night. He had no business—or desire—meddling in the Crown's finances.

King Eadwine hated nothing more than to be woken up before he was ready. After that, he hated having to physically get out of bed. Then to be met at the breakfast he'd been dragged out of bed to go to, to be forced to sit and listen to the bad news being delivered? *Outrageous.* Because gods forbid good news arrive at the crack of dawn.

Mosley, after much insistence, took the seat across the table from the king in the suite attached to his bedroom. This table was small and intimate and was meant to be used to enjoy languid, post-copulation pastries. Instead, he and the king were nearly knocking knees trying to both fit under it. There was hardly any room for the coffee and the tea and the breakfast plates and the *Herald* splayed out over it all, smearing ink onto unsuspecting napkins.

Reading *The Harking Herald* was seen as a vulgar pastime by the previous king, but Eadwine believed it was the surest way to absorb feedback from the general mass. Between the financial page reporting the costs of goods and the opinions columns sent in by commoners, to the gossip page submitted by sleuths, it was easy to gauge what the state of the kingdom looked like to its citizens, and the king could see where leaks needed to be sealed in terms of privacy and scandals.

"Get on with it then," King Eadwine snapped, slapping closed the paper.

Mosley pulled out his notes and attempted to end the meeting in record time. "The valuation has been confirmed. Two hundred gold coins each. I also discovered that there is a broom shop on the north side of the city that used OCCs to purchase new brooms from a manufacturer."

"Was this before or after my meeting with the mints?"

"Before."

The king gave a dismissive wave. "Irrelevant. I need to know the ramification of this, *now*." He jabbed a finger into the paper as if it would puncture, deflate, and dissolve the whole mess. No luck.

Mosley flipped the page in his notebook and froze. "Oh, wait. Also after. But by a different company. It looks like the dealership changed owners."

"You're saying that a manufacturer of broomsticks is accepting fake coins? What does it think it will do with it, pay off its debts to the Aluminum Mint with that nonsense?"

"It seems so."

"That's preposterous. The Aluminum Mint won't accept fake coins from its debtors."

"Sir, you could...ask them."

"I'm not spoiling another breakfast."

Mosley looked through the doorway and nodded to the mirror in the king's office. It wasn't an ordinary mirror; it was a mosaic of mirrors, each piece able to peer into one of the five-dozen high-profile homes and businesses in the kingdom that was infiltrated by this creation. It was created back when a mirror had to be linked to another one to communicate through it, and it could only scry its pair. Since then, mirror magic evolved to allow a mirror to scry into any mirror, if the right rune was drawn. "What about...?"

"Oh, right." The mirror craze took off in this kingdom as an initiative by his father-in-law, who needed eyes in every home in his kingdom. King Eadwine, on the other hand, found it an excruciating invasion of privacy. Rather than monitor through the mosaic mirror, he still relied on getting his intelligence reports from the Secret Agency of Watching, the spy network that Mosley had curated. Still, having a mirror to contact anyone anytime was convenient. Anyone except the Heads of the Mints, he discovered. They could afford to enchant their mirrors to be rune-locked against infiltration, even by the king. The king could still ring them, and they were mostly still obliged to answer, but at their own leisure.

Mirror magic came in handy at times like this, when Eadwine needed an impromptu meeting. "Alright, ring the mints."

Mosley went over and drew on one surface. He waited a moment before he moved to the next one. As he began to trace a finger, Sir Nilman's face appeared in the first one, and his wasn't the only one. Lady Silversmith's profile was behind him. Sir Nilman swiveled his mirror around and took in the whole view of the room he was in, revealing all the other Heads—including the elusive Head of the Aluminum Mint.

"Your Majesty! Look, everyone!"

A groan resounded and was immediately stifled as Count Goldstem's face appeared, and then everyone else's in turn, a polite greeting muttered by each.

The king stood and stepped closer to the mirror. "Can you...?" He gestured to the small mirror, then the mosaic as a whole. Mosley understood. He pinched two fingers onto the glass then flicked them apart, and Sir Nilman's face blew up into all the mirrors. It was the view an insect would have, and the king felt as if he were a fly looking in on them...having breakfast together? "Where...?"

"Count Goldstem's winter chateau," Sir Nilman explained, grinning. "An annual tradition."

Those in the background dropped their heads guiltily but didn't make to move away from the spread they were enjoying.

An odd pang of envy hit the king and he thought, *Why wasn't I invited?* It was a silly thought, a thought he often had in his youth, being left out by the bigger, older boys. It was a feeling that as king he didn't think he would ever feel again.

King Eadwine mustered a polite smile and said, "I would like to discuss business. Much has happened in the weeks since you all vanished."

"That's my fault," Count Goldstem apologized, doing his best to look sheepish. The mirror panned to him, Sir Nilman eager to give him the blame. The king saw the earl sit beside Lady Silversmith, then realized that wasn't her, couldn't be her because the lady was sitting across from the earl. The woman Eadwine had mistaken for Lady Silversmith was the earl's wife. The resemblance, King Eadwine marveled, was discomfortingly uncanny. "We escape here every year for winter play. I saw no reason to break tradition."

"At a time like this?" King Eadwine chided.

"At a time like what?" the countess asked and got a glare from her husband. Spouses were discouraged from having a say in business, at least publicly. In fact, they would have been able to perhaps ride out the entire fiasco if Sir Nilman's new wife hadn't broken the cardinal rule of no mirrors on vacation. And so, she would be shunned by everyone for the remainder of the trip, which was probably not going to be for long, they realized, now that they were most likely being summoned back to deal with the king's mess.

"Mosley will fill you in," King Eadwine said and poured himself a fresh cup of coffee. He leaned back in his seat and attempted to read their faces from the poor angle Sir Nilman held the mirror, trying to pan it around the room constantly so he didn't feel singled out and lectured at.

In truth, all the Heads had heard bits of rumor; it was impossible to hide completely from the world in a time like this, when their servants had mirrors and read papers and whispered news and gossip that no wall was thick enough to stifle. In fact, the Heads had conversed long into the night over what had to be done. Even the Head of the Aluminum Mint made an appearance, joining in the evenings in the post-meal smoke-choked cigar room as the other Heads lamented to him. Atticus had sat rigid, politely holding the glass of liquor handed to him, abstaining and listening. That was why he was ready with a solution when Mosley gave a little bow to indicate he was finished filling them in.

Atticus motioned to Sir Nilman to pan to him. "We do nothing."

In his surprise, Sir Nilman nearly threw the mirror at Atticus, who finally ripped it out of the jerky hand and held it before him to address the king directly.

"Greed will ruin this. It will go out like a spark. It went up so fast, it will plunge just as quickly. No one is to accept the coins, pure and simple. All those small businesses that are so pro-OCC? They don't sell wares worth hundreds of golds. As for our friends selling homes and brooms and magical appliances and luxuries, we tell them to simply refuse to accept the coins. We will be the ceiling they can't break. They will get discouraged soon enough, passing the OCCs between themselves, each trade diminishing their worth. Once the surfaces of those coins are worn away from exchanging hands so often, they will tire and give up."

The king looked at Mosley, impressed. "And this will work?"

"Aye," came the chorus through the mirror.

Lady Silversmith spoke next. "Make the Chamber of Commerce's recommended worth at one gold again. Eventually, it will reflect the true price, when they're done squabbling amongst themselves. Allow anyone to bring the coins to our banks and exchange them for official tenders. Then we'll sell them back to the Crown for one gold apiece, ending this madness."

Making the Crown pay for its mistake. They would feast over this glory tonight.

"When will this go away?" King Eadwine asked.

"In the blink of an eye," Atticus promised, because to him, everything did.

The mirror flickered and went back to reflecting the pair having breakfast at the tiny table. King Eadwine looked away from his reflection and said, "Is that all?"

Mosley wrung his hands anxiously. "One last thing...the representative for P.U.K.E. has presented a counter-offer—"

The king cut him off with a wave. "Accept it. All of it. But weave into the clause that I own their absolute loyalty so long as they are employed by the Crown."

Mosley nodded. That, at least, he could do.

34

Price Correction

It took a few days for the boycott to take effect. The Heads had to finish enjoying their vacation, after all. They knew what the ramifications would look like. At least, they could imagine. Their kingdom had been peaceful for quite some time. It was hard to see the betrayal implode from within.

The effect didn't unfold immediately. The orders to stop accepting OCCs first circulated through the highest ranks. Loose ends had to be tied off. Unloading of useless coins happened swiftly and quietly and trickled down to the lowest level of the richest businesses. Then as one caught wind of another selling off, the effect ripped like wildfire through the business world. Panic selling began, as no one wanted to be the last one holding the bag of potentially worthless coins. Luckily, there were always hopeful individuals ready to catch the coins below.

It didn't affect the general population until about a week later, when someone tried to buy a necklace for his wife for their anniversary with OCCs. The jeweler refused, and the man smashed a fist through the glass, grabbed the necklace, and threw the coins on the ground before he fled. He didn't make it off the bridge; the guards were trained to catch any and all suspicious behavior, down to the subtle shifty walk trying to conceal stolen goods. But a man barreling through the crowd, shopkeepers shouting after him? Now that was too easy. He was quickly tackled, stripped of the stolen necklace, and publicly scolded. Mirrors appeared in onlookers' hands, capturing and projecting the scene to anyone who happened to be flipping channels on their own mirror. In that moment, the news broke.

Everyone rushed to trade OCCs for jewelry, desperate to exchange them for something expensive, but no shop accepted the fool's gold. Bricks and rocks smashed through glass windows that weren't warded tightly enough by magic until finally the Midnight Brigade arrived to break up the scene. Gilded Bridge was closed except by appointment.

The pawn shops still accepted OCCs, but their ware was second-hand, and even the most extravagant enchanted weapon peeled from the coffin of a dead relative was worth only so much gold. They sold out of their most valuable items quickly, before they, too, caught on to what was happening and stopped accepting OCCs, fearing they would be saddled with loads of diminishing return coins.

It was a group of riled-up pawn shop owners who sent a pile of excrement to the palace steps as their official complaint about the "meddling of the Crown."

Remember who serves who, the attached note read, which seemed comical to the king. What did they think this was, a democracy? He laughed out loud and crumpled the smelly parchment.

"Sir, we haven't had a revolution since...oh, since the dungeons were still equipped to be used as dungeons, and they haven't been that in..." Mosley's eyes rolled up into his head, trying to remember. He was a lot of things, but official royal historian he was not. Sometimes he felt it was the *only* hat he didn't wear.

"Send a note to the Chamber of Commerce. Instruct them to update the new price of OCCs. One gold."

Mosley gulped. "Y-yes S-sir."

Bane saw it all unravel in the blink of an eye. After payday, he sold one OCC to Amos for forty gold and kept the others in reserve in his tiny chest. He watched the price climb. He cheered on his fellow collectors channeling optimistic fore-casts through their mirrors to anyone who bothered to scry in. They spoke openly about investing in OCCs. They were now *investors*, not just collectors.

These coins were something to pour your hard-earned money into that was sure to pay off five, tenfold. They were the best retirement plan. *Just hold.*

But after the stolen necklace incident, Bane had no idea what they were worth, and he was frantic to find out.

Price correction, voices soothed through the mirror. These voices contradicted what *The Harking Herald* printed, but what did the *Herald* know? It wasn't fast enough; it couldn't print a new issue every hour to update the tumbling prices. Their official mirror correspondent rapid-fired updates to anyone who scryed into the channel, but was *that* fast enough? Bane flipped between Heathrow, the *Herald*'s Head Finance Writer, to the mirror in a pawn shop trailing the parchment tacked to a wall. It had so many numbers written then scratched through it, it was hard to tell where to find the current price of OCCs.

When the Chamber of Commerce declared they were only worth a single gold, Bane refused to believe it. Once Lusine left for work, Bane put one mirror channel on the big mirror in their bedroom and flipped through others in his hand mirror, trying to decipher which number was more current and correct. Frantic, he remembered the piece of paper Vito gave him. He hunted around the loft until he found it, stuck like a bookmark into one of Lusine's boring books. He traced it onto his hand mirror and the face of Harper appeared. "Oh." She looked surprised. "Got another kingdom-shattering bit of news for me?"

"Apparently *you* do," Bane said dryly. "Please, you need to fix this. You need to just print another article that says everything is fine, that the price of OCCs is back up. You're the reason this happened. Your words, they are like magic. Wave it around once more, would you? For the poor ones like me? Just print in the paper that it's worth, oh, twenty gold!'

"I'm not the market maker. I don't have the authority to just walk onto the printer floor and print a bogus story."

"Let me publish an opinion piece," Bane begged. "That I think it's going to go up. That I think it's going to be worth a thousand gold soon!"

Harper couldn't laugh at this, no matter how comical it sounded. It dripped with desperation, and she felt it through the glass. She herself hadn't invested in OCCs; she found a few coins on her routine pre-dawn exercise flight and immediately sold them and filled her coffers with gold to pad her emergency fund. She hadn't believed its value would soar so high as to make paupers kings. There simply did not exist enough gold in the kingdom to pay out all those coins. The numbers just didn't make sense. Besides, why would the banks pay them out? What did they owe those coming up with fake coins, demanding a sum that they had collectively made up? Where did their worth come from, but hopes and dreams?

Harper had seen all the good and bad these coins brought on. Some people made sound choices, while others dug themselves into financial graves. From one moment to the next, some lives did, in fact, change. She saw the ramifications unfold now, the sobbing faces in the mirrors, the rage and anger and regret. She avoided opening her mirror and wouldn't have for perhaps days more if it hadn't chimed, alerting her of the direct call, which she always dutifully answered.

"I can't fix this," she said softly.

"Then who can?" Bane wailed, tearing his hair. "Is it worth nothing now?"

"I'm sorry. I have to go."

Bane's mirror went back to reflecting his face. His eyes were shiny with tears of frustration. This *couldn't* be happening. He tugged on his tight shirt and flew to work.

At the dealership, the mood on the sales floor had completely changed. Some customers who bought brooms just the day before were loudly arguing with Marvin, demanding refunds for brooms they hadn't been able to afford in the first place. They had been persuaded to take out a loan for a broom outside their price range instead of paying for one outright with the OCCs in their hand, having been assured that the price of OCCs would keep going up. Now they couldn't afford the payments on the loan.

Salesmen buzzed around the angry customers, trying to placate them with cups of coffee, trades for cheaper models, or a trip across the lot to Used Brooms. That was where many already were, selling back brooms that had been bought with cash from a retirement fund that suddenly found itself worthless. Coppers were being paid for what had been worth golds last week.

Bane sipped his coffee, listening as first shift updated them on how chaotic the morning had been. The veterans took the news with stony faces.

Bane felt the stress emanating off Ezra, who tried to stay jovial. But Bane knew he, too, had taken his pay in OCCs, and had been collecting them even before that. Finally, unable to bear it, Bane asked him for advice. "Should I sell while it's still worth something?"

"If you sell, you've definitely lost that money. What you have now is *unrealized* loss. It means potential loss. It's not actual money lost until you sell and there's no hope for it to go back up." Ezra tapped his temple. *Think about it.*

That made sense to Bane. The coins were worth nothing and one gold and a hundred gold all at once. He just had to wait until the right time to sell came. It was definitely not now. It was down now, but what went down had to go up, didn't it?

Ezra looked around as if to make sure no one was eavesdropping and added, "If I were you, and this isn't financial advice, I would get my hands on all of them now while people think they're worthless and are dumping them."

"Are you saying the price will go up?"

"All I'm saying is...I like the coins." Then Ezra stalked away to stand before a different window and plot his way out of this mess.

It was the spark of hope Bane needed to hear. If everyone went and bought them back at this cheap price, why, the demand would go up and the price would, too. And he didn't need it to go up a lot—just to, say, ten golds. Yes, he would *definitely* sell when it went up to ten golds. He was suddenly very sure that would happen overnight.

During his lunch break, Bane jumped on his broom and flew to Amos's. There he presented the five gold coins he had left to his name. "Sell me your OCCs."

It was a bold demand, one Amos hadn't expected to hear. As it were, Bane was the first and only person to make this request all day. Amos would have sold Bane all the OCCs he had just to end the anxiety it all caused, but if Bane was here to buy some, surely more would come, and he needed to keep the price reasonable. "One gold apiece."

Bane narrowed his eyes, seeing the problem. If he demanded more, he would be cheapening the worth to less than a gold each, and then it would take more to dig itself out of that hole to be worth ten golds. "Deal."

Bane felt good leaving the shop. So good that he didn't mention a word of it to Lusine, who seemed completely deaf to the whole mess that was exploding all around her. It was as if all the coin drama was taking place in a parallel universe, nowhere near her own. And so, she slept soundly that night as her fiancé wrestled with excitement beside her.

The next day, OCCs were worth a single silver.

35

P.U.K.E.

The pigeon shifters of P.U.K.E. were called to assemble bright and early the next morning. They lined up to sign their contracts, still rubbing dreams from their eyes, assured by their union representatives that this was a fair deal, a very good deal, *for the love of all the gods please sign and let's get back to work.*

And the first order of business was to be carried out that very day.

Brand new, beautifully embossed leather shoulder harnesses were issued to each member, riddled with a dozen pockets to carry multiple letters to multiple doors. This should have been their first warning that their workload was about to increase exponentially, but at that moment, they were too distracted by the shiny new brass buckles. Each accepted their harness and eased it on, helped each other fasten those clasps, already smudging the shine from them. They were funneled toward the window, stacks of pamphlets piled everywhere, and they were ordered to stuff each pocket with as many as it would carry.

"Fly your usual routes and disperse them into the wind. Our mission is to target every home in the kingdom. For you long-haulers, there's overtime to clock, so don't dilly-dally. Newbies are to hold back to be assigned your route."

Enchanted quills scribbled furiously on the pamphlets, signing the king's signature on those freshly printed pages.

Some members paused to read the pamphlets. Others were so close to retirement they couldn't care less, puffing on fat celebratory cigars. They snuffed out their cigars on the windowsill before they jumped out, tumbled, and transformed midair. They flapped to catch an air current and soared their routes, pulling parchments out with their beaks, sprinkling generously as ordered.

That was how the city of Citeel found itself showered from above once again, this time with pamphlets that did not hold good news.

Official Order of the King:

Each official commemorative coin is hereby worth one silver. Exchanges may be made at any bank. Value is subject to change at any moment by order of the Crown.

It went on to explain that the reproduction or even the attempt of reproduction of the coin was illegal and liable to be punishable by several years in the dungeons (which was now a knitting center, but no one knew that) and a severe fee. Of course someone had already mass-produced them and was on their way to deliver a wheelbarrow of the fool's gold to a bank. They were arrested and tried for the obscure crime of alchemy. But since there weren't any actual holding cells in the dungeons, they were eventually fully pardoned and employed by the gold mint. They still work there to this day.

It was a Saturday, a day Bane usually worked but Lusine did not, and so they both slept in, nowhere to rush to that morning. Lusine woke first and decided to go out and grab fresh pastries.

As she walked down to her favorite little bakery, with its cinnamon twists that weren't too heavy and pillowy doughnuts drizzled with hazelnut spread, there was a spring in her step. While Bane waged his silent war, her worries were lifted. She earned more than enough at her new job to pay their bills. Better yet, since today was her birthday, her trust fund was due to begin distribution. Though she was locked in a silent dispute with her parents, they could go nowhere near her trust. It had been set up generations ago with iron-clad rules that protected the offsprings, no matter the troubles that inevitably manifested between them and their parents. And each generation certainly had its quarrels.

Lusine wasn't spared the sight of the swarm of pigeons overhead, the fluttering of pamphlets like leaves releasing from a mighty oak. She, like everyone else, snatched one. She dutifully read it and overheard the excited chatter in line at the shop as to what it all meant.

Bane was awake by the time she got back, though he had meant to be the one to wake up early and get breakfast as a surprise for her birthday. He grabbed her by the hips and pulled her in, kissed her. "Happy birthday." He tasted the sweetness on her lips. "You stole a bite," he accused and peeked into the bag she held.

Lusine handed it over willingly, along with the pamphlet. She set his coffee on the bedside dresser that barely fit in the tight space between the bed and the wall and took a seat on the bed beside him. This was their nest, where they made love, watched the mirror channels, ate, and confided all their secrets.

"What's this?"

"It's littering the streets," was all Lusine said. She wasn't sure if it meant anything to him. She watched him read it, saw his face morph from curious to devastated. When he finally looked up at her, his eyes were haunted.

"It's all gone," he whispered.

"What is?" Bane dropped his face into his hands. Lusine had to pry them away so she could hear what he was muttering. "Speak up."

"All of our money is in OCCs. I got paid in the stupid coins at work. Then I took whatever wasn't fool's gold and went to Amos's and exchanged them all for OCCs. We're doomed. We have nothing now. Sixteen silvers, technically. That's it."

Lusine sighed before confessing, "You didn't exchange all of it."

"Where...where is the money?"

"In the bank, of course."

Of course. Now he remembered that she got the OCCs to spend at the coronation festival from her bank. Relief flooded through him. "We have more money!"

She nearly said *I have money* but then remembered their engagement. What was hers was his now.

He grabbed her and kissed her gruffly, and from the way he did she assumed they were putting a pin in this conversation. Her hands roamed southward, the kiss having the effect it always had on her, but he wasn't in the mood. He pulled her hands back up out of his lap and kissed the palm of each, squeezed them to try to get her to see how serious he was being. "You must promise never to let me be in charge of our finances ever again."

Lusine frowned. "You never were."

"What do you mean?"

"Have you never noticed who pays the rent and the bills on time? Sure, you get the coins to me eventually, but we'd be out on the street if I waited on them. Did you never wonder how the ice box is miraculously full every month? You certainly never questioned where the money you kept finding in your pockets came from."

Bane burned with shame. "I've just lost a great deal of money."

"We're going to the bank today and exchanging whatever coins you have left," she announced. "*All* of it."

"What if the price goes up?" he whispered, but that sliver of hope was so thin it was translucent.

Lusine shook her head. "It's not worth the trouble." She placed a hand on his chest, over his heart. "I can see the turmoil it's caused you. The fickle hope, the soul-crushing disappointment. It's the aches of gambling, my love. You cannot live like this. It's a fool's hope for fool's gold. It is worth nothing and we don't need it."

Bane threw his hands up and around, motioning to the tiny room that was their home. "We live in a pigeonhole. We can't bring children into this."

So he *had* understood her that night in the woods.

"It's all a game," he said to Lusine. "Money. All of it. If you have it, the world's your playground, isn't it? You own the pawns. You can direct them to go wherever you like. If you don't have money, you're the pawn being barked around."

Lusine's heart broke, hearing this. "Is that how you really feel? That you're controlled by money?"

"You can't understand," Bane snarled. "You're rich."

Lusine slid off the bed and took a defensive step back. "*I'm* not rich, my parents are. They hold their coffers in iron fists. I hated begging them to give me money for anything, and so I stopped. I have funded my own education. I paid for my exams, my books, my meals, my clothes. They have contributed nothing. *I* built myself into who I am."

"That you have. And that's grand jolly, but here's the difference. If you fall ill or get run over by a horse or scorched nearly to death by a dragon, your family will save you. You may not ask for it, and you can denounce them after for doing it, but if and when you truly need it, they will make sure you are alright and taken care of. Me? I've got Mum, who's got a meager pension. She can afford a doctor, now. But what if she becomes feeble? Blind and crippled? Who will take care of her while I have to work to pay my bills?

"And if I fall off my broomstick and break my back and can't work, who feeds me? Will you? Sure. Until you decide it's no fun anymore. Without you, I have nothing. And I have worked myself to the bone trying to find a place in this city to become useful. Appreciated. Compensated my worth. But I don't think I'm worth that much, I'm afraid. Realizing that has shaken me to the core. Who will take care of me, the werewolf? Do you know I have to pay a premium at the doctor? For the only one in the city who will even see me? And he's a fair ride away. What if he leaves? Who will take care of me?"

Lusine's eyes shone with tears. She had never thought of it that way because she was so proud of what she accomplished by actively rejecting her family's help. But he was right, she knew. She had a whole system of support her lineage wove around her, ready to catch her in its soft netting anytime she really, truly needed it. And now, through his love and the ring he had placed on her finger, she was pulling him into that safety net.

"*I* will." She kissed him softly, then fiercely. She held his gaze and forced him to believe her. He understood the look, and he felt a fracture in his fears. "You are mine, and I am yours, and what's mine is ours." Lusine reached into the bag and produced a sweet, flaky roll and pressed it into his hand. "Speaking of what's mine...my mother reached out. I sent her a letter informing her of our engagement."

"And?"

Lusine paused for effect. "She's thrilled."

Bane threw his head back and howled with relief. Lusine laughed then reached to pinch his lips closed so she could finish. "She gifted us quite a large sum of money."

"How much?"

"Enough. And you're signing a prenuptial."

"What's that?"

"Let me take you out to dinner. Somewhere nice. Lots of meat. It's the sort of thing you discuss over a meal."

"But it's your birthday. I've already planned a place to go to."

"Alright, then I'll get cocktails first, you get dinner after?"

Bane eagerly agreed, wholly unprepared for the heavy conversation that took place over the exquisite steaks and exorbitantly priced wine that he paid for with his final fistful of silvers, which he asked Lusine to carry for him.

He didn't mind though, in the end. Bane signed the agreement on the spot, before the check even arrived and their dessert was only half devoured, grateful that Lusine still found him worthy enough to marry after the fool he had been.

Thanks to that prenuptial, they lived happily ever after.

Epilogue

While many, like Bane, lost a great deal of money from the crash of the OCCs, there were a few who made out like bandits. Some of the lucky ones included Marmie Woods. She found her son's mirror conversation odd and so went forth and did her own investigation into what, exactly, those coins resting in her kitschy new teapot were all about. She suspected amulets charmed with magic and was confused when instead she discovered she could exchange them for gold. *Lots* of gold.

In the tourist town of Bambrough, news was slow to arrive, but this bit of information miraculously made it over. She went and found a shop that exchanged the fool's gold coins for a staggering amount. She arranged to have the rest of her belongings delivered to her seaside home. Then she paid to fix up the city house, which she gifted to the newly engaged couple with the condition that she could drop in anytime. They were more than eager to accept. She never told anyone about her sudden fortune and even Bane didn't dare ask how much she made. But it was enough that she lived out the rest of her days in moderate comfort. Her son never had to worry about her again.

Others were not so lucky.

Many people held on to their OCCs, believing the dip was a fluke, but it was not. Soon after, the Chamber of Commerce posted a notice that each was worth only a copper, and then nothing at all. Banks refused to accept them, and soon so did every other establishment, with or without an official royal seal. Those that held onto them until the very end were mocked as *coin holders*. They are still out there, somewhere, and they are the most optimistic people in the world. At least they have that going for them.

Mel's Deliveries is still around, though Bane is no longer employed there. Mel secured an exclusive contract with the Apothecary Guild and they do business delivering medicine around the kingdom. Thanks to new hires who are trained healers and qualified to administer the medication, the service has been lifesaving on several occasions. Mel's daughter was born happy and healthy at a whopping 10lbs, a blessing Mel attributes to a hearty diet of Toby's turkey legs.

Brooms of Van De Besens went out of business. All four locations closed, and their entire staff was laid off without severance pay. The Van De Besens are fine, of course; they filed for bankruptcy, sold off what they could, restructured their debts, and opened a new broomstick dealership in another kingdom. They have since opened two more.

Bane felt an immense relief to no longer sell broomsticks. The shuttering of the dealership doors gave him the chance to do something new. He was surprised that it wasn't Jaymie, but rather Dante who refused to hire him back at Copper University.

"If we take you back, you'll never leave," Dante explained.

"So? You won't, either!"

"No, but I don't have a fiancé, I will never have children, and I am happy living in the loft above. Would you be so happy here?"

While this initially ticked Bane off to no end, he finally conceded that it was the nicest thing a friend had done for him.

Bane currently works as a Stardust Sales Representative, a job Ezra got him. It's infinitely worse than being a broomstick salesman, and Bane swore to Lusine that as soon as something better comes along, he will jump ship. He doesn't know that Lusine has already accepted a job offer at the very prestigious Law Offices of Bonadona and Bartlebaugh. Her start date is after their upcoming spring wedding. Bane will be promoted to house husband, and shortly after that, to stay-at-home father, which will be his life's calling.

They go on to have three perfect children, each conceived under a full moon.

The End

Acknowledgements

I had a ton of fun creating a broomstick dealership that parallels a car dealership! I want it to be known that while I have (as of this moment) a real-life full-time job working in the auto industry, I'm not criticizing my actual job (I am a sorceress). The industry itself? Well... some of my tiffs with dealership practices are in here, but they are my own opinions (please don't fire me).

A huge thank you to my editor, Sarah Faeth Sanders, who continues to be my cheerleader. If your editor doesn't make you feel brilliant, get a new one. Just not mine, I'm keeping her.

Shout-out to my wonderful husband Benjamin, who beta reads my work, criticizes my timeline for dragon vaccines (it's not even real!) and takes my works as seriously as if I were a real historian of Everdorne.

Many thanks to you, dear readers, who have come along on this silly adventure into the whimsical world of Everdorne. It's by your enthusiasm that I keep writing, and I hope you enjoyed this book as much as I loved writing it!

About the Author

Bo Huffman lives in a cottage overgrown by roses and overrun by perfect pets. A lifelong writer, she has also held several dozen very weird jobs, including self-employed baker, wedding officiant, and tea specialist. You'll find remnants of these past lives sprinkled in her stories. When she's not writing fantasy books, she reads romances and dark fairytales, hunts for speakeasies, and takes up space in local coffee shops. She is still on the hunt for the perfect croissant.

Follow her work on Instagram: @authorbohuffman
Or via her website: bohuffman.com